# The Shadow of the Raider

by

## Caroline Phipp

## The Conrad Press

*The Shadows of Mystic River*
Published by The Conrad Press in the United Kingdom
2024
Tel: +44(0)1227 472 874
www.theconradpress.com
info@theconradpress.com
ISBN 978-1-916966-00-0
Copyright ©Caroline Phipp 2024
Typesetting and Cover Design by: Levellers
The Conrad Press logo was designed by Maria Priestley.
Printed and bound in Great Britain by Clays Ltd, Elcograf
S.p.A.

The Shadows of Mystic River
by

Caroline Phipp

# Chapter 1
## A fresh start

It was a beautiful summer's day.

The sun was beaming through the windshield of our car my father was driving, with the windows rolled down to the maximum, the wind blew strong as my hair swung across my face, the cool breeze weaving around my extended hand as I sat looking out the window towards the horizon, taking in the scenery for the fourth time this year.

We are the Fortmans. My father is a district attorney but for the navy, causing us to travel to where the work is.

My mother died in an accident a couple of years ago and we've been on the road ever since, my father is still unwilling to talk about what happened, moving us from place to place, never settling, just the endless turmoil of starting my life over again.

I don't usually bother making too many friends in my schools, because when you move, they don't stay friends for very long, the distance created between us with the pointless social phone interactions, that they keep missing or avoiding was hard to swallow, so after we moved to avoid my embarrassment, I cut ties completely.

We were moving to our new house but only some of us were excited about it.

We were moving from California to a small town in West Virginia called Mystic River.

I wasn't sure what was so mystical about it, I was sure this town would be much like the last, tedious, and boring, with an endless cycle of fake friends, everyone out for themselves kind of town. It would be fitting seen as this is what I was used to.

My father was a tall man with a dark moustache, his hair was dark on top but greying on the sides. The saying 'scared straight' comes to mind when you look at him due to his ghostly appearance and serious features, his need for privacy overshadowed by his self-loathing and guilt that he carries alone on his shoulders.

Turning around I look at my younger sister and brother who are in the back of the car, their names are Payton and Ethan.

Ethan was the youngest he was four years old with bright blonde hair, he has something called heterochromia which meant he had one blue eye and one brown eye making him unique and positively beautiful.

My sister on the other hand was the same age as me, don't get me wrong we aren't twins she was born nine months after I was, I think our parents didn't get the memo about a fertile window or they did they just didn't listen. You would think being so close in age we would be the best of friends, but nothing could be further from the truth.

Turning back and looking at my sister was amusing, Payton can literally sleep anywhere, I'm sure she would sleep on her head if she could. Mouth wide open, dribble flicking down her chin as my brother attempts to chuck popcorn in her mouth, unsuccessfully I might add as he is a terrible shot. I watch in amusement as it bounces off of her forehead and chin landing in a neat heap on her lap, as he re-arranges it into a line for her. I watch on as she doesn't move a muscle quite satisfying actually, given the fact she is a bit of a moody cow at times.

Payton has light features brown eyes and deep brown curly hair, built like an ironing board, so she says, giving me satisfaction that we are nothing alike.

As for me, well my name is Annabeth, my mother seemingly couldn't decide which name she liked better for me, so I guess she chose both. I have blonde hair with an annoyingly thick grey streak running through the front, however much I try and dye my hair it just simply will not take. My mother always said it's because an angel kissed me before I was born, which of course I believed for quite some time.

My sister's snores distracted me from my present thoughts, the last snore awoke her as she jolted up in her seat, her attention quickly turning to the rows of popcorn on her lap, pinching one she raised it to her mouth.

'I wouldn't eat that if I were you,' I said, smiling at her, knowing she wouldn't believe me.

'Luckily you aren't me!' she said, in an annoyed tone, picking the pieces from her lap.

'Well don't say I didn't warn you,' I said, my smile wide as I turn again to look at her, Ethan chuckles in his seat rubbing his little hands together.

I watched him as his devilish smile got bigger, knowing he had licked every one of those popcorn that Payton was about to devour, he was painfully adorable and has the sweetest little face you just couldn't stay mad at. If his little smile didn't get you then his adorable little dimples would, that I could say without a doubt he certainly had a little sparkle about him.

'How much longer?' I asked, tapping the dashboard.

I looked towards my father as if I knew he wouldn't reply, he simply sighed and looked at me pointing right. As his arm stretched over me his musky cologne wafted up like a wave hitting my nostrils causing me to choke, it was the smell of Joop mixed with old spice, but its potency was alarmingly strong today. How in the world did I not smell this? He smelt like a pimp in a brewery!

'Totally gross,' I thought, holding onto my nose, trying to avoid his scent.

As I looked out into the distance there was a sign that read *Mystic River 50 miles*, as the car slowly drifted past it. At this speed we wouldn't be getting anywhere soon.

'Oh great, another fifty miles in the car,' I said, mistakenly out loud, bringing my hands to my face I tried to silence the words that had already formed.

My father tutted at me instantly as he started to fidget slightly re-adjusting his chair whilst reaching for the radio, my eyes widen as I lift my arm and rest it on my window continuing to flash my eyes between him and the radio, he was switching back and forth through stations to find nothing he liked.

My body began to shudder as I looked on in horror, I saw him reaching for his personal mixed tapes collection, which by the way no one makes anymore or probably even knows what it is. But my father was old school, pushing in his CD it began to load, with wayward son now playing in the background Dad's mood shifts, I began giving him the side eye. It was my poor attempt at being inconspicuous, he looked at me through the corner of his eyes as the sweat formed his brows, biting down on his lip he desperately tried not to break into song, he taps the steering wheel with his right hand whilst bobbing his head back and forth.

Payton tutted heavily behind me growing tired of Ethan throwing things at her, snapping her head around she put her headphones in his ears in an attempt to shut him up. Putting on the dreaded song 'Baby Shark,' even with earphones and wayward son playing I could still hear that damn song, it was like white noise, highly annoying. I knew exactly where he was in the verses as he made the different expressions and gestures, my sister was still growing impatient with him by the minute. The funniest one was watching him do grandma shark as he tries to make it look like he has no teeth, attempting to curl his lips inwards to achieve the desired effect. It was much funnier watching in person, as his little nose scrunches up in anger as he is not able to keep his front teeth shielded whilst moving his mouth.

After another ten miles or so had gone past, my father had to stop for supplies, although I will admit he could have stopped somewhere better than this place, everyone looked super scary and territorial like they didn't like outsiders, the feeling of all eyes on you was creepy. An eerie feeling that would be everlasting as the people stopped and stared, creating a different meaning to the word uncomfortable.

Walking into the diner was like walking back in time, a little spooky. Diners were not made like this anymore, it looked like an old American diner that hasn't seen a renovation in decades. To tell you the truth it was a bit of a dive, in need of some desperate attention. Crossing my right leg over my left I began to bounce, I could avoid it no longer, the urge to use the toilet was all I could think about, sliding past my family I made a break for the toilet.

The toilet was interesting to say the least, as you walked in there was a giant hole in the floor that you had to bypass before reaching the actual toilet, it was green and overflowing. I was not using this! I wasn't sure I could hold it for another forty miles, but I was not balancing to use that thing. Clamping hold of my nose to shield myself from

9

the eye-watering stench, I backed out slowly trying to avoid the hole.

Returning back to my seat I turned to my father, looking at him for a moment as he looked around.

'Can we get this food to go?' I asked, with a smile. Looking up at me I could see the relief on his face, he nods sheepishly looking around for the waitress, bringing his hand to his neck he clears his throat.

'Ma'am,' he said, still raising his hand, only to be ignored once more.

'Excuse me, ma'am,' he said, his voice louder, and noticeably more irritated.

I sat awkwardly still bouncing in my seat, my bladder was strong which was helpful.

'Ain't no ma'am around here, sonny,' she said, refusing to look at him, her attitude towards us growing the more we was in her presence.

Finally snapping her head around to look at us her attention diverted as she focused in on me, her scowl was frightening as she looked me up and down.

'Can we get that to go please?' he asked, pausing for a moment. His hesitation confused me, as I tilt my head to the side looking at him.

'If you don't mind,' he added, looking up at this woman with the angry face. She had dark curly hair, frown lines and a slightly curvy frame.

'Sure, where you headed?' she enquired, turning to the counter behind her, only to return holding our food in paper bags, the grease soaking through the bottom and dripping to the floor. That is so gross, I thought staring at this heart attack waiting to happen.

'We're heading to Mystic River,' he said, proudly taking his change, and began ushering Payton and Ethan out of the diner.

'Good day to you all,' he said, very politely as they exited. I slowly began to raise from my seat, turning to walk out the door I was greeted with a sudden coldness washing over me, which quickly followed by pain. The waitress had gripped my wrist tightly pulling me closer as she leaned into me, I looked down at my reddening skin as her clasp got tighter and she got closer.

Feeling her breath hit my face was eye-watering, the smell of cigarettes filled the air as the stale cigarette smoke oozed from her pores.

'You don't want to go there, nothing but sadness awaits you there,' she said, her eyebrows furrowed with concern, and her eyes were wide and worried.

I could have sworn I saw her eye colour change, but I was more focused on the painful strong hold she had on my wrist, the bell rang as my father came back in to see what was taking me so long.

I wiggled my wrist with worry, looking up and back at my father. With her attention now averted I quickly swiped my wrist away rubbing it as I backed away from her, the cold imprint she left was like the feeling of darkness loneliness and regret all mixed into one.

'Mark my words child, your troubles are only beginning,' she said, pointing at me with her eyes still squinting at me.

Turning around I rushed out of the diner, making it outside I jumped into the car and took a shaky breath in.

Her words echoed in my ears for the next few miles, as I recalled the terror on her face.

'Annabeth, what's wrong?' Dad said, glancing at me. But I was unable to put into words my exact thoughts,

picture this, Dad the creepy diner lady with the killer grip, told me nothing good will await me in our new home, I'm sure that would go down so well.

My father's great idea to get me to eat something was shoving a grease filled burger under my nose, which I politely declined as I looked at the aged soggy bun.

As the morning drew in Dad put on his headlights to increase vision, as a deep fog had set in, in the early hours looking up I screamed.

'Stop!' I cried, holding onto the dashboard.

My father slammed on the breaks, the wheels screeching across the gravel and grinding to an abrupt halt.

'What is it?' he yelled, rendering me speechless for a moment, completely frozen to my seat as the colour began draining from my face.

'Annabeth, what's wrong?' he snapped. Worry filled his face as he sat looking at me.

I was lost for words, finding myself unable to answer him. He reached for my arm and began slowly shaking me.

'Annabeth, will you answer me?' he said, holding my hand.

I glanced quickly over my shoulder at Payton. Ethan looked at me in horror, Payton remaining as dramatic as ever as she sat clutching her chest.

'It was nothing, I just thought I saw something,' I said, shrugging my shoulders.

'Well don't do that again,' he mumbled, reaching for his chest. 'I nearly had a stroke,' he added, taking in deeper breaths to calm himself.

'Okay I'm sorry, maybe I just need sleep,' I replied, tapping my head to try and centre myself.

I chuckled a little to hide my true feelings, he started the car again continuing down the dark fog filled road.

'Do me a favour, don't do that again I nearly wet my pants,' Payton said to me, rather sarcastically.

Glaring at her I poke my tongue out forcefully in pure frustration, I am eighteen in a couple of weeks and in all honesty, she still knows how to bring my immaturity out in me, which bugged the hell out of me at times. Not wishing to stoop to her level, I ignored her as we continued the rest of the journey in silence.

# Chapter 2
## The home from hell

When we finally arrived, it was quite clear our father had not done his research properly on the house. Pulling up the drive I stuck my head out the window. It was like looking into a dark scary graveyard, everything was wilted as far as my eyes could see.

'Oh, so this is where everything comes to die?' I scoffed, looking out the window, whilst taking a closer look at everything.

Every plant was dead apart from a big bush to the right of our drive which was the only life I could see, apparently even the birds had migrated.

'Annabeth, do you have to?' he tutted, clenching his fists in anger only to loosen them again.

Deep down he knew I was right. Does anything even grow here? Who even sold us this house?

The paving leading up to the house was cracked, uneven and raised, this was extremely funny to Ethan, as he leant down wiggling his little bottom before pouncing onto each crack individually like a little frog.

The picture we saw of the house was not completely accurate, this house was dull lifeless and boring,

given the fact we actually didn't see the house in person as it was so far away. My father was obviously desperate to move for reasons unknown to me, it was unlike him to not completely vet a place before moving to it though.

'Hmm looks like it could use some doing up,' he said. Bringing his foot up he kicked the front step, causing a crashing sound to occur as the railing fell off, rolling my eyes I look at him in disbelief.

'It's going to need a lot more than just doing up,' I said, making sure he caught my sarcasm.

I began walking towards this death trap of a house, slowly scanning my surroundings to avoid injury.

Pausing for a moment my ears focused, hearing my little brother Ethan counting the steps behind me as he climbed them. My father quickly reminded me that I would need to go into town and look for a job, this was apparently to teach me valuable life lessons that nothing in life is free.

'Got it?' he said, holding both thumbs up at me.

'I sure do Dad, no worries,' I responded, attempting to raise my thumb, but much less enthusiastic. Like it was back in the old days of the Coliseum, as soon as his back was turned, I lowered my thumb to the ground.

'Kill him,' I thought, sniggering to myself.

Luckily for him we are in no such time, so my extremely fortunate father was quite safe.

I had only one year of school left and truth be told I didn't even know what I wanted to do after, I was however saving everything I could for when I gained some independence, how I longed for this day to come.

Plus, a job would stop me from having to help with this house.

I sighed as I finished climbing the stairs to the front porch, running my hand up the side of the wood noticing it was chipping on the banister as damp and rot had set in. The front door was a dusty blue with cobwebs nestled in its corners, hanging baskets either side of the door frame with dead overgrown weeds laid inside.

It was quite obvious no one had lived here for quite some time, it was no surprise my father was mailed the keys; so when we arrived we could go straight in. However, when I got closer the rickety door handle opened with ease with a creak as it's desperation for repair was quite clear, that even the house was screaming. Isn't that going to get annoying?

Walking in Ethan latched to my legs, refusing to loosen his grip I stumbled through the door onto the welcome mat in the front entrance, a puff of dust clouded my face as I spluttered struggling for breath, looking up to my surprise was a woman standing in a black suite with welcome cookies.

'Who are you?' I asked, standing to my feet, pulling Ethan closer.

I tried asking as politely as I could as I glared at this stranger in my kitchen, I'm not sure it was really the tone I was actually going for, but it will do.

'Yeah, who are you?' Ethan said, his tone less intimidating, but equally extremely sweet.

'Hello my name is Katrice,' she said, raising her eyebrows. Her smile instantly annoyed me, quickly followed by a sneer from me. What is she after?

'I am the local real-estate agent here, I'm responsible for selling you this lovely home,' she said, folding her arms together as she stared at us.

'Hmm, fascinating,' she said, smiling at me.

She unfolding her arms and reached behind her, picking up a plate filled with fresh cookies.

Looking down I see Ethan beginning to fidget, licking his lips in a round-circle desperate for a cookie. I scoffed accidently at the notion, before I knew it the words flew out in an instant.

'Lovely hmm, needs some serious work,' I said, bringing my fingers to my mouth, to try and shush myself. Her eyes dart towards my forehead as she looks me up and down, I waited patiently for a response.

16

'What an unusual hair style,' she said, taking a step forward, I proceeded to move backwards as my father walked through the front door.

'Hello Katrice, how are you?' he asked, his smile widened, as his eyes became lustful.

I glared at him, wondering why he was so friendly and where in the hell that smile came from. My eyes traced back towards her in anger as I eyeballed her closely. Who in the world is this woman? I'm quite sure she can't just be an estate-agent.

'I'm fine thank you, Clay. I know the house needs work but I'm sure you are up to the job,' she said, her eyes wide and lustful, as she pushed out her chest.

'Well, I like it,' Payton shouts, putting her earphones back in. Her smile becomes wide as she goes to explore the house before I could, winking at me as she dashed out the room in a hurry. What a total cow, I thought, knowing full well I was about to do the same.

'I am more than sure you will be happy here,' Katrice said, leaning forward, smiling sweetly, she flicked her red hair over her shoulder as she laughed with my father.

'Would you be interested in a movie sometime?' she said, balancing her arm on the kitchen counter, pushing her chest closer towards my father.

'Hussy!' I said, with wide eyes.

My thoughts were uncontained as I spoke out-loud again, honestly, I really have to stop doing that. I move back slightly with some resistance adjusting my stance, readying myself for the telling off of a lifetime and bracing myself for its impact.

'Annabeth,' he said, in a disappointing tone.

Oh lord, I know that look I'm in trouble now. I tried to move further back in my attempts to create more distance between us, earning me another glance, stopping still I waited for my punishment.

'Curse this woman!' I mumbled, in a low tone.

Luckily it was low enough not to be heard, I smirked pleased with myself for not projecting loudly for once.

'It's fine really, I had better be going anyway,' she said, lifting one shoulder.

She quickly started walking towards the door, her heels tapping on the hard wooden floors as she made her way to the front entrance. My brother still clinging to my legs as I tried to take a step forward, I had almost forgotten he was there, lifting my leg I began shaking it in attempt for freedom.

'Will I see you again?' Dad said, his tone shortened and to the point.

He was like a lovesick puppy, causing a little sick to rise to the back of my throat as I rolled my eyes.

'If you would like, there is always that movie,' she said, turning back and smiling politely.

As she turned, she batted her unusually long lashes at my father. Lowering my gaze, I looked at Ethan, he did his best imitation of his little pukey face where he rolls his eyes back and pretends to wretch, he is literally my favourite little human. Our father looking back giving us the evil eyes, before turning back around and waving goodbye to Katrice, taking a deep breath as he closed the door. Taking a fighting stance, I pushed Ethan backwards freeing myself from his grip, I crouched down low looking Ethan dead in the eyes and whispered.

'Run!' I said, laughing a little.

His little legs instantly moving with neither one of us knowing where we are going, but knowing I had the unfair advantage over him as his legs are so small.

'Too easy!' I said to myself smugly, as I dart in the opposite direction.

His playful little screams echo through the front room as my dad chased after him, gently bringing him to the ground and tickling him to the point of barely breathing, I came back into the room and trapped my foot under the sofa causing me to fall on my face, my motion felt slowed down, a sick cosmic joke meaning I could watch it more closely, I face planted the floor causing them both to laugh hysterically.

Did I forget to mention how incredibly clumsy I am?

But that laugh was worth it as it was a laugh I had not heard in a while, the laughing stops and my dad looks at me with his tickling gradually slowing.

'What's wrong?' I said, with minimal eye contact.

He pressed his lips firmly together causing his chin to bunch and tighten, leaning forward I rolled onto my stomach looking on at him with anticipation. Knowing full well I'm not going to like what he is going to say, I eagerly awaited my fate. Or was I, maybe I might be wrong?

'You have to be more respectful of other people Annabeth, Katrice is a nice and kind woman and I'd like to get to know her better,' he said, with another deep breath and a change in posture.

Nope I was right I didn't like it. Get to know her better? Is he joking! I thought to myself as my eyebrows pinched together. But I nodded out of respect.

'Daddy, can I go play?' Ethan asked, with an impatient smile. He rose up to his feet tapping on the spot trying to contain himself.

'Of course, you can,' he replied, nodding for him to leave. Thinking dad was finished with both of us, I got to my feet ready to leave too. I soon realised he wasn't done

19

with me as I watched a free Ethan rush off through the house. 'Lucky little devil,' I thought, as the jealousy flushed my cheeks. Looking back at my father I noticed his expression was pained, seeing the wheels turning as he chose his words carefully.

'Now you have school on Monday, so that gives you the weekend to find a job,' he said, nodding in my direction. Of course, how could I forget? It's not like I need a life.

'Yes, Dad,' I said, in a weary tone.

I go to turn moving towards the stairs to see what room Payton had left me with, my father called to me stopping me in my tracks.

'Annabeth,' he said, in a lightened tone.

I stopped on the spot, kicking my foot out I slowly turned around to see what he wanted.

'I will be going into town in a minute, did you want to come?' he said, with a wide smile.

Is he serious right now? I had to seriously resist the urge to say no, I haven't even looked at the house yet and already we have to go into town.

'Sure,' I said, shrugging both my shoulders.

I know it's annoying but what was I going to do? I slumped against the kitchen counter awaiting further instructions, as my father ordered a dancing Payton to watch Ethan. Her smile soon vanished as she glared at me.

'Right then, she is watching Ethan, and you're coming with me,' he said, slightly giddy, with a newfound spring in his step.

I followed closely hunching my body forward dropping my hands to my sides, I made my way to the car dragging my heels behind me. Climbing back into our little estate car as if I hadn't already spent enough time in it already, I realised there was more on his mind, he began stroking his moustache and curling it at the corners.

'Can you just try?' he said, looking at me with a saddened expression.

Pinching between my brows I look to my left, my eyebrows furrowed as my expression dulled, folding my arms I looked back at him in anger.

'I am trying,' I said, through gritted teeth. Knowing he would respond with.

'Well try harder,' I said, at the same time to try and lighten the mood, well it didn't work, it only made his eyebrows raise and then lower, as if he was surprised and angry at the same time.

'Okay, I'm sorry,' I said, reluctantly as we set off.

'It really doesn't seem like you're trying, Annabeth,' he muttered, looking out to the road.

'I really am Dad, but who knows how long we will be here for this time,' I said before thinking.

'Please I plan on making this the last stop for a while,' he said, half smiling at me.

'Do you really mean it?' I said, looking on in shock.

'Yes of course I mean it, well this time at least,' he said, gripping the steering wheel firmly.

That was his first mistake, I roll my eyes in a bigger circle this time as the images flashed through my head rapidly, recalling every time my father had said those words to me. Each time I had forgotten like a dream that never came to pass, and I forgave just as quick as the last time he spoke those words. I folded my arms again and just agreed, by this point I was so done with this conversation.

The journey into town was quiet, you could hear our tired car rumble and clang, we had money for a new one, but my father wouldn't part with this old girl as it was my mother's favourite model, and they don't make these anymore. Even though there was a hole in the footwell, and you could literally see the ground rushing past through it, my father loved it all the same.

'Funny, I thought the years of the Flintstones were long past,' I joked, chuckling a little to myself.

Making my father roar with laughter, my laughs matching his as we giggled away, looking over at my father's now softened features I couldn't help but think this town might be good for him.

'Better start running then,' he said, as my sides began to hurt. Sitting back in my seat and re-adjusting my seat belt, I looked out the window at my new home, longing for something more and itching to see the world.

My father pointed out the school me and Payton will be attending, just outside of the school the plaque read.

'Everbeam High,' I said, as I spoke the words.

'What a ridiculous name,' I added, nudging my father a little with a grin.

'Yes, but nevertheless that's where you're going,' he said, with a slight smile.

We continued on the road a little longer till we got to the towns peak, we pulled over into a designated parking space and my father missed the curb by inches on account of his awful parking skills. The town was big with greenery everywhere, flowers remaining in full bloom surrounding you with bright and beautiful colours. The shops were all at the front in an oval shape, it was a bit of an oddly shaped town, but it was appealing.

The houses were at the back of the shops in separate little dwellings, quite confusing but weirdly beautiful in their individual plots. Getting out of the car we walk towards the middle of the town, there was a little seated area like a park but completely open, looking closer the houses were everywhere with seemingly separate ways and backstreets to get to them. As I look further up and into the distance there is a trail that goes up and off into the mountains, I can't quite contain my interest as to where it goes, as I continue to stare my father snaps me back to reality.

'Did you see the fountain.' he smiles, pointing right at it. Given the fact you can't really miss it as it is right in front of us, still I shook my head staring at him blankly.

'No I didn't, must have missed it,' I said, with one eyebrow up and my cheeks raised.

He of course knew I was lying as you could not miss it as it was so big, with a beautiful stone angel residing in the middle. When suddenly it was turned on, water shot out from the angel's mouth, but something was weirdly off, as it started to shake slightly.

Bubbles soon started to rise and fall off of the sides, rising before our very eyes as it began to spill over, me and my father stood staring.

'Kids,' we heard below from behind us.

Turning to face the voice we saw a little old man approaching us with a limp, his face pains with every step he takes.

'Kids did this, but why it's so beautiful?' I asked, as the chords in my neck tightened.

'Not from around here, are you?' he said, tilting his hat at us.

'How could you tell?' I said, with my teeth clenched. My forced smile causing my face to ache, earning me a look from my father that suggested I should stop.

'We've actually just moved here,' my father replied.

'Well sir, there is plenty more where that came from,' the old man responded, as he quietly moved past us.

'Good day to you,' he said, tilting his hat at us.

'Good day to you, sir,' my father politely replied.

'Welcome to Fenby,' he said, continuing his walk.

I watched as the old man hobbled away, when he was finally out of ear shot, I looked at my father.

'What the hell is Fenby?' I said, staring at him as if he could actually give me an answer.

'He said Fenby, are we somewhere else?' I added, confusion laced my face. Unsure if I heard him correctly, I searched my father's face for clues. He didn't answer right away, why would he. The pause in his response was agitating me, why is he so quiet all of a sudden.

'I don't know, I'm not quite sure if he's alright. Should we get him help?' he said, looking around for him.

I staired at him some more completely clueless as to what had just happened.

'What the hell is Fenby?' I thought, not wanting to ask any more questions. Where they hell are we? The flaming towns people don't even know where they are! Granted he was old, but he's been here longer than anyone. Oh lord, things can only get better.

# Chapter 3
## Ask and you shall receive

My father decided he would be going to the store alone, sending me off in another direction to start my search.

'Annabeth start going store to store, whilst I go food shopping,' he nodded, shooing me away.

I stood on the spot as he gets further away from me, my stare confused as I watch him abandon me in a town I barely knew. Walking down the streets I worked on my speech, I began trolling the stores with help wanted signs in the windows, only for them to quickly be removed by the shop assistants soon after my visit. Why is this so hard, I thought heading to the next one with sheer determination.

'I've been here for a matter of hours, and already I'm job hunting,' I thought, as I stomped down the path.

Making my way from store to store getting rejected everywhere I turned, it became obvious people didn't want to hire someone they had just met. Walking closer towards the bushes my hands brushed across the soft leaves, I continue walking as I intertwined my fingers around the leaves for comfort. Walking across the road I noticed a restaurant with a help wanted sign in the window, getting closer I noticed the sign said restaurant sixty-six. The writing on the door was slanted and the outside almost looked brand new, with a black exterior and half frosted windows just enough to cover the guests whilst they dined. When you walk inside there are private booths situated all around, black décor with a hint of white to brighten the place. To my right was a girl at the entrance, her eyes were wired as she watched me closely but before I could utter a word.

'Hi my name is Shay, are you here to make a booking?' she asked, twiddling her hair.

Her beauty was intimidating, she was that beautiful her face should belong on the front of vogue; I quickly shook my head smiling politely at her.

'No actually I'm here about a job, you know the help wanted sign?' I said, pointing towards the front window.

'Owe how exciting, did you just move here?' she said, moving towards me quickly.

'Yes, how did you,' I said, before she cut me off.

'Well you don't scream town girl, and I would know you if you was from here,' she said, tapping her cheek.

I realised she was actually from here, turning back around heading back to her desk she sat and began shifting paperwork through her fingers, looking back up at me she flicked her long shiny hair out of her face and over her shoulder.

'Okay I will let the boss know,' she said, as she began to move.

'Cool should I come back or?' I said, standing awkwardly in the doorway.

'No, wait here,' she said, holding her hand out for me to stay. 'Quick thing though,' she added, with a worried expression.

'Yeah, what's that?' I said, furrowing my brows at her.

'Don't stare,' she said, with serious eyes.

Before I could ask her more, she hoped off her chair and ran to the back, she can't have been gone for more than a couple of minutes when she skipped back towards me.

'The boss will see you now,' she said, with a big grin.

'Oh so quickly, why?' I said, anxiously.

'I said you are pretty,' she said, quickly without hesitation.

'You said what?' I snapped, pulling my jacket closed.

'Relax I am only joking, I just said a girl was here for the job. What's your name by the way?' she said, as she examined me closely.

'Erm, Annabeth,' I said, tugging at my jacket.

Taking hold of my arm she pushed me in the direction of his office, my mouth was now drier than the Sahara Desert, it's complete lack of moisture meant my tongue was now sticking to the sides of my teeth. Seriously, why am I so nervous.

'His office is down the back, take a left and it's at the end of the hall,' she said, with a beaming smile.

The corridor suddenly got longer, the walls felt like they are closing in yet getting bigger at the same time, standing beside me she continued pointing down the gloomy looking corridor. Turning to face her I noticed she was a very tall girl, she was muscular but not too muscular, her hair is a mismatch of colours, mousy brown on the top and then medium brown towards the ends.

With a real preppy spring in her step, she turned around to walk away, looking over her right shoulder she said in a much quieter voice.

'Good luck,' she said, bouncing when she walks away.

'Why do I need luck?' I thought, as my face saddened.

Thinking about it I'm probably much happier that she didn't say 'break a leg,' because as my luck would have it, that actually sounded more plausible than me getting this job. Looking around I inhaled loudly, I walked down the hall doing as she said, having no time to prepare anything made my anxiety higher, everything was screaming at me to just leave but before I knew it, I had taken a left and was already at the door. I knocked twice and waited for a response, anxiously I knocked again to be met with silence once more.

'Am I being punked?' I said, out loud kicking myself for doing it again.

I took another deep breath and opened the door, swinging it open with force which of course I didn't mean to do, banging into the wall as it opened, crashing into something hard as it bounced back slightly hitting my arm.

'Wow that door is really light,' I said, with a worried expression. Trying to make sure I had not damaged the wall, I ran my hand against it checking for any defects.

'That was quite the entrance, is my wall okay?' I heard this voice bellow from behind me. That gruffy tone sent butterflies rushing through my stomach, it was a deep voice and slightly raspy, I jumped slightly making my knee hit the cabinet, I yelped accidently moving forward I knocked it again, sending a vase crashing to the floor as it shattered into small pieces.

'Clumsy, aren't you?' he said, as the corners of his mouth pinched outward.

'I am so sorry,' I said, as I turned to face the voice I had heard.

Seeing instantly why she told me not to stare, blinking twice I then smiled. The man before me had four evenly spaced scars running across his eye and halfway down his cheek, he was devilishly handsome even with his scar, but he was far too old for me. Or was he?

'If I ask you to sit, will you break anything else?' he said, showing his perfectly straight teeth. His smile got me, he is absolutely too old for me but equally exceptionally good looking. I took in a gulp as he started to ask me questions, it was more of an interrogation really, as he leaned towards me his elbows rested on the desk in front of him.

'Take a seat,' he said, gesturing in front of him.

'Where are you from?' he asked, in a formal tone.

'California,' I said, answering as quickly as I could.

'How old are you?' he asked, as he staples his hands in front of him staring at me.

Not answering him right away I rubbed my clammy hands together, wiping them on my jeans to dry them.

'How old are you?' he said, as his face narrowed.

'Seventeen,' I responded.

I will admit though, I wasn't entirely sure why that mattered.

'What's your name?' he said, clamping his hands together, and cracking his knuckles.

Of all the questions he should have asked first, surely it should have been that one?

'Annabeth,' I replied.

These questions continued when he finally smiled and it quite literally nearly floored me, how was he so beautiful, it should be a crime against humanity to make a man that perfect. My mouth finally moistened, catching myself drooling I wiped my mouth before he noticed. I patiently waited as he continued to look at me when a smile arose from the corners of his mouth.

'You're hired, go and see Shay, she will show you the ropes,' he said, dismissing me with a wave.

I hesitated for a moment worried my legs might give out before replying. 'Thank you so much,' I said with excitement. Springing to my feet I tried to remain cool, brushing my jacket off and pulling at the corners to close it backing away from him slowly, his laughter filled the air. What a wonderful sound.

'Oh gosh,' I said, as my knee buckled, as I attempted to close the door.

My stomach now full of flutters I closed the door behind me, as soon as I was out of ear shot, I ran back up to Shay excitedly.

'I got the job,' I said, bouncing on the spot.

'Well now, we had better get you a uniform,' she said, visually scanning over my frame.

Her eyes checking over me slowly, getting to my chest she reached for me.

'Absolutely not, hands off,' I said, slapping her hand away.

'Relax would you, I am trying to figure out your size, not trying to get into your pants,' she replied, in a shocked voice.

She was about as shocked as I was at this point, I have to admit now she mentioned it that actually made a lot more sense.

'Why is there something wrong with me?' I asked, my smirk small and barely present.

'I am only messing with you,' I said, holding eye contact for a moment longer.

I leaned against the front desk exhausted from my interrogation, she walked back around and flopped into her chair sighing in relief.

'Hmm you're a size eight,' she said, looking me up and down again like a prized cow.

'Wow you're good,' I said, leaning over the desk slightly.

Her smile began to beam, and her body language finally settled, it was far too easy to rattle her cage given the fact of just how preppy and upbeat she was. Mental note if I want to be her friend, I shouldn't do that again. I laughed to myself, as if I didn't already come across as a perverted weirdo.

'You will be working every other evening with me, as I'm sure we will both be going to school together?' she said, raising her brows whilst clearing her throat.

'Only if you go to Everbeam High?' I asked, quietly. She nodded excitedly, I still stood awkwardly in front of the reception desk unsure on what I should do, when suddenly it dawned on me.

'I had better go and tell my dad,' I said, bolting upright.

'Our shift starts tomorrow at 5:30pm,' she smiled, nodding for me to leave. I nodded in response as I turned on my heels still excited rushing out to find my dad, I tripped on the matt at the entrance in a fluster, causing me to fly out the front door and into the street straight into oncoming traffic. As I crashed to the floor my father screamed as a car grounded to a halt, it was a black Mercedes and it was perfect, I almost felt like I'd have been horrified if I damaged it.

Sitting for a moment I stared into space when the door to the car flung open, and out came this boy causing a flash of wind to sweep towards me, with it brought the smell of sunshine and fresh rainwater. My head was all in a daze and my adrenaline was pumping, unable to move completely frozen to this spot, I felt around the ground making sure I was still alive. Looking up I saw this handsome boy before me, he was like nothing I had ever seen before but his face was angry.

'Maybe I should listen to him?' I thought, as I looked at him more closely.

I continued to lay on the floor with this boy now towering over me, letting my ears adjust I looked up to him screaming at me. Why is he so damn angry?

'I could have killed you, you idiot!' he screamed, bringing his face down to my level.

This was not the welcome my mind had concocted, or indeed longed for.

'What the hell is the matter with you?' he added, lowering himself further to my level.

'Bub?' was all I could say at this point.

I was too busy examining his face and taking in that scent, my nostrils began to flare as I inhaled deeply.

How could one person smell this amazing? He is cute too with black hair, hazel eyes, a chiselled jawline with a slight stubble and he was impeccably dressed might I add with a black tailored suit and red tie.

'Oh great, are we sure I didn't hit this clumsy girl?' he snapped, looking around for answers.

'No sir, you didn't hit her,' Shay replied. I saw Shay bow before him with her head low to the ground.

'What kind of shit is this?' I said, in a daze blinking quickly.

'Oh lord, I've broken her; it was her fault!' he said, pointing at me frantically.

My father got in my face trying to pull me back to normality as he bent down in front of me, completely shadowing that scent made things easier to concentrate.

'Excuse me! I fell I will have you know,' I snapped, his rude behaviour was now fully vexing me.

'On what, you silly girl?' he said, his tone becoming more aggressive.

'Your flaming front welcome mat!' I said, as my anger began to boil. My father tried to make me stand, I sat for a moment longer still in shock as my hands trembled.

'Oh yeah because that's better, isn't it?' he said, his tone was sharp, and his tongue venomous.

I know he is shouting at me but oh lord that face has me weak, it's a good job I'm on the floor already if I'm being honest. A thousand thoughts rush my mind at once, all of them were of a potential future and what our babies would look like.

What the hell was this? I barely know this boy and already I'm running off into the sunset with this arrogant git. Breaking my trance my father's voice echoing beside me.

'We are leaving, please move out of the way sir,' he said, in a polite tone.

I could tell by Shay's face he had never been spoken to like that before, I stood to my feet still a little shaken but the further away from him I got the better off my thoughts became.

'What a weird experience that was,' I said.

'What do you mean?' Dad asked, his voice guarded.

'That boy smelt like rain and sunshine,' I said, aware of how crazy that sounded.

Looking at him I tilted my head to the side, usually even with my wildest thoughts he would have appeased me by answering, but today he remained completely silent all the way home not uttering a word. I was too confused and still too fixated to care, my mind was running wild as that boy kept popping in and out of it.

The car wasn't small, but I began to feel claustrophobic, the feeling of being unable to breathe came on quickly like someone had just placed a weight on my chest. Opening the window fully I stuck my head outside to try and clear my thoughts and calm my nerves, but it didn't work, to avoid panicking I counted the seconds before we would finally arrive home. A little while later we finally approached the gates to our drive, my father got out to open it when it fell off of its hinges.

I snort trying not to laugh as I watched him drag it across the ground, his face turning a strained red as his lips curled under, his feet stamped into the ground as he leaned backwards making him give up. When an overly excited Ethan and a slightly less enthusiastic Payton met us in the front drive.

'He isn't cool to hang out with for long you know! next time I'm coming to town and Annabeth can look after him, got it?' she said, putting her earphones in and returning inside. The question was more rhetorical she was great at those, never willing to give you the last word.

'Finally, Dad can I see my room now? Payton has probably got the best one,' I said, frowning at him from the car.

'Of course, just help me with these bags first,' he said, lifting one from the boot of the car.

Reluctantly I helped unload the bags from the boot, looking inside I realised he had brought his favourite ingredients, I frowned angrily now searching for snacks, only to be disappointed by what I found. Apples, since when do we buy those?

'Oh lord this only means one thing,' I said, bending down in front of me. Whispering loud enough to Ethan who was trailing behind me holding some crisps, blissfully unaware with his mouth wide open as he pummelled as many crisps as he could in.

'Company,' I said, as he began to chant and repeat everything I just said.

He's the type of little boy who will tell your secrets to anyone who will listen, once Ethan told a man I was on my period because I was being grumpy, to say I was mortified would be an understatement.

The kind of child who pokes holes in his Christmas presents because he cannot wait to see what Santa has brought him, very impatient but equally adorable.

'God, I hope Katrice isn't coming for dinner,' I thought, thanking the heavens that my inner thoughts finally remained inwards.

Finally getting inside I placed the shopping on the kitchen counter, disappointingly reaching for an apple as it was the only thing to snack on as my father unpacked the shopping. Before he could interrupt me, I silently backed away to try and find my second-rate room, I should have run for it when we got here.

Stupid Payton always getting the upper hand as my father rarely made her do anything she didn't want to do, the-apple-of-his-eye you might say. However much trouble we find ourselves in Payton always manages to escape unscathed, but as for me well I'm never quite so lucky. Never mind, I'm sure whatever I'm left with will be worth it.

# Chapter 4
## Dinner for two

After finally finding my room I walked inside, I was on the third floor making me feel like Cinderella banished to the attic, of course I'm being dramatic but climbing these stairs after work or one too many is going to be interesting. Do not get me wrong we are not rich, it was a slender house that just had three floors.

Walking into my room I looked around, the window caught my attention straight away as it gave me a direct view across the lake that runs down the back of our home, I paused for a moment as I took in its beauty,

looking back to my room I decided to only unbox the essentials, as I am not totally sure how long I would be here for, sad but true as the nature of my father's job can take us anywhere at any given time.

After opening some of my stuff and placing it strategically so if my sister even so much as touches it I will know, I now felt like a total master mind that I finally went downstairs.

Peering through the door, I saw my father panicking as he had forgotten one of the main ingredients to his masterpiece.

'Dad when's the guest coming?' I said smugly.

'Read me like a book you can,' he said, half smiling at me, as he continued his search.

'Dad when you buy your best dish, I know somethings up,' I laughed, waiting for him to confirm what I already knew.

But he didn't he just stood adjusting his tie and shirt, sweat filling his forehead, as he uncomfortably tugged at his fingers. Unable to take much more I placed my hand on his arm, to stop his fingers from tapping loudly on the kitchen side, that he was now slumped over.

'Look you go and get what you need, I will continue to prep,' I said, through gritted teeth.

He looked at me so grateful, it was sweet at how nervous he was. After all this time, it was apparent this was a massive step for him to do.

'Oh, thank you,' he said, as he grabbed his keys off of the side going to run out the door.

'Remember I need the car later for work,' I said, quickly to grab his attention, making him pause and turn to face me.

'Work?' he said, looking at me puzzled.

'Oh shoot, yeah I completely forgot, I got a job at that place I fell out of yesterday,' I said, smiling awkwardly.

'That's brilliant, congratulations,' he said, pulling me into a hug. Why can I feel a but coming on?

His hesitation filled me with unnecessary hope that for once he would just let it go and leave without words.

'But please hear me' he said, staring at me.

'Ohh there it is,' I thought, my smirk getting bigger.

'Please be careful, and watch where you are going,' he said, with a worried tone.

'Okay I promise, be quick I start at five sharp,' I said, as I reached for the ingredients he did have.

This was indeed a lie, but I didn't know the place and I needed to get there early, as being new meant I knew nothing so I had to try and learn at least my way around so that I will not be in anyone's way.

A little while had passed and I finally finished all the prep work, it was now just up to him to cook it. After hearing the car pull into the drive, my father came through the door beaming from ear to ear.

'Pleased with yourself, are we?' I said, smiling at his happiness, not fully wanting any details or information I quickly interrupted his thoughts.

'Remember I will not be here for dinner tonight.' I said, thankfully as I didn't need to see my father flirting with anyone, especially Katrice.

'Oh, but I thought you would be here?' he said, with saddened eyes.

'Well Dad, whoever this mystery person is, you will just have to invite them again won't you,' I said, my eyes now wide and bulging.

After I spoke those words, realisation hit me that I had well and truly screwed myself over, let's hope I don't regret it.

'Right Dad I have to go, I'm not sure when my shift finishes but I will be home soon after it does,' I announced, grabbing my coat. Desperately trying to hurry out the door before Dad could say anything else.

'Don't forget your phone, I don't accept that, you text me as soon as you know, okay?' he said, holding my phone out for me to take.

'Okay Dad, I will text you as soon as I know,' I said, shooting him a reassuring look.

'Deal,' he said, as he reached in for a big hug.

As he let go my legs were taken out by Ethan as he tackled me to the floor, his spirit was bright and bubbling, after giving his hair a ruffle he let me up, bending down he picked back up his plane and flew off in a flash.

'Damn that boy is fast,' Dad said, watching him run out the room.

'Bye Dad, I will text you later,' I said, waving as I backed out of the door. His gaze soon turned to fear as the stove caught on fire, fear flashed as he desperately tried to put it out. I made my way to the car placing my hands on my hips as I stared at it, realising I can't park this outside as it is quite beaten up, tutting I rolled my eyes as I would have to walk some of the way after parking it. Climbing into the car I adjusted the seat as my legs were not as long as my father's, I pulled the seat forward so I can reach the peddles. Pulling away I make my way to work with mixed feelings about my new job, who on earth is that boy that is now etched into my brain. My thoughts got me all the way to town, as I think about where I'm going to park this absolute death trap. After I got out and walked around for a while not fully know where I was, I managed to make my way back to town with only ten minutes to spare. I found myself running, my feet carrying me faster than my thoughts could travel. I originally left enough time to get to work and get settled, but now sadly I am just going to have to wing it.

Finally finding the restaurant I walked through the door noticing something had changed, I looked down to see the carpet had been removed.

'Oh great,' I sighed, as I continued through the door. Shay immediately snaps her head up so fast I half expected her to get whiplash, she was approaching me with my name badge and new uniform, holding it out like a trophy. The restaurant closes after lunch and then re-opens later to allow for turn around and no walk-ins.

'Why are no walk-ins so important?' I enquired.

'We just don't accept it, it's one of the rules,' she replied, annoyed as if I should have known.

'Rules?' I said, blinking at her in confusion.

'Don't worry, you will learn them with time,' she said, shoving me to the back room to go and put my uniform on.

I went out the back to the changing room, it was quite creepy in here without anyone coming in and out, I put on my uniform it wasn't much just a pair of black trousers a white shirt and a tie, unlucky for me I realised I am wearing my pink converse's.

'What an idiot,' I thought, as I stare at my shoes. Getting myself together I walk out before walking back into Shay, my shoes are aluminous and shining.

'What's on your feet?' she said, staring at them.

'I'm sorry I forgot my work shoes,' I said, swallowing hard and avoiding eye contact. Shaking her head she pulled me towards the front desk, sitting me in her chair and showing me how to deal with customers and how to search the system for reservations.

It was <u>about 6:40pm when</u> the smell of sunshine and fresh rainwater hit my nostrils, what an unusual feeling. Pushing those feelings to the back of my head the door opened, Shay instantly stood up as I awkwardly stared at him, my face flushed as his eyes connected with mine.

'Mr Grayson,' she said, as she bowed at him.

Was this going to be a thing because I certainly was not going to bow at this man, I remained in my seat and continued to push papers even though I had no idea what they were, or currently what I was doing other than making a mess. The scent hit me again as he was standing right before me, leaning in his heated breath inches away from me as he closely examines my face.

'Personal space, if you please?' I said, with furrowed brows. I lean backwards creating distance between us, the look of horror on Shay's face was a picture.

40

'I will do as I please, are you that clumsy girl from yesterday?' he said, still staring at me.

'What if I am? Were you the one driving?' I replied, my face hollowed, as my expressionless features watched his every move.

He smirked at me and walked away.

'Are you stupid?' Shay said.

'What do you mean?' I said, my anger now growing.

'You of all people should know,' she said, her expression now blank.

I saw a tiny light bulb go off in her eyes as if someone had replaced her thoughts rendering her useless, I sat waving my hand back and forth in front of her frozen motionless face, but she didn't move. I was about to call the emergency services when she finally came back around, carrying on with her work as if nothing happened.

'I should know what?' I said, trying to push the issue, still wondering what the hell just happened.

'That it's not a good idea to annoy your boss's son on your first day,' she huffed, looking at my face to see if I believed her.

'He's the boss's son. Woah!' I said, very sarcastically throwing my arms in the air.

'Oh lord, are we going to make it through this shift?' she said, with a worried expression.

I laughed but I got the sense she was not joking, I kept my head down and continued to do my job.

'What time does our shift finish?' I said, tapping her shoulder.

'Ten-thirty, why?' she said, with an inquisitive look.

'It's okay I just have to message my dad,' I said, smiling politely reaching for my phone.

The evening went much quicker than usual by now I have learnt the basic stuff on reception, everyone else had to remain behind to close up but I was allowed off shift early, this was unusual, but I wasn't about to complain. It was pitch black outside I rushed to my family car to find that the old crapped out thing wouldn't start, giving it a swift kick, I hit the bumper and a sharp pain ran up my leg, it was the type of unexplainable feeling when you stub your toe.

'Are you kidding me!' I said, slamming my hands on the bonnet. Getting under the hood I attempt to diagnose the problem, I don't know why I thought I could.

A black Mercedes drives past me at speed before screeching to a halt and slowly reversing back in front of me, the window winds down slowly revealing Luca Grayson's grinning face.

'Need some help?' he said, slowly scanning my car.

'Not from you, the car is fine,' I said, tapping the bonnet with a grimace smile.

'Oh no, your cars in need of some serious help,' he laughed, pointing his finger at me.

'Listen here bud, if you have stopped merely to make funny jokes then hit the road!' I said, pointing in the opposite direction not fully knowing where I planned on sending him. His angry eyes stared at me for a moment, I could have sworn they were black, I rubbed my eyes for a second looking at him again.

'Get in!' he said, with a slight growl.

Before I knew it my feet were moving as I sprinted to the other side of his car, as the door opened, I hopped in.

'What the hell is this?' I thought, completely stunned.

'Now I don't need to ask where you are going, your house was the only house on the market and has been for some time,' he stated, rather happy with himself.

I was sat with my arms folded annoyed at how quickly I ran into this damn car, my thoughts muffled as I kept darting my attention to his hands, his veins were bulging, he had the kind of veins a nurse would love to get her hands on and resisting the urge to hold his hand was torture.

'Why so sour?' he asked, with an aggressive tone.

'I am not sour, I'm just not in the right company!' I said, noticing him pulling up my drive.

'Hmm sure you're not, lighten up a little would you,' he snapped, gripping the steering wheel.

That fresh rain smell hit me again, my eyes widened when I finally knew for sure it was coming from him, I opened the door and fell out the car, absolutely mortified I slammed the door closed behind me.

'A thank you would be nice?' he said, as he watched me scurry away, completely ignoring him.

My father was standing in the doorway ready to fire a million questions at me for being late.

'Dad that was a boy from work, the car died so he gave me a lift and that's why I'm home a little late.' I said, rendering my father speechless, as he blinked at me.

'Right, well don't let it happen again,' he said.

'Ohh believe me it won't!' I said, with such assurance that even I believed me.

# Chapter 5
## Time for school

After getting home late last night I could feel my father's eyes on me when I walked into the kitchen, he fixated on me like a leopard trying to catch his prey.

'So how was your date last night?' I said, trying to find out what he wants.

My poor attempt at communication did not work, I'm thinking the date didn't go well, in which case we can expect this mood to last a little while by the looks of things.

'It's school day today for you both, how are you planning on getting there?' he said, through gritted teeth.

Payton walked through the door with not a care in the world as she listens to her music, I must admit for the first time in our lives it was a relief to have her come through that door.

'I can't take you without the car,' he said, darting his eyes towards me.

'It's not my fault the car died Dad,' I said, a little annoyed at him for even saying it.

'Yes well, how am I going to get you there?' he asked, whilst pouring orange juice into glasses.

Suddenly I heard a car horn from outside, a welcomed reprieve from my father's current mood.

'That had better not be that Grayson boy!' he snapped, with a clenched fist. Closing my eyes, I hoped for the best praying to the heavens that it wasn't him, as if I need to explain anything else to my menstruating father. I know it's not possible for a man to menstruate, but I'm convinced they get something at least once a month. Anxiously looking through a crack I had made through the window, lifting the dusty curtains I saw Shay in the driveway, relief washed over me as I opened the door to Shay yelling at me.

'Heard you might need a lift?' she said, in her normal preppy tone.

'Thank you, hold on a second,' I said, closing the door again. 'Dad that's the girl I work with, she's offered me a lift,' I said, shouting at him as I ran back to my room to collect my bag.

As I stormed past them aiming not to be late on my first day, my mind was heavy as I couldn't help thinking I was forgetting something.

'Erm, Annabeth,' Payton snapped, tapping her heels on the floor.

'What is it? Can't you see I'm going to be late!' I said, furrowing my brows at her.

'You mean were going to be late?' she snapped again.

'Dad, can't she walk?' I said, with a slight stamp of my foot.

'In these shoes, you have to be kidding!' she yelled, pointing at her shoes. Shifting her stance, she folded her arms in front of her scowling at me.

'Annabeth please, I will take her as soon as the cars back,' he said, staring right through me.

Sizing my father up I detected that I didn't have a choice, she was coming with me whether I liked it or not and in all honesty I would prefer not.

'Fine,' I said, sighing heavily at him.

Me and my sister don't have a great relationship I don't know why but we have simply never gotten along, we barely speak and that was how we liked it without the added pressure to be in each other's company.

'Come on then, Payton,' I said, as I flung the door open.

Her wedged high heels clicking behind me as we left the house, my anger boiled anytime I was in my sister's company.

'Shay, can we possibly take my sister with us as well?' I asked, as my lips curled inwards.

'Twins?' she said, her eyes widened in shock.

'No not twins, plus we look nothing alike!' I said sharply, as I spat the words out.

'You can get the non-identical kind ya know!' she snapped, with a vein now appearing on her forehead.

'Oh, how silly of me,' we both laughed, but Payton just remained silent in the back seat.

'How did you know I needed a lift this morning?' I questioned, even though I think I already knew the answer.

'Who care's!' Payton said, irritated by the company.

'Mr Grayson, he told me your car wouldn't start last night and that I should come get you,' she said.

'He told you to come and get me, why do you listen to him?' I asked, not fully wanting a response.

Her lips began moving but I was no longer listening as my mind put me in a deepened daydream, my thoughts were getting the better of me, images raced fast paced through my mind that they are the local Mafia. A powerful family with no limitations, or they were the C.I.A and that they had some serious reaches. Oh maybe he's royalty?

'Gosh my imagination is wild, I need to chill myself out,' I thought, trying to slow my breathing. I've clearly spent too much time with my sister!

'Because they are important to me' she replied.

Now I know I should have left this here and just taken her at face value, but something bothers me about that family and I want to know what there deal is.

'Important are they your family as well? Are they part Chinese? Is that why you bow before them? Blink twice if they have abducted your family!' I said, frantically winking at her. Shay erupted into laughter, sensing it was an awkward laugh as she was obviously not sure if I was joking or not. Well I'm not, I want to know what is going on here, but I sense I will have to wait and see,

plus, her poker face is so good that she certainly wouldn't be giving up any information without a fight.

'They are like family to me yes,' she said, as her smile faded.

With her eyes now fixated on the road she was no longer making eye contact with me, sensing her tension I watched her fidgeting reaching for her necklace, placing the beads between her lips, and grinding it back and forth between her teeth.

I expect that's enough questions for today.

Pulling up to our new school Shay pulled into a spot on the parking lot which she claims is hers, the school was alive with students like a thousand hungry locusts, it certainly was wild, getting out of the car attracted even more attention as we walked towards the school. We cannot seriously be that interesting, everyone's eyes darted towards us making me feel like a bit of meat has been dangled before the lioness and they were blood thirsty and ready to pounce.

'Can we all agree they all look pissed?' Payton said, and for once I'm inclined to agree with her.

'Maybe they're just not use to new people?' I said, side eyeing everyone.

'Or maybe it's because your both fresh meat?' Shay implied, her grin now growing.

47

'That's it, I knew it!' Payton said, shaking her head and stepping backwards. 'Dad's brought us to some backwards, back alley carnivorous town, and we are going to die!' she said, her breathing now heavy.

I look upon her face as panic slowly sets in.

'Payton will you stop it, you watch too many scary movies! You need to stop with those as they are sending you mad,' I said, looking at Shay for reassurance.

Shay leaned against the car her face remained calm and her back arched, licking her hand she wiped the mud from her jacket that collected at the bottom of it, she stood rolling her tongue across the inner side of her cheek still remaining silent much to my dismay.

'Hello, help me out here?' I said, giving her a little shove.

Payton started to cry, her whaling now attracting more attention for all the wrong reasons, Shay roared with laughter as I tried to snap Payton out of it.

'Silly girl, no one is going to eat you,' she said, taking Payton's arm.

'You're too skinny. Not scared, are you?' Shay added, as she began tugging her in the direction of the school, Payton desperately trying to resist her.

'Who me? Scared, absolutely not,' she huffed.

As we continued walking towards the school a boy and a girl slowly approached us, Shay's feet were getting lighter as she began to bounce towards them.

'Shay, how you doing girl?' came this light-hearted voice with a beaming smile.

She was wearing low rise jeans a tank top and a leather jacket, her hair was ombre and slightly wavy with a bright smile, slightly crooked with a minimal overbite.

'Hey, Sis,' he said, as a husky deep voice rumbled from within him, peaking my sisters interests immediately as his tall muscular physic was on full show, his arms suffocating from the tight shirt he was wearing.

'Payton, Annabeth, this is my brother Paddox and my best friend Addison,' she said, pulling her brother in for a tussle, bringing her arm around his neck she dragged him down sharply whilst ruffling his hair.

'What a name,' I thought, as I watch my sister drool all over him.

It was like watching a documentary on a mating ritual gone wrong, stalking towards her prey, getting down low puffing out her chest and snapping up straight as she ran her fingers up his arm. Unable to contain my laughter as I looked at her with a raised eyebrow, partly cringing whilst I watch the scene unfold before me. I so wish David Attenborough wasn't in my head right now, it's making it so hard to concentrate, running my fingers over my eyes I let out a loud laugh.

'What's so funny.' Payton demanded.

'Oh sorry, absolutely nothing,' I said, as my smile turned upwards in an attempt to hold in my laughter.

It wasn't working, I had to somehow figure out a way to prevent my rumbling laughter from exploding. Thinking quickly as my attention was still fully on a mating ritual, I definitely had no interest in witnessing, I changed the subject quickly.

'So where are our first lessons?' I enquired.

Still trying to not look at my sister and her new boyfriend, although I have to admit he doesn't look the slightest bit interested in her which is a shame as I could do with her being out the house more.

49

'I can take you to reception, they will have all your information there,' she said, smiling sweetly at me.

'Sure thanks.' looking back I notice Payton still hanging from his arms, feeling his biceps whilst giggling like a child.

'Payton, move your arse!' I snapped, waving for her to come. If looks could actually kill you then I would have died a long time ago, seriously for a girl who says she is fine she needs to have a word with her face seen as that tells you a significantly different story.

After getting my stuff from the abnormally cranky receptionist, I finally found my first class. Mr Bleak was our English teacher, honestly if all the teachers names are like this I'm doomed.

'Can I have your attention please?' he announced to the class, 'We have a new class member,' he said, with a whistle to his voice.

As the loud whistles come from the Neanderthals in this class, I rolled my eyes in annoyance shifting my balance to my right hip as I crossed my arms.

'Please take a seat, Miss?' he asked eagerly.

'Annabeth,' I replied, not willing to engage too much in conversation as the whistling got louder.

'Okay take a seat, Annabeth,' he said, gesturing to the one at the back of the class.

I sighed in relief knowing I could hide out of the way and hopefully be left alone, seen as one of our teachers is unwell today so we are going to be in here for the next few hours, so a window seat is perfect for me.

Hours went past and I could hear the teacher speaking in the background, but my mind took me elsewhere, a tingling ran over my ears as they rang like a bell.

50

'Annabeth?' I heard, as my ears focused in bringing me out of my daydream.

Shocked I looked at him and realised his mouth was moving, I thought for a second on how long I must have ignored him for.

'Huh, erm yes sir?' I said, my eyes widen, as I realised, he was asking me a question, and I had outright ignored him.

'A speech from Romeo and Juliet, if you please?' he said, knowing full well I was not listening.

Closing my eyes as I desperately searched for a worthy chapter to recite, my eyelids flickering beneath closed eyes as I began to panic. Soon soothed as I found the perfect one, standing to my feet with confidence I cleared my throat before reciting the verse.

'Come gentle night, come loving black-Brow'd night, give me my Romeo; and when he shall die, take him and cut him out in little stars and he will make the face of heaven so fine, that all the world will be in love with night, and pay no worship to the garish sun,' I said, with a smug grin.

Jokes on him my identic memory made that speech flawless, a speech recited to perfection so that even he couldn't argue with that.

'Shall I recite another?' I said, knowing full well he would leave me alone for a while now.

'No, but nice save,' he said, smiling at me with a crooked vicious smile, as if I was invisible to him a mere shell unworthy of his presents.

The day was finally over, and it was time to go home and get ready for work, Payton of course being the social butterfly that she is made friends very quickly, as she tried out for the cheerleading squad and of course was accepted, she now has a newfound purpose in this forsaken school. Coming out of the school gates we sat and waited for Shay by the unkept willow tree that towers over the entrance, my sister sits relishing in her new freshly pressed uniform, it was a yellow and white striped top with separating black lines, and a yellow skirt with a white trim. She is going to look like a giant bumblebee, I scoffed looking at her as she waved it around in victory. The school's mascot was a Falcon instead of Everbeam it should have been called Falcon High, but the founders seemingly went in a weird direction, heavens knows why.

Suddenly shouting caught my ears, startling me slightly as I looked up, I saw Paddox and Shay having an intense argument just outside the school's entrance, standing to my feet I rush over to them.

'What's the matter?' I said, as the arguing continued.

'I said what's the matter?' I demanded, pulling on Paddox's shirt.

'We will continue this at home!' he said, puffing out his chest and raising his posture. I have actually heard of this on a documentary, where they would make themselves look bigger to the opposing animal to scare and intimidate them, I let out a little chuckle by mistake making big foot stomp towards me.

'Something funny, squirt?' he said, looking at me with intense anger, making me recoil inwards.

His breathing became laboured as he reached for my arm gripping it tightly, he went from a cool temperature to red hot in a second, his touch began to feel like fire as his grasp around my wrist tightened further.

'Paddox, let go you're hurting her,' Shay yelled.

Shay's words didn't seem to make a difference, his eyes blackened bordering on homicidal as he pulled me in closer, the heat radiating from his breath and body encapsulated my face as he exhaled heavily.

Fear radiating from me as I shivered on the spot feeling goosebumps rise up my arms and stopping at his grip, sweat began to fill my brows as he was inches away from my face, sending me a burnt red colour as his temperature warmed me instantly. Shay pummels into the side of him knocking him backwards, getting up he shakes himself off before he lunges for her, followed by a shove from Addison sending them tumbling into the trees beside the school.

The rustling stops, looking forwards it would seem that Paddox and Addison are gone. Where the hell are they.

'What the hell was that about?' I demanded.

I clutched my wrist, praying it doesn't bruise as that would be extremely hard to explain to my father, people really have to stop using that as their first attack as my fragile wrists can't take it.

'Oh that, that was just male hormones,' she said, sheepishly pointing in the air with her finger.

'Hormones huh, well then where are they?' I said, knowing she was hiding something from me.

'I'm sure they are around, now we had better get you home as we have work in a couple of hours,' she said, with a smile, realising I had to let it go I agreed as she changed the subject.

'So, I heard it's your birthday next week?' she announced, whilst we walked back to her car, I kept turning my head as my attention was still on the woods that remained perfectly still.

'Annabeth?' she said, shaking my arm a little to get my attention. Still startled I dragged my arm away as the imprint left previously was causing some discomfort, a sudden sadness appeared on her face.

'I'm sorry, yes it's my birthday soon,' I said, still unable to focus.

'We should do something for it?' she said, excitedly looking for approval. I agreed nodding my head with a wide smile, anything to stop this current conversation as I really was not a fan of birthdays let alone all eyes on me, but for now I was going to have to accept it.

The journey home was blissful, getting home I got out of the car said my goodbyes and thanked her for the lift. From the moment I arrived home there was visible movement in the house, dragging myself up the steps I couldn't help thinking about my long shift tonight. I saw what I was dreading.

'Company,' I thought, why today of all days.

Opening the door my father instantly greeted me, waving my hand back at him I made my way to the fridge and pulled out a bottle of water.

'Hello, Annabeth,' she said, holding out her hand for me to shake.

Ignoring her I continued swallowing my water taking longer sips between breathing, earning me a look from my father which meant I now had to interact.

'Katrice,' I replied, in a monotoned voice, I could claw her eyes out.

'Were going out for dinner,' Dad announced.

'Dad, I have work in a couple of hours, what about Ethan?' I said, pointing to the little troublemaker pulling out threads from the rug in the lounge.

'Payton?' he said, looking at her hopeful.

'Oh no, I'm going to a party tonight! There is a guy there that I desperately want to see again,' she said, pulling a nail file out of her bag, as she began scratching at her thumb nail. I hated that sound, not to mention the damn nail dust she creates, for them to only snap days later what a waste of time that is.

'You're not going to a party, you're going to look after your brother,' he replied, I stood and waited for the scream that didn't come, my smug grin was now fading.

'Fine but next time I'm not missing a party,' she said. And that was that, not so much of a squeak. How disappointing was that? She didn't explode at all. Am I missing something? Did my dad have something on her, as previously any slight inconvenience to this girls life and you would hear about it for days.

My father turned around and left feeling enormously proud of himself, however I can't help thinking that her not reacting was going to cost him big time.

# Chapter 6
## Be still my beating heart

I had arrived a little earlier for work today, I scanned the restaurant looking side to side and looking back again hoping my eyes were not deceiving me, Shay is nowhere to be seen and I couldn't help but hope that maybe she was just running late.

'Annabeth, the boss wants a word,' Paddox said.

Mr Grayson Senior summoned me to his office, and I will admit I was both intrigued and terrified. This man gave me butterflies in all the right places, but his age made it very inappropriate. Getting to his door I hesitated before going in, knocking on the door twice I heard that familiar raspy tone.

'Come in,' he said, as his voice rumbled from within.

'Gosh that voice made my heart race,' I thought, trying to contain my thoughts, I gave myself a pinch.

Opening the door, I tried to poke my head around it in my attempt to not break anything, but having not opened the door wide enough upon entry I slammed my head into the door frame, a belly curdling laugh came from within as I came crashing to the floor landing on my stomach.

'Are you alright?' Mr Grayson said, I could hear the sincerity was not real, as the held back laughter was still on the tip of his tongue.

'I'm fine,' I said, rubbing the largely forming egg on my head. 'You wanted to see me, sir?' I added, looking up as my head began to grow two sizes.

'I did indeed, we will be having slightly different guests in tonight, so I will need you to remain on reception,' he said, as I tried to concentrate, but all I could see was dancing fish singing everything little thing is going to be alright. He stared at me for a moment before moving towards me, he knelt down in front of me before clicking beside either side of my ears.

'Annabeth?' he said, louder and much firmer.

'I stay, yes,' I said, shaking my head trying to

re-scramble my brain to recognise what he had just said to me, when I finally could comprehend what he was saying I responded. 'Uhem, yes sir I will stay at reception of course,' I said, smiling politely as my head starts to pulse and throb.

'Okay good, and you are not to talk to these guests. Do you understand?' he said, with his piercing eyes now glaring at me.

Well now that confirmed it he's a mafia boss, I'm sure of it now, but why can't I talk to them.

'Can I say hello?' I enquired.

'Yes, you may,' he said, nodding at me.

'Can I ask them if they have a reservation?' I said, with caution.

'Yes!' he said, his tone now weary and impatient. Sensing I'm trying his patients I try one last time, it was one of my many flaws, I just never knew when to stop.

'Can I tell them my name?' I said.

'Annabeth, your to say the bare minimum understood!' he snapped, his eyes zoned in on me, I could sense he was staring at that monstrosity growing on my forehead as the veins in my head bulged with it.

'Yes sir, may I leave now?' I said in hope.

'You may go. Annabeth, put some ice on that,' he said, with a scoff.

'Hmm yes funny man I see,' I thought, as I left his office. Well let's see what this shift brings.

Sitting at reception that familiar scent of fresh rainwater and sunshine filled the air, but this time it was mixed with something awful, it smelt like sour lemon and damp washing. As the door opened their he was an absolute godly vision, my heart began to palpate as he got closer. Looking down I saw his hand gripping another, she was tall blonde and a total cow, why on earth is he with her.

'Who does she think she is!' I thought, as they approach me.

I painted a smile on my face as his attention diverted to me, a smug grin formed his face as he pulled her in closer, her stupid little giggle made my belly fill with rage. They both walked past me not even acknowledging me, looking back over her right shoulder at me she shot me a smile that was indeed deadly. My eyes followed them through the restaurant, her laugh was hyper like she was trying too hard, oddly getting louder the further away they got from me. Why was I so mad it's not like he's mine?

A while later another face came through the door, I had not seen him before, and he looked angry.

'Name?' I said boldly, trying to get his attention as he scanned the restaurant. I Snapped my fingers at him, as being ignored was not my thing, and I certainly was not going to accept it from someone I didn't know.

'Hey, name please?' I said, his eyes flash red as he looked at me.

'Jason!' he replied, closing his eyes, and taking in a deep breath.

'Well Jason, looks like you're not on my list therefore you're not allowed in,' I said, pointing for him to leave.

'I'm not here for dinner, I'm here to deliver a message!' he said, as he searched more closely around the restaurant.

'Oh goodness theirs that puffing of the chest I have seen already today, honestly it's like a zoo here,' I thought, as I dragged my hand down my face.

'Well sir, they are currently busy can't this wait?' I said, trying to calm the situation.

'No, it cannot!' he said, as his eyes captured that for which he had been searching.

Barging past reception he walks straight up to Luca, bring me to my feet as I followed close behind him tugging at his shirt, trying to re-direct him towards the front door unsuccessfully might I add.

'A meeting has been requested, for your pack to attend. Do you accept?' he said, staring intently.

My eyes widen as I try and listen in, Paddox stands in the way pushing me towards reception completely out of ear shot making the conversation harder to hear.

'What do they mean by pack?' I said, as his shove gets more aggressive.

'Paddox, what do they mean by pack?' I added, attempting to shove him back as he kept resisting me.

'Wow this boys built different,' I thought, moving backwards.

'They said group!' he said angrily.

'No they didn't, he said pack!' I replied, trying to peer around him.

'No, it's just a meeting!' he said, sternly whilst blocking my view.

Knowing I was getting nowhere with this I went back and sat down, he smirked walking back towards them all.

'Hi, sorry I didn't mean to frighten you,' Jason said, with a smile, as he came back to reception.

59

'Frighten me? You big idiot, annoyed me more like!' I said, with my nostrils flaring in anger.

'Oh, how so?' he said, completely shocked by my manors.

'Well for starters, you weren't invited; I was under strict instructions you big baby, now I'm probably going to get fired!' I said, snarling at him over my desk.

'Well, you just might if you talk to people like that,' he said, with a devilish smile, as he leaned into me.

'Oh funny, you're a funny guy,' I said, shooting a glare in his direction.

'Fiery, aren't we?' he said, leaning even closer.

'I suggest you leave,' I said, standing to my feet and creating some required distance between us.

'Oh yeah what are you going to do?' he asked, standing up straight and moving back, his smile getting bigger as he folded his arms.

I must admit he got me there, I was in no fit shape to fight him for anything which I'm sure he was blissfully well aware of.

'I will, I will scream!' I said, taking in a deep breath, as my face started to turn red with a hint of purple.

'Wow, wow relax I'm going,' he said, as he tilted his head waiting for me to breathe again.

Nope not doing it because I have got some stamina in me, sure I'm no athlete but I sure as hell am good at this game. He smiled shaking his head as he turned and left, I let out my breath and continued with my work feeling proud of my achievement, which was quickly diminished by Luca as I saw him stomping towards me, with the stench of that woman's scent gripping his clothes as it wafted towards me.

'You weren't supposed to let anyone in without an invitation,' he snarled.

'I could hardly stop him could I, you saw the size of him,' I said in confusion.

'Don't let it happen again girl!' he sniped, looking at me in total disgust.

I have to admit I'm not sure what hurt more, the fact he looked at me the way he did or the patronising tone of his voice, either way I wasn't sure why he was able to bother me so much. Why did that hurt me so?

'Sir, with all due respect,' I said, but before I could utter another word, he cut me off.

'Listen all the time you work here, you work for me! You will do as you are asked, and you will do as you are told,' he said with a smirk.

'But if you would just listen!' I pleaded.

'I'm done listening to you, look at you you're nothing!' he spat.

Yet another blow as I felt my heart twinge at those words, how could he be so cruel what did I ever do to him. Why did my presents aggravate him so much?

'Yes sir,' I responded, with sadness filling my heart.

'Now get back to work!' he yelled, throwing a piece of candy at me from the dish on the front desk.

Taking my seat, I continued to work as the angry tears filled my eyes, desperately trying to push them back down again, my chest rising and falling. Picking my manual up I disguised my face burying my head into it.

'What an asshole,' I thought, as I tried to ignore the scent that was in the air.

The evening drew to a close and everyone left, I was relieved by Paddox who came up to me in a hurry.

'Listen I'm sorry about earlier, it was just a little heated in here,' he said, with sincerity.

'Okay I forgive you,' I said, as a little smile appeared on my face.

'Honest, do you really mean it?' he said, with excitement.

'I do mean it yes, otherwise I wouldn't have said it,' I said, as I half smiled again with exhaustion.

'Hey erm, Shay might have mentioned your birthdays in a couple of days,' he said, with an alarming grin.

I must admit I didn't like where this was going, but still I remained at my desk pushing papers, messing everything up that I had done today in an attempt to look cool or organised, something I was sure was going to cost me later but in all truth I didn't care.

'Yes, it's nearly my birthday,' I said.

'Well, we had better get you ready then?' he replied.

'Ready for what?' I said, pushing to see if he would tell me.

'Your party?' he said, without hesitation.

I watched as the realisation of what he just said hit him like a ton of bricks, shock and fear appeared on his face.

'Was that supposed to be an inward thought?' I asked, as he nodded frantically.

'Don't tell Shay, she will literally kill me!' he said, in a state of worry.

'So where are we going?' I smiled, politely leaning in.

'We are having it at our house,' he said, as I giggled knowing he was in the mist of telling me all his secrets. One more push and he would be done for.

'No more questions, you can't ask anymore, you will get me in trouble,' he said, as we both laughed in unison.

'Okay sorry,' I said, rolling my eyes at him.

'How's your surprised face?' he asked.

I proceeded to show him just how shocked I can be, like a chameleon with ever changing faces.

'That last one is the one for me,' he laughed.

'Okay well, it is time for me to go home,' I said. Moving to the staff room to gather my things I tried to move quickly to get out before something else is needed, opening the door ready to leave I heard Mr Grayson arguing with his son Luca, keeping the door open a jar I listen in.

'You need to be more polite to her, you know what's at stake,' Mr Grayson said, waving his fingers in Luca's face.

'I know, but we don't know it's true,' he responded, scrunching up his face.

'But we do, and you will act accordingly from now on!' he roared.

His roar took me by surprise and completely startled me, my body trembled slightly knocking my bag into the door with a bang, so I just walked with it as if I had just got to it praying it wasn't noticed.

'See you tomorrow,' I said, politely after already agreeing to work two days in a row.

I mean honestly who does that? Leaving with my eyes down at the floor, avoiding eye contact with them both.

Walking to my car I take in the night air exhaling and inhaling that cold swift breeze that flowed around me, sending a chill down my chest as the freezing air filled my lungs, my tension eased the closer I got to the car as I practiced my breathing. What in the world have I got myself into.

# Chapter 7
## The surprise

A couple of day's had passed, and it was finally the weekend, that double shift has murdered me and all I wanted to do was sleep, knowing that would not be the case as it is in fact my 18th birthday today. With those thoughts it was like the universe was speaking to me, almost laughing in my face at the notion of having a silent lay in that was never going to happen.

My door flung open crashing into my cabinet as Ethan fly's in with a half-eaten cup cake and a present with tiny holes in it, well that's one way to tell me you don't know what it is, I guess. Also why has he only got on one sock?

'Happy Birthday, Annie!' he said, excitedly throwing the box at me.

This boy watched the film *Annie* once and decided he liked that name better for me, so in doing so he now just called me Annie and out of greatest respect to my father and my mother I actually totally preferred it.

'Open mine first,' he said, eating the rest of my birthday cupcake.

With his mouth open wide I stared at him as the food went around it like a washing machine, crumbs flying out of his mouth with every word spoken and falling onto my duvet. I strategically distract him as I swipe the crumbs off of my bed. Opening his present first it was a handmade lump of clay, he was not the best gift giver, but I always appeased him by keeping them.

There was another box that he presented me with and upon opening it up I looked at it confused, it was a pair of keys. Do not tell me dad has brough me my own car for my birthday, as I will quite literally die. Unable to contain my excitement I leaped from my bed, hooking my foot under my duvet sending me plummeting towards the wooden floor, but something weird happened I didn't hit it. What is wrong with me am I still sleeping? Shaking the feeling off I lunged for the window and their she was, a VW yellow beetle classic it was my absolute dream car. I could literally die go to heaven and be happy right now, I jumped up and snuggled my little brother to death before I ran out of my room and downstairs to see my father in the kitchen. I rushed to him and flung my arms around him, bringing him into a bear hug that was designed to cut off air supply to anyone who receives it.

'Thank you so much,' I said, as the smell of blueberry pancakes filled the room.

'Annabeth, I can't breathe,' he said, tapping my shoulder for air, to only make me squeeze him harder.

'Hmm maybe I shouldn't have got you something bright yellow,' he said, as he choked a little.

'If you wanted it to be a secret then no,' I said.

Going over to the table I reached for a nice glass of orange juice, stretching out I took my napkin and placed it on my lap, I sat and patiently waited for my pancakes that my father made me every year. They smelt divine.

'It is to my understanding that you have plans tonight?' he said.

'Apparently so, but who?' I said, before realising.

Looking up I noticed Payton making her way down the stairs with her stupid grin, I knew full well she told him because her smug expression said it all.

'I do have plans tonight, I have been working so hard Dad please,' I begged.

'Listen I don't mind but you stay away from that boy, he's nothing but trouble do you hear me?' he said.

I agreed, still salivating waiting for those pancakes he was still flipping around. If only I was a bird right now, I'm so hungry.

'So why can't I come then?' Payton piped up, showing the food in her mouth as it looks like it's on spin cycle, every chew visible making me want to vomit, it was very classy, maybe her and Ethan have more in common than she realised.

'I didn't plan it,' I said, quickly so I didn't get in trouble.

'I didn't want to come anyway!' she insisted.

'Then why did you ask?' I said, as her stare ran through me, feeling the frostiness in the air my father introjected.

'So will you be going shopping?' he said, trying to change the subject.

'Yes, with Shay,' I said, in a cranky tone.

I wondered why no one actually invited her. And how in the world did she actually know? Still seething with Payton for telling dad my plans, she sat glaring at me over the table. Surely, I should be the angry one.

The frost between us was next level today but I was on top of the world and wasn't going to let anything stop me, after breakfast I went upstairs for a boiling shower, I looked in my wardrobe to be met with nothing I liked, I settled for a cropped jumper, black jeans and a pair of black doc Martens and just throwing my hair up in a messy bun. Now I was ready all I had to do was wait for Shay to arrive, playing hide and seek with my baby brother until she pulled up. He was an excellent hider, by that of course I mean I walked into his room to see him half hidden under a blanket in the middle of the floor with his little bottom poking out.

'Oh no, where oh where is Ethan,' I said, toying with him until he responds.

'I'm in here,' he squeaked.

This goes on for a few more moments until I get in the other side and looked at him.

Lifting the blanked I grinned as his high-pitched scream filled my ears, almost deafening them as I lunged for him, bringing him into a bear hug and blowing raspberries onto his neck and tummy, he screeched and squirmed as dad started to call for me. Staring down at Ethan I gave him a little kiss on his head.

'Eww that's gross, you're a girl you got cooties!' he said, wiping my kiss away.

What in the world is this new school teaching him? Girl's do not have cooties and he never said that to me before, I huffed at him out of frustration mixed with a little sadness, he's growing up too fast for my liking.

'Annabeth?' Dad yells, in a clearer tone.

Leaving my room, I descend the stairs ready for my shopping trip, it would have to be a short and cheap one though as I was working on a budget. Shay stood at the door greeting my father, he turned to face me and Shay points at my father behind his back and mouthed the words. 'He's hot!' she said, as I screwed up my face in utter disbelief. Is she joking? Going over to the sofa I grabbed my bag, and we rush off.

'Is that yours?' she said, in amazement.

'Yeah it was for my birthday, do you like it?' I said cautiously.

'Love it!' she said, in her usual preppy voice.

'Are we going into town for a dress?' I enquired.

'I know just the place, you will absolutely love it,' she said, as we drive down the road, listening to songs and catching up.

Who knew birthdays could be so fun? Usually, we have a tradition in my house that involved presents movies and snacks, it was what I was used to, as we never had parties anymore because we never stayed in one place for long enough.

When we eventually got to the shop, on the window in slanted writing it read.

'A little for a lot,' it said. It was quite the moto, and some of the stuff in this shop was vintage and incredibly old looking but still in pristine condition, I picked up a black dress with tassels hanging from the hem.

Shay's was of course white but I'm far too clumsy for white, but I must admit something about her seemed different somehow, but I still haven't forgiven her for abandoning me at work however she is slowly winning me over.

'Hey, shall we pop into work?' she said, as we walked back to her car.

'Oh no thanks, I've had just about enough of their for a while,' I said shily.

'Okay listen I'm sorry I deserted you the other day, it really wasn't cool,' she said, bringing her hand up and tapping my shoulder.

'Shay honestly it's fine, it was just a hard shift is all,' I replied, knowing how hard she is trying.

'So shall we go in?' she said, pulling me towards the doors, pulling back slightly I soon agreed, after all what was the worst that could happen.

Upon walking through the door everyone was present jumping out before me trying the art of surprise, they really should have been quiet if they wanted to scare me.

'Surprise!' they all yelled.

I have to admit it was quite lovely, they had set out lunch for myself and Shay, the smell was enticing as we sat down to see fruit and fresh bread baskets laid on the table, this restaurant isn't usually known for cooking normal dishes, but the chef made us homemade beef burgers and chips just the way we like them, medium rare with American cheese. Why do you ask? Because American cheese is the only cheese that doesn't split when cooking it. The burger was dripping with juices as gravity pulled it down our arms and onto the table, this is what heaven was made for with every bite came blissful satisfaction. After we had finished it was time to leave but not before thanking the chef for our delicious meal, after we gathered our stuff and headed for the front door. The door opened and in came Luca. The usual smell hit me but this time it was much more powerful, its potency had me floating towards him, he looks right at me and says the word. 'Mate,' In a low whisper.

Walking with my hand out for him he went to pull away, but his father was in close proximity glaring at him with a frosted stare. Shay looked at me and half smiled as the corners of her mouth turned inwards, my attention is distracted as the smell of him begins to encapsulate me as the air around me became lighter. Reaching for him I touch his arm and an electrical surge coursed through me, seeing it did him too made me happy as the power of our touch kept zapping at our fingertips, it was the kind of feeling you wanted more of and would die to feel it again.

'Annabeth?' I heard his father say. 'We need to talk.' he added, directing me towards his office.

Following on down the corridor I looked back for Shay, but she was nowhere to be seen, I followed sheepishly worried about what was happening but all I could think about was Luca. Why did I want to be so close to him all of a sudden. It was totally bizarre.

'Annabeth, would you take a seat for me please?' he said. I instantly sit on my hands, as the feeling of being in trouble was overwhelming.

'Did I do something wrong?' I asked, worried about what he might say. 'I think whatever it is it wasn't me,' I added, as awkward laughter escaped my lips.

'We need to tell you something, and we need you to understand, okay?' he said, with a worried look on his face, as he took a seat Infront of me.

'Okay,' I said, with fear in my voice.

I'm not sure I like where this is going? I don't think I've done anything wrong surely someone would have told me, lifting one hand I begin biting the skin around my nails as the anticipation put me on edge.

'We aren't what you think we are,' he said.

'Oh yeah and what are you?' I smiled slightly.

'We're wolves!' Luca blurted out.

'Ohh, sure you are and I'm a unicorn,' I scoffed.

Luca looked at me displeased with my behaviour, his eyes blacken, blinking at him I reached up with both hands rubbing my eyes, completely shielding my face to feeling a sudden heat at the back of my hands. Moving my hands and opening my eyes I saw something that looked like Luca, but his eyes are pitch black, with sharpened teeth into points as the dribble oozed from his mouth.

'What the F...' I screamed, shoving my chair backwards in horror.

'Wow calm yourself child, he will not hurt you!' Mr Grayson implied.

'Sure he won't, look at his damn teeth,' I screamed, tilting further back on my chair, trying to distance myself from him. 'Why am I attracted to this wolf?' I thought to myself. I never imagined he would actually answer me.

'My name is Blane, it is because you are our mate,' he said, in a sexy low and menacing voice.

I opened my mouth and at first the scream was silent, but he made the mistake in grinning at me with sharpened pointy teeth, I soon screamed my head off as my chair gave out with one last jolt backwards, I tumbled out of my chair and rolled backwards into a heap on the floor.

'Clumsy girl, aren't you?' he said, as I hear his wolf chuckle.

'Who am I to you why do you want me, oh you're going to eat me aren't you?' I said, starting to panic.

'I'm not dog food you know, I'd taste bland too; Also, I had garlic for lunch so I'm not sure if that counts?' I added, as I reached out for anything I could grab hold of.

'We are not going to eat you, you're our mate,' Blane said, with passion.

Oh lord this wolf is too damn sexy. 'Annabeth focus!' I thought, wondering how I avoid this.

'You could reject us, but that would be a mistake,' he said, with a hint of caution, as they leaned against the wall totally fixated on me.

'Blane, that's enough!' Luca demanded, pushing him to the back of his mind.

'What exactly do I do now?' I asked.

'I'm glad you asked, you will be my Luna; you will deal with all pack affairs and will help me lead them, it is also expected for you to move with us and leave your family, you will also need to cease all contact with them,' he announced, as if it was nothing.

'I can no longer see my family?' I asked, shocked that he would even ask that of me.

I stared blankly at him hoping he would change his mind, but that gravitational pull I had for him was luring me in.

'You have two weeks to say goodbye to your family, after that your father will be relocated and you will not see him again,' he said, so quickly as if it was that easy, I nodded at him as if I partly agreed, before the realisation hit me and I shook my head.

'Absolutely not, my family are everything to me!' I said, trying to stand my ground.

'You will do as you are asked, our pack is your family now; they should be the only thing that concerns you!' he said, banging his fist on the desk.

Getting the sense that if I did not comply something bad might happen, I nodded for real this time and I meant it.

'Now you will be a good girl, go home and tell your father you are moving in with Shay in a couple of weeks!' Mr Grayson said, the pressure was overwhelming I nod holding back the tears.

'Can I leave now?' I said, lowering my head.

'You may be human, but you are my mate, should you run or try and leave I will know got it?' he said, with a hint of disdain.

I couldn't tell if he was lying or not because I didn't know a thing about his kind, I lowered my head in shame. I had no choice, the only hope I had was that I would wake up soon and this would all be a dream. If only I would be so lucky.

# Chapter 8
# The longest goodbye

With my head a mess and my heart pounding I made my way to the car park, Shay was waiting for me outside, but the gravity of my situation weighed heavily on me and began to cloud my judgment.

'What am I going to do?' I asked, as I turned to face my friend. 'Shall I run?' I added, but she shook her head.

'Relax its you're birthday my Luna,' she said, as she bowed at me. A bad feeling filled my stomach as she uttered those words, it was the feeling my life was about to change forever, my thoughts shifted back to the woman in the diner.

'Mark my words, your troubles are only beginning,' I recalled. My throat became strained, as I tried to swallow the thickened saliva in my throat.

'You knew, you knew the whole time?' I said, as I found myself beginning to yell at her.

'I didn't know straight away, I only had a feeling you might be,' she said, as she started to cry a little.

'But you could have warned me, now I have to leave my family; this is officially the worst birthday of my life!' I screamed, as I slowly began to pace up and down.

'Would you like me to come and help you tell your father?' she said, I nodded before I had even had a chance to think about it.

'We are still going to have to go to that party, it is at the pack house; it's a chance for you to meet your people, okay?' she said, with caution.

But my ears are still ringing from my earlier conversation, my head trying to think of a thousand different words I could say to my family to somehow try and explain how I'm feeling right now.

'The party, are you joking?' I said.

'Annabeth, it is expected!' she said.

I nod as my eyes widen; I try rubbing my eyes again, but nothing changed other than my entire life of course.

'Tell me more about being a Luna?' I asked, to try and calm my nerves.

'You will be in charge of pack affairs and us, and you will be Luca's wife,' she said, those words dried my throat immediately, I tried to gather whatever saliva I had left to help facilitate in swallowing, my mouth opened and I'm sure if my jaw wasn't connected it would have fallen off.

'Wife!' I yelped.

'Why yes, he will mark you as he sees fit and will go about your days together fulfilling your duties,' she said, causing my head to become heavy, as it started to spin.

'I need to sit down!' I replied, as I lowered myself to the ground.

'Okay why don't we start with getting you some Dutch courage?' she said, walking towards her car and pouring me a questionable shot. I necked it without hesitation, as the heat warmed my core, and a cough escaped my lips.

'What is that?' I said, with a strained voice as I try to breathe. It was like drinking hellfire, burning my throat and stomach simultaneously.

'Another!' I said, shoving it back at her knowing full well she had no choice but to comply, I shot another in an attempt to warm my breaking heart.

The drive home was completely silent, for the first time ever in my life I could with confidence say that I didn't want to go home.

'You have to do this,' Shay insisted.

She pulled into my drive, and I could feel the alcohol rising to the back of my throat making me completely sick to my stomach, Shay nods and I resist the urge to slap her for not telling me the truth straight away.

'Do you want me to come in with you?' Shay said, I shook my head as I got out of the car. Carrying my bags for tonight's party I approach the house, I let out a light whimper and next thing I knew Shay was right beside me.

'I can't do this,' I whispered, as my legs started to tremble and drag across the ground.

'Believe me you're stronger than you think,' she said, gripping my left hand. She looks at me as she wipes my tears away. 'It is for their own good, the moon goddess blessed us with you; but your family would be forever in danger if you don't this,' she said. Those words were seemingly all I needed to hear to help me make my choice, I dried my eyes and walked into the house.

'Hey birthday girl, did you have fun?' Dad said.

'It was great, thank you. Dad, can we talk?' I said, trying to get myself together, and get out as quickly as I could.

'Sure pumpkin, what's wrong?' he said, his smile hurt my heart, knowing I had to lie to him filled me with shame, I had lied to him before but not like this.

'Nothing's wrong I just have some news, me and Shay are doing really well at work, and well we have found an apartment and are moving in together,' I said, holding my thumb in the air, watching as his face turns from happiness to sadness in an instant.

'What about us?' he asked.

'We will still see each other, I just won't be living with you guys anymore,' I said, closing myself off from him. My words hit my father like an arrow through the heart, taking a step back he leans against the kitchen counter for support.

'Oh okay, well I just figured it would be a while before I had to say goodbye to one of my girls,' he said, in a saddened tone.

'Aren't you happy for me?' I said, looking on at him desperate for his approval.

'Of course, sweetheart,' he said, bringing me into a tightly gripped hug, my emotions took over and I sobbed unable to fight them off any longer.

'It's okay you won't be far away, right?' he said, pulling me out of the hug, and slowly scanning my face.

'Yes Dad, we will still be living here,' I said, as I faked a smile. I knew the minute I left here I would not be seeing them for an awfully long time, it crushed my soul as I look upon my baby brother's face seeing his tears trickling down his little face ripped my heart out.

'Why is everyone crying?' Payton asked, as my father dried his face.

'Your sister is moving out,' Dad said.

'Great can I have her room as a walk-in wardrobe?' she said. My sister is so sympathetic and caring that instead of sadness, she showed bitterness and resentment.

'Payton!' Dad yelled.

'It's fine Dad, let her have whatever she wants,' I said, taking pleasure in knowing she wouldn't have it for long.

'I won't change it, much!' she smiled, with that shameless wink she gives.

God she really is a bitch! my body shifted as I was about to swing for her, but Shay placed her hand on my right shoulder dragging me towards the stairs.

'Okay well we have a party to get ready for,' Shay announced, pulling me further away from my father's clutches and my sisters impending doom.

'Now girl we don't have long,' she said, as if this was going to be harder than she first thought.

'Okay let's get to it then,' I replied, with a sigh.

After having a shower, she pulled me into my chair and blow dried and curled my hair, pinning each section little by little drowning it with hairspray to the point of me actually tasting it. Moving to my face she began by applying skin care, apparently, it's rather important to prep the base, I of course had no idea what she was talking about. She applied the smallest amount of each product giving my skin a radiant glow before moving on to make-up products, strategically placing it without me being able to see I felt like a thickly layered oil painting. We were in my room for an hour and half, she urged me to get dressed, so I stood to my feet grabbing some underwear out the draw and moved towards my bathroom, soon after climbing into my party dress I came back into the room.

'Wow, you look stunning,' she said, jumping up and down.

'Thank you,' I replied, readjusting it as I wasn't used to wearing dresses.

'Now the hair!' she said, reaching for it.

She carefully re-sprayed each section and removed the pins. 'Turn you head upside down and shake' she said, in a playful manor, feeling a fool I did as she said.

'Right, I do believe we are ready,' Shay said, with sheer excitement as she stared at her masterpiece.

We begin walking downstairs as my father greeted me with a 'Wow! you look positively beautiful,' he said.

'Thanks Dad,' I replied, my cheeks flushed a deep red from embarrassment, as my little brother did a little wolf whistle, that child watches far too many films.

'Not too late!' Dad said, with a warning.

My father wasn't big on rules but the one rule he did have was not to be late. I wasn't the one who usually broke the rules but on the odd occasion such as a party I might.

If anything, I was going to try and stick to it as it would probably be the last time I ever heard those words. I so wish my life was different, I could attempt the art of manifestation to save me from this life, but alas like Cinderella I would be leaving the ball early, hopefully not in a shrinking pumpkin but the night is still young.

# Chapter 9
## The world as I knew it

Leaving the house, I still had to keep up the façade of being excited, but truth be told I was anything but. I had to make the journey not only to a house I had never been to before, but to be introduced to my future pack. I feel positively sick, if it wasn't for the makeup covering my face, I was sure I was turning green. Sitting in the chair I continue to fidget and flounder around.

'Calm down will you, your making me nervous,' she said, giving me the death stare.

She finally smiles at me easing my nerves slightly, I must admit that quote didn't go with her accent.

'I'm sorry,' I said.

As I was about to open my mouth further, she took a left turn up the hill towards the mountains, I had been so curious as to where this leads to. Moving further up the drive it was as if we had entered into another world, palm trees with a beautiful spring running down the side of the mountain with a separated village from everyone else.

Beautiful little houses like something from the movies, Shay peered out the window, sticking her arm out she waved through this gate that was electrically operated, the gate opened, and my fidgeting got worse as we approached the house.

'Erm Shay, who's house is this?' I said, looking out the window expecting to see a smaller house around.

'It's yours silly, that's the pack house; this is where you will be moving too,' she said.

She has got to be kidding, that's enormous.

'How many pack members are here?' I said.

'Around two hundred,' she said, with a smirk.

'How many!' I said, as my breathing became erratic.

'You need to calm down, the pack will sense you and think something is wrong just breathe, breathe slower!' she yelled. I must admit shouting at me was not helping.

'Okay I'm sorry, I just can't help it!' I said.

I sat fidgeting with my dress, thinking I should have chosen a longer one.

'Look the sooner you accept this, the better off we are all going to be!' she said, signalling for the guard.

I climb out of the car and begin walking towards the entrance, noticing lights above my head, hanging like little diamonds designed to glimmer as if lighting the way of royalty. I was neither royalty nor a diamond.

The house stood tall there must have been more than seventy rooms in this house, and I was expected to live here. Coming through the door the party came to a standstill with everyone now looking at me, I walked slowly through the hall praying I don't fall on my face. Looking up I saw Luca stood waiting for me, he was not happy I could see this on his face, but I wasn't sure why. I hadn't done anything to him, and from what I gather wolves wait sometimes forever to find their mates. The strong bond that brings you together like an unmatched unit, stronger together and together forever.

'What a magical place this is,' I said, as I staired at the hand painted and hand carved ceilings, each painted to perfection. I look back down to see Mr and Mrs Grayson stood Infront of me, fully believing I would never bow to these people I felt my body lowering to the floor. Remaining calm Luca took my hand as a forced smile arouse the corners of his mouth, his father shot him a look making Lucas sigh and relax fully.

'Hello my dear,' he said, making my stomach flutter.

'Hello,' I said, fluttering my eyelashes at him in surprise.

'Would seem you are mine now,' he said, pulling me into a dance.

'For now, and forever, you are mine,' he whispered in my left ear, making my legs buckle, I believed every word he was saying to me.

'You will be with me soon,' he whispers.

What is this magic, this is like a dream that I was hoping that I would never wake from, his touch made me feel like I was floating on a cloud, a cloud I wasn't ready to fall from just yet. The evening got away from me, and I realised it was time to go home.

'You can't take her home, her father thinks she will be living with me; otherwise, he might not let her leave,' Shay said, pushing him back slightly, realising she had made a mistake she dropped to her knees.

'Shay, it's fine get up,' he said, as he looked at her and smiled.

'Okay I will see you soon,' he said, reaching for me as Shay moves past him, he took a couple of steps backwards gazing into my eyes.

'Until tomorrow my dear,' he said sweetly.

'Oh my gosh what a fantastic night,' I thought, longing for him to touch me again.

He is just what dreams are made of, that lady in the diner was wrong. Maybe it was just nerves I was seeing on his face, because his love for me is quite clearly real.

'He loves me,' I said, as if I was a child.

'Well of course he does you're his Luna, a strength and bond like no other; you will see what I mean,' she said, smiling as she took me home.

Rolling up my drive I saw Katrice leaving quietly, I was no longer angry with her as I figured my father would need her now more than ever. I waved as I walked into my house, I would be spending the morning with my father and there was nothing I wanted more than to get memories in before I had to leave.


It was the next day and I have never looked at my family like this before, it was as if I was seeing them for the first and the last time. It was an odd numbness that my mind couldn't comprehend, I loved them whole heartedly and the fear spiking in my heart at the thought of never seeing them again was astonishing.

'Hey pumpkin,' Dad said, as I walked into the lounge.

'Hey, do you need any help today?' I asked.

I know I said I didn't want to help, but spending as much time with them was crucial for me now.

'Sure, if you like?' his replied.

My father was no builder that became clear when he was trying to use a trowel as a sander. God only knows how long he has spent doing that for.

'Oh Dad, didn't you do any research?' I said, as my hysterical laughter grew louder.

'What, this is the thing you use for the,' he said, as he tried consulting the manual. 'Oh,' he said, as we both erupted into laughter, I dropped to the floor cradling my stomach from the aching, my face now hurting from my stretched-out smile.

'Right, it's okay we can fix this!' I said, picking up brushes still laughing to myself.

'Maybe we should just start with some paint?' I said, waiting for an answer.

'Maybe you're right,' he said, smiling in defeat.

'Oh lord!' I said, raising my eyebrows in confusion.

'This isn't what I ordered!' Dad said, in annoyance.

'What was the number you said?' I asked, trying to figure out who's fault it was.

'485, it's supposed to be grey!' he said, scratching his beard in confusion.

Either the person was colour blind or my dad ordered the wrong thing, seen as the colour was green and not a nice green either.

'Who am I kidding, I'm better off hiring someone to do this for me!' he laughed. 'Shall we go out for lunch?' he added, rather calmly considering this morning's antics.

'Okay if it means no more injuries?' I smiled.

'Sure, let's go into town, we can dine at your work maybe?' he said, open heartedly.

My smile faded as I knew I'd be watched their.

'Okay,' I said, as hesitation filled my voice, my father searches my face seen as my tone of voice didn't match my grimace smile.

'Are you okay?' he said, with raised eyebrows.

'Yeah, I was just thinking what todays menu was,' I said, with a slight stutter.

I lied of course I wasn't sure work was the best place for me right now given the circumstances but still I agreed.

Going into town was always like its own separate adventure, listening to the birds in the tree's without a care in the world was amazing to me, that smell of fresh air accompanied by the scent of freshly mowed grass was my favourite. Pulling up to restaurant sixty-six blew my mind, it was as if they knew we were coming. Paddox came out of the restaurant and opened the door for me, I glared at him as he opened my side only.

'What a nice boy,' Dad said, lightly as he nodded at him.

'Hmm, yes he is,' I said, pushing past him, to get in and out as soon as possible.

'The chef will prepare something special for you,' Paddox said, as he showed us inside.

Luca and his father Mr Grayson were sitting at the table opposite us; both of their attention had directed at us as they sat watching our every move.

'So does your father know the good news?' Paddox said, looking at us both, my father looked confused.

'Yes, I told him I was moving in with Shay, and he is happy for me,' I replied, giving him a glare. Paddox seemed confused, but it is an extremely hard choice! Imagine this for a moment.

'Hey Dad, got to move out because a family of werewolves have chosen me as their Luna, I'm expected to live with them now. Have a nice life!' I thought.

That would go down so well wouldn't it, so yes, I lied but it was for their own good.

A couple of moments later Paddox returned with our food, the smell was so enticing as the steam filled my face, with a lift of the lid the food was finally unveiled. It was Lobster Linguini the smell was enough to make your mouth water. Obvious much? Especially when I wouldn't be expected to pay for this afterwards,

my eyes flash towards Luca as he sat smiling at me. Honestly, these next few weeks were going to be trying. Looking back over at my father seeing the joy on his face as he slurped up his Linguini, I had to say it was not received well by anyone in this restaurant, but my father didn't care, he was enjoying himself so what did it matter. He was however making a complete mess, with every slurp shot off little droplets of tomato sauce onto the freshly pressed white tablecloths. What an experience this was. I look up at my father and laugh as he tried to tackle the lobster, a towel placed beside us was to facilitate in cracking open the shell of the lobster. But what does my father do, he begins banging the lobster with no cover over it, so it's shell proceeded to fly around the room, looking back at Luca I burst into laughter as the shock on their faces was so amazing.

'Dad?' I said, looking on at him, as he massacres his lobster.

'What is it pumpkin?' he said, holding up his tiny hammer.

'You're supposed to cover the Lobster,' I whispered, throwing the shell back onto his plate.

'I see, well I erm,' he said, as panic starts to set in.

It was the first time I had ever seen him speechless but at least he got it half right, his face flashed red, so I decided to join him, I took my tiny hammer and smashed the hell out of my lobster. After the next few weeks, my life would have to be monitored forever so why not engage in a little fun now.

'Thank you,' he whispered, as we finished our meal.

'Excuse me, can I get the bill please,' Dad asked.

'Mr Fortman that is not necessary,' Mr Grayson said, standing to his feet.

'Sir, surely this was expensive for your company?' he said, attempting to pay again.

'Dad isn't the weather lovely today; shall we go for a stroll?' I said, placing my hand on his trying to introject into the conversation, but I was ignored.

Distracting my father was never an easy task, but this time I was desperate for him to stop talking.

'Mr. Fortman,' Mr. Grayson went to say, before my father introjected.

'Come now, how much?' Dad said.

'Nothing it's on the house,' he said, his voice became more threatening.

'But why?' Dad asked.

'Well Clay, your daughter is a much-valued employee no payment is required,' he said, adjusting his cufflinks. Making it perfectly clear no payment would be taken.

'No payment is necessary, good day to you,' Mr Grayson said, dismissing him with a wave.

Looking around my father stood to his feet as embarrassment crossed his face, he began scanning the room at the people now staring right at us.

'Thank you, good day,' Dad said, taking a hold of my arm, and pushing me towards the door.

'What sort of arrangement do you have with that family, do they think we are poor?' he asked angrily.

'Dad no one's family pay's to eat here, it's one of the benefits of working here,' I said, feeling proud of myself for thinking on my feet, but at this point the lies just kept coming.

'Why?' he said, scratching his beard.

'I don't know, it's just the way they reward us I guess,' I replied, shrugging my shoulders.

'Hmm I must admit, that was the tastiest bit of grub I've had in a while,' he said.

We laughed together as we slowly began our journey home, not before stopping for more supplies from the local store.

'Dad seriously, you need a more positive attitude!' I said, toying with him.

'I am positive somethings wrong with that family, how is that for positive?' he said, pushing me towards the car.

'You need to chill Dad honestly, the Grayson's just look out for their staff,' I insisted.

'Well, are they good to you? do they use you? are you a mule?' he said, stopping and folding his arms together.

'Answer me!' he snapped.

'You think I'm a drug mule?' I said, as I burst into laughter.

'Well, I will take that as a no!' he said, as his face softened.

'Dad seriously, I think like Payton maybe you watch too many movies,' I said, teasing as I leaned into him.

'Right, let's go home,' he laughed, stretching his arm around me pulling me closer.

# Chapter 10
## D-day approaches

The days were beginning to fly by and getting closer to me leaving, today was the day I packed up my stuff, luckily however I hadn't actually unpacked anything anyway, the irony was I wasn't sure how long I would be in this state not that I was moving across town to be relocated here indefinitely. My little brother walks into my room, his pouty little face pulling on my heart strings. This was all I needed right now.

'Why you leaving us?' Ethan said, with a quivering lower lip.

'I'm not leaving you silly, I will still be here; I just won't live with you guys,' I said, pulling him into a hug not wanting to let him go, he was like my little best friend and brother rolled in to one.

'But you're not far away?' he said, with a glum expression.

'No sweet child I will never be that far away, if you look up at the stars at night and the brightest one will be where I am,' I said with sadness.

As I brought him into a smothering hug, I hold on for dear life with him trying to escape my grasp.

'You're squishing me!' he yells loudly.

'Oh yeah, well what about now?' I said, as my lips twitched slightly, as I tried to hold back my smile.

'Your squishing me, you're really squishing me!' he screamed.

Turning him around I begin to tickle under his arms and down his belly, as he shrieked fighting to get out.

'I love you, Annie,' he said, completely melting my heart, I reached for my face wiping my tears.

'I love you too,' I said, pinching his little nose as tears filled my eyes again, I look away trying to calm them, but when I turn back around, he was gone.

I now only had one more day left in this house, and I hadn't even had a chance to make it look like home yet, Payton on the other hand had, and her room looked like a boyband shrine.

There came a knock at my bedroom door and without waiting the door swung open, with a prepared Payton coming through it.

'Oh, are you still here?' she asked, in a bitchy tone.

'I still live here for another 24hours, remember?' I said.

'Well can you hurry up I need this space,' she said, rolling out her measuring tape, before marking the floor with frog tape for her new wardrobe.

What an absolute cow. Why does she hate me so much?

'Don't worry, it won't be long now, and you can have this space,' I said, still packing my things, as her tongue clicked at me.

'Good luck, hope independence is all you thought it could be,' she said, before leaving my room.

If she wasn't my sister, I think I would have floored her by now, for someone so intent on me leaving you would have thought she would have at least helped me do it, I smiled at the thought, it certainly would have been done quicker.

'Kids, dinner!' Dad said, as he bellowed up the stairs.

My father had set out a lovely meal for us, but I of course was leaving early in the morning. I planned on driving first thing to prevent anyone from coming to collect me. Dad made us his favourite; it was a beef hotpot but his contained some family secrets that just made it the best you ever smelt and tasted. How was I going to learn this now?

'Shall we say grace?' he said, holding out his hands.

'Dad, we have never said grace, why now?' Payton said, as we all looked at him as if he had gone mad.

'Come on Dad, you can't be serious?' Payton asked, in hysterics.

'Fine, let's just be ungrateful and eat our food,' he snapped.

'Thank goodness I'm starving!' Payton said, as my father glared at her.

'Dear lord, we thank you for this food, for our family friends and companions. May you continue to bless us with what we truly deserve; Amen,' I said.

I know I humoured him, but I could at least honour him with something he genuinely wanted just to see him smile. Opening our eyes my father had prepared quite the feast, chicken, sprouts, carrots, sweetcorn, parsnips, Yorkshire puddings, stuffing.

'Piggies in blankies!' Ethan yelled.

'Annabeth, how about I come with you tomorrow to help settle you into your new home?' he said.

My hands began to warm, sweat filling my pits, I was in a state of panic as all eyes now focused on me.

'Dad can we at least let me do these first steps alone, then you can come visit once everything is sorted and perfect?' I said.

How was he ever just going to go and just leave me here? I watch as his eyes look over to the grandfather clock in the corner, as he watches the seconds turn to minutes, the clock sounded louder as the deafening silence beckoned for me to fill it.

'It's okay Dad, as soon as everything is perfect then I will send for you?' I said nodding.

'Send for me? Who are you the queen of Sheba?' he said, making everyone laugh at me.

I push backwards adjusting my seat to create a little distance from them, I of course was not the queen of Sheba, but I was now the queen of dogs. Ironic huh?

'Can I go now?' Payton asked, removing her napkin from her lap, as she pushed her chair out rising to her feet.

'Where are you going?' Dad paused.

'Sit down please!' he added.

'Dad there is a party at Sarah's house. You don't need me here do you, Annabeth?' she enquired, with a stone-cold expression.

'But this is a goodbye dinner for your sister?' Dad insisted, as his face drew in becoming more disappointed by the minute.

'Okay goodbye, there you happy?' she said.

My dad's hands balled into a fist, I reached for him, causing him to relax again.

'Dad it's fine, let her go,' I said.

Leaning in I put my hand on his nodding as it would be easier if she left, his lips pursed under as he agreed, making Payton turn on her heels and run for the door.

'Goodbye Payton!' I said, knowing I would be gone before she got up in the morning.

'Yeah, yeah, see you in the morning!' she sneered, leaving as she waved a peace out sign to us all.

'Annabeth is there something I should know?' he sighed, raising his eyebrows.

'Like what?' I replied.

As I reached for another piece of bread, I begin breaking it into bite-size pieces, I pummelled it in to give me time before answering his questions.

'Well, you are still planning on going to university, aren't you?' he asked.

'Of course,' I sighed with relief.

Not entirely a lie but not completely the truth.

'Great, I was afraid you changed your mind,' he said.

'Nope just gaining some independence,' I smiled.

A feeling of shame washed over me as lying to my family didn't come naturally, I always made sure I was completely honest with him most of the time anyway, a welcomed distraction comes when the bell rings twice. I jump for the door to avoid any more uncomfortable questions; I swing it open putting a dent in the wall behind it. It's a good thing this house does need renovating because I keep breaking it.

'Annabeth, what was that about?' Dad asked.

'Hi Katrice!' I said, as I invited her in.

He can tell me off later, her keeping him busy was just what I needed. Turning back to face the table I noticed Ethan began yawning, I scooped him up from his seat cradling him to his room for the last time, getting him ready for bed slowly to not wake him, I gazed upon his face realising he will grow to be a big and strong boy. Feeling the tears welling as I realised, I would not be around to see it, I peeled back the covers and place him inside, pulling the covers back over him I put on his night light giving him a kiss on his forehead before I snuck out of his room.

'Would you like some help loading up your car?' Dad asked.

'No Dad it's fine!' I said adamantly.

Some help would have been great seen as my boxes where heavier than I first realised, I resorted to dragging them outside as lifting them certainly wasn't an option. Getting to my car I heard a rustling come from the bush beside my house, I picked the first thing up I could think of that would potentially hurt.

'Need some help?' a voice bellowed.

I began looking around frantically, as Paddox soon appeared from the bushes.

'Jesus, are you trying to make me bludgeon you to death?' I said, clutching my chest.

'With that thing, I don't think so!' he giggled.

His chuckle caught my attention as I realised, I was holding a wooden coat hanger, embarrassment filled my soul as I continued pointing it at him.

'Please don't shoot me!' he cackled, holding up his hands.

'What are you doing here?' I said, dropping the coat hanger to the floor.

'You didn't think we would leave you unattended, do you?' he said, grinning smugly.

'You've been following me?' I said in shock.

'Of course, you are our Luna now; certainly not going to leave you defenceless!' he replied, looking around.

'Fine grab that box and put it in there,' I said, pointing him in the direction of my car.

'Hey cool car, why haven't I seen you drive it?' he enquired.

'It was a birthday gift, my last one from my family,' I replied, with a vague expression.

'Oh gosh you're not going to cry are you, I don't handle crying very well,' he said, cautiously holding his hands up to shield his face.

'No Paddox, I am not going to cry!' I snapped.

'Okay, no need to shout!' he said, pulling on his ears.

'Do you need anything else?' he asked, as I shook my head.

'Okay if you do just yell,' he added, backing into the bushes.

'Might be better to just have your number, screaming attracts attention you know,' I said, rolling my eyes.

'Oh, okay sure,' he said, handing his phone to me, so I can retrieve his number.

'Don't you know it by heart?' I said.

'Who knows their number by heart?' he replied.

'Surely he's joking,' I thought to myself.

'Everyone?' I responded in shock.

'Oh right, well I don't,' he said.

'Obviously I got that, right I'm going to bed I will be with you in the morning,' I said, handing him back his phone, he nodded and collapsed into the bushes.

If he's going to have to stay their all night, I have to do something nice.

'Paddox!' I whispered, walking towards the bushes. His head poked through a hole in the bushes to meet my eye level, even though I knew he was in their it still frightened me half to death.

'Yes Luna?' he said, with leaves in his hair.

'Want some tea?' I said, laughing a little.

'Love some!' he said, as his head disappeared again.

Heading for the house I went straight to the kitchen made some tea and put it in a heated flask, turned back around I carried it outside. Hearing my dad leaving with Katrice, I launched it out of pure panic.

'Ouch!' Paddox said.

'See you soon, Annabeth,' My father called.

'Bye Dad, have a lovely time,' I replied.

Katrice was the perfect distraction; I wasn't happy him dating again but I was happy that he was happy.

'Oi, that hurt!' I heard Paddox voice rumble from behind me, as my father drove away.

'Ohh stop being a baby, you're a big bad wolf, aren't you?' I laughed.

'Why yes my dear, what big teeth I have!' he said, as he shifted slightly, his eyes were glistening in the moon light.

'All the better to eat you with,' he added, causing me to laugh on the spot, noticing he wasn't wearing much I grabbed a blanket from my car for him to sleep on.

'I'm a wolf, we don't get cold!' he scoffed.

Like I was supposed to know that? Looking again I gave him a glare for his rudeness.

'Thank you, Luna,' he added, adverting his gaze.

I smiled politely as I walked towards the house, things are going to be so different come tomorrow and to tell you the truth I wasn't ready for it.

# Chapter 11
## A new life begins

I laid awake all night as the moonlight shone through the cracks in my curtains, darkness soon became light beckoning me to get up. I watched as the sun rose; the light emitted through my curtains letting me know it was time.

Dragging myself up I walked to the bathroom with the strangest feeling, everything I was doing would be for the last time. Soon my dad would be getting the orders to move on, while I remain stuck contained to a life, I didn't choose which instantly filled me with dread.

Finally ready I attempted to move downstairs slowly praying that everyone was asleep, grabbing my keys I walk down the hallway through the lounge to the kitchen, opening the door it creaked and I cursed it.

'You wasn't going without saying goodbye, was you?' I heard my father's voice calling to me, hurt and unsure.

'Who me? No, I was just doing a final check of my car,' I replied, but I was trying to escape the dreaded goodbye.

'Come sit, let's have breakfast before you leave,' he said, waving me to come closer.

My father of course longed breakfast out by making blueberry pancakes from scratch, knowing I couldn't resist; I really was starving at this point. Not bothering with a knife and fork, I slammed those babies into my face faster than I could chew.

'Slow down pumpkin,' he said.

'I'm all done Dad thank you, I really must be going now,' I said, wiping my face, pushing my chair out from under me, with one final stretch I stood to my feet. Ethan was not awake yet sneaking in his room I gave him one last kiss goodbye, before returning to the kitchen.

'Come here you,' Dad said, with arms open wide, I nuzzled my face into his neck, trying to commit his scent to memory.

'I love you,' I whispered, still holding him.

'I love you too,' he replied.

Pulling myself away I walked to the front door, I turned to look around before saying a final farewell. Tears ran down my face as I made my way to my car, this gut wrenching feeling I had in the pit of my stomach was awful, fighting the urge to run and tell my father the truth about everything was painful, knowing in my heart that distance is what I required.

Whilst driving my memories went into overdrive, flashing me images of my life with my family.

Driving towards town the tree's beside me started rustling, I knew who that was, pulling over unwinding my window I yelled at him.

'Paddox, just get in the car!' I said, before blinking twice, he was suddenly beside me.

'Wow, that was quick,' I added.

'You're not going to cry again, are you? you know I don't do crying,' he said, with a crooked smile.

'No, I'm not going to cry again,' I laughed a little, pulling back into the road we continued the journey.

'Okay you promise no crying?' he said.

'Relax Paddox, I'm not going to cry!' I snapped.

'Well, you are a bit of a cry-baby?' he said.

'Do you want to walk? Or run? Or whatever it is you do!' I said, my grouchy tone getting more frustrated.

'I'm quite comfortable actually,' he said, sitting back in the chair, holding onto the door handle.

'Something the matter?' I asked, noticing his hand placement.

'Nothing Luna, I'm sure you're an excellent driver!' he said, now holding on for dear life.

'Paddox, one more word from you and you will hit the ground running!' I snapped, waving my finger at him.

'Okay noted,' he nodded.

My frown took over half of my face, soon softening as we got closer to the pack house, it had only been a couple of weeks, but I had already forgotten it's beauty.

'Welcome home, Luna,' Paddox said, as we made our way up the drive.

'Thank you Paddox, I hope it's worth it,' I replied.

An on-duty patrol man approached my vehicle, bending down was a big guy called Boid, which was ironic because he looked like he should have been called roid. His shoulder muscles joined into his neck, making him look like a giant floating head.

'Hello, Luna,' he said, as his voice did not match his physic.

I looked at him blinking for longer than I should have, all this Luna business is going to take some getting used to.

'Hello,' I said, pausing for a moment.

'Boid, madam,' he said proudly.

'Oh gosh, did he really just call me that?' I thought, turning to look at Paddox who was smirking beside me. Boid stood to the side as the scent of rain and sunshine filled me with joy, a wonderful smell that intensified the closer he got to me. The door opened and I stepped out.

'What is all of this?' Luca said, staring through the window examining my belongings.

'My things?' I replied awkwardly.

'You won't be needing them!' he said, flicking his hand for it to be removed.

'But they're my things?' I said.

'Fine you can take your things into the house. But some of it will need to go into storage, understand?' he said. Reluctantly I agreed, climbing in the back of my car I sifted through my things, pulling out what I wanted to take in with me, before stepping to the side as I watched my car being removed.

'Come my dear,' he said, holding his arm out for me to take, linking it with mine, causing that familiar electrical surge to flow through us, pausing feeling grounded we both took in a deep breath. Infront of us was a girl that was fast approaching, finally reaching us she bowed down on one knee.

'This is Orion, she will be your guide,' Luca said, retracting his arm from my firm grasp.

'What, where does he think he is going?' I thought, attempting to grab his arm again, only to be dismissed.

'Hey Orion, it's nice to meet you,' I said, shaking her hand.

'I have business to attend to. Orion, please show her the grounds,' he commanded, disbelief hit me as it was my first day and he is already leaving.

'This way, Luna,' she said.

Thank God, she didn't call me madam or worse ma'am.

Walking through the halls each room was bigger than the last, the kitchen was one of the biggest rooms on the ground floor, as it was pack tradition to all dine together. The games room was also an exceptionally large room, where pack members would come to relax after combat training.

'Erm Orion, sorry forgive me but where are all the pack members?' I asked, in hope they had run away.

'Out on patrol, Luna,' she said.

'Ah of course, how silly of me,' I said, uncomfortably moving forward.

It dawned on me just how little I actually knew about werewolves; I would have to brush up on a couple of things if I was going to help lead them.

There were seven floors, the first was for the Omega's, second the Beta's third floor was for guests from other packs, the fourth was for business containing four offices, Orion begun showing me down the corridors, each room was strategically placed the further away you are the harder you were to get to.

'This one's yours, Luna,' she said.

Of course mine was the first room, typical if you ask me.

'Orion, please stop calling me Luna; My name is Annabeth,' I asked politely.

'Oh of course thank you, Annabeth,' she smile.

'Right this way,' she gestured, as I trailed closely behind her, out of fear of getting left behind.

The fifth floor was for unmated females, sounds funny but for two weeks in a year they have to be separated from other pack members, due to being in heat apparently. The sixth floor was mine and Lucas.

'Wait, the whole floor is ours?' I asked.

'Yes of course,' she replied.

It was like a dream, one big apartment just for us, the only thing it didn't have was a kitchen. The bed was queen sized with black silk bedding, hand crafted wolves carved into the bed posts with a massive walk-in wardrobe already stocked, a spa bath with a separated shower two toilets and two sinks, the colour scheme was grey and black. I looked around in awe of my surroundings it would seem that privacy wouldn't be an issue for us, as the only one allowed on our floor was cleaning staff, guards, assistants and of course Luca's beta, no one however was allowed on the seventh floor, as that belonged to Mr and Mrs Grayson. Leading me to wonder why?

Walking all the way back downstairs was challenging, I wasn't unfit, but I wasn't physically fit either. Finally reaching the bottom floor, I was oddly out of breath as I hunched over gasping for air.

'All those floors and no one thought of an elevator?' I said.

Orion scoffed. 'Yes it's rather a lot isn't it?' she said, moving through the kitchen to the back garden.

The grounds were big, just on the outskirts was a 12ft fence with barbed wire running over the top of it.

'What's the wire for?' I asked, tilting my head.

'To keep any unwanted guests out, the wire is tripped when touched, alerting the entire pack to intruders,' she said proudly.

'I see, so does that work instantly?' I said, receiving an excited nod from her.

Peering around the corner I saw the sparring ring and the young Omega's training.

'Orion, who's your fit friend?' he said.

She went to answer but I shushed her, looking up at me she backed away.

'What is your name?' I asked, the boy fully aware of what I was about to do to him.

'Connor,' he replied, proudly taking off his shirt and flexing his pecks.

'Well Connor, my name is Annabeth. I am your new Luna!' I said with force, dropping him to his knees in an instant.

'I'm so sorry Luna, please forgive me!' he begged.

I looked at Orion who smiled, not knowing what my next move should be I improvised.

'Rise, next time you will show some respect!' I said, in a firm tone.

'Yes Luna!' he said, putting his shirt back on.

Holding out my hand behind me, Orion gives me a low five for my efforts, my face remains strong not wanting to push my luck I instruct. 'Carry on!' as they scattered. What a frightful feeling this was, I'm not sure I'm ready for this.

# Chapter 12
## Oh Luna, my Luna

It had been six months since I joined the pack house, my Luna training started shortly after I arrived and it was intense to say the least, the mountains of paperwork I was expected to sift through daily blew my mind. I didn't have time to think about my old life as my new life was so tasking. I got out of bed looking around for Luca to see him coming out of the shower, oh what a vision he is, my mouth watering at the sheer sight of him as my eyes stalked him to the wardrobe.

'Stop it!' he said playfully.

'Stop what?' I look at him more closely.

'That! I have business to attend to, we can continue that another time also we are going out tomorrow,' he said.

'Do you mean it?' I replied, almost bouncing.

'Yes!' he sighed, rolling his eyes at me.

'Promise?' I asked.

'Yes, I promise,' he said, in a teasing manor.

Delighted I jumped out of bed ready to start my day, with my new positive attitude in tow.

His father was forcibly trying to get him to mark me, he said he would do it when the time was right, so I suppose I just have to accept that patients is something I really need to learn and fast. Going to my study Shay is in the chair waiting for me, with her mud ridden boots dripping on my desk as she flicked them about.

'Hmm, still no mark I see,' she said slyly.

I approach her and kick the bottom of my chair, that she was sitting in with her legs raised balancing on my desk.

'No, now get up!' I snapped.

I was not in the mood for this today, my spirits were high, and I was going to keep it that way.

'Move,' I ordered, as she tutted standing to her feet.

'Can we not do something fun today?' she pleaded.

'No Shay, I can't I have work to do,' I said, sitting down on my chair, attempting to clean the mud off my desk. Shay starts moaning loudly as she throws herself down on the chair opposite me, huffing and puffing in a displeasing and annoying manor.

'Ohhhhh,' she said, closing one eye but keeping the other on me, I ignore her and continue my work.

'Ohhh,' she said again, but this time more winey.

'Alright! if you let me finish my work, we will go into town later, okay?' I snapped.

'Yes!' she replied, her mood improved drastically hoping up off the chair, she walked out of my office.

'See you later!' she said, shutting the door behind her.

The Silence was deafening, it was that blissful time of the day where no one bothers me unless it was an emergency, I finally settle back and get to work.

Opening book after book I began looking over pack law to familiarise myself with it, nothing however made sense when it came to human involvement. If a pack member were to expose who they are to a human and the founding families found out, that human would have to serve the family forever, but should they refuse they would be sentenced to death. Gosh, this is all a bit much isn't it? The door creaked open, I peered up over the abnormally large book I was reading to see Luca heading right for me, his eyes as black as night. I had never seen him so angry.

'Luca, what's wrong?' I said, as I arose to my feet taking a step back.

'The silver moon packs treaty is coming to an end, why wasn't I informed of this?' he said, slamming his hand down onto the desk beside me, this was the first time I had actually feared him.

'Luca, please calm down!' I said, cowering slightly.

'I don't have to do anything!' he growled, making me flinch slightly, grabbing my throat he dragged me from my seat and slammed me against the wall as my head collided with it, I winced in pain struggling to gain freedom as he pinned me in place.

'Luca, please?' I begged, clawing for him to loosen his grip, but he only tightened it further.

He looked me in the eyes with a cold frosty stare, a psychotic look I would not be forgetting anytime soon. Pressing me further into the wall he wrenched my head to the side with his canines protruding, my eyes widen as I struggle for breath. Whipping his head forwards he sinks them into my neck, I let out an almighty scream as the venom entered my body. Hearing him laugh was horrifying, loosening his grip he let me fall to the floor with a bang, clutching and clawing at my skin as venom surged and coursed through my veins. This wasn't what the book said it was supposed to be like, even for a human, this was supposed to be the best feeling of your life. So why did it feel this way for me?

Still on the floor I was expecting him to seal the wound, but he didn't he just watched on grinning at my pain. I was seeing stars with a mixture of shock and pain. Rolling onto my back I clawed at my face and sides as his venom ran through me burning my skin, the sweat pouring from me like someone had just torched my soul.

The pain soon subsided, but the shock did not.

'You are mine now I didn't want it, but now you are you will do as you are told, got it?' he yelled.

The shock continued as his attitude towards me had now changed.

'Get back to work!' he instructed, pointing towards the mountains of paperwork on my desk. Not wanting to make him angry I did as I was told, pulling myself to my feet I winced again as I wiped my bleeding neck from my wound that remained unsealed. What did I do wrong? Why didn't he seal it? Trying to avid crying I emersed myself in my work, that was what I was good at.

A year passed by in an instant, Luca was constantly on business, which meant I would spend the majority of my nights alone longing for comfort.

But something would happen each and every night, a searing burning pain that would start off as light cramping in my abdomen, before traveling everywhere and taking over my entire body, I would lay and scream into my pillow for sometimes hours unable to cope, writhing in pain as I thrash around on my bed with my pillow pressed against my face to help silence me. Standing to my feet pacing up and down, I was unable to sit and unable to settle, biting on my hand to prevent my cries from being heard. Too afraid to tell anyone in case I was rendered weak, this was something I couldn't afford to be branded as. The pain was long lasting, some nights I would pray for death, a death that never came.

It was a new day, upon going to work I decided to consult the pack history to figure out a way of finding out why I was feeling such pain, as if someone were pulling on a piece of string and cutting into it with blunt scissors, toying with my lifeline and there was nothing I could do to stop it. After consulting the book for a number of hours, I stumbled across what I had been looking for, and I so wish I hadn't.

Luca returned to me that evening, now it was official the book said he would come and claim me and claim me he did. There was nothing romantic about that experience, I figured the sooner it was over the quicker he would leave and thankfully I was right.

He left me feeling ashamed and used, I was grateful for the silence but the minute I tried to fall asleep the pain started, my life now revolved around not sleeping and working long hours. The bags around my eyes had their very own bags, my skin was dry, my nails were frail and were cracking. Had my life really come to this?

The working day began again like clockwork, I continued my studying as the door opened silently revealing a smiling father-in-law, well I wasn't married just mated, so I am not sure if that counts for anything.

'Mr Grayson,' I said, rising to my feet.

'Part of the family now I see,' he said, looking at my neck happily.

'Yes, Mr Grayson,' I bowed.

His smile was making me angry, but I now had to contain my disdain as the whole pack would feel what I am feeling, it was not long before the voices echoed through my head of thoughts from the other pack members, my head pounding as I try and concentrate.

'You'll be needing this,' he said, handing me a bottle of liquid.

'What is it?' I asked, with a wary quaking voice, trying to be grateful at the same time.

I looked up at him half smiling to avoid detection of my hatred towards this family, my emotions contained as I stared at him for a moment longer.

'That is for you to mask your scent, can't have people knowing you're our true Luna now, can we?' he smiled.

'Hmm I suppose we can't, is this for when I leave the grounds?' I said, trying to show gratitude.

'It is yes, you will be needing it tomorrow,' he said, with a sickening smile.

'Where am I going tomorrow?' I enquired.

'Silver lake pack, you know you're supposed to sort out the overdue treaty, right?' he questioned.

'Of course, Alpha, I obviously forgot,' I said, nodding as he leaves me be.

Tomorrow was another day in this hell hole, if the last six months have taught me anything it is that true love does not exist, it was something meant to lure young girls into doing as they were told. A dream told to little girls during story time with fairy-tale endings, a lie told by many and believed by all. Hope is something we all want to believe in, but not something we all get to believe in. Leaning back in my seat I cry heavily into my cup of tea, dripping my tears onto the pages in front of me as I consulted the book. It has however taught me how to tune into my senses, which meant this time I could feel him approaching, numbed by the constant voices in my head I massaged it gently.

'Tomorrow you are to go to silver lake pack!' he announced, as the door opened quietly for once.

'Yes Alpha!' I bowed, refusing to call him Luca ever again, as the love I had for him was being burnt out night after night.

'Put make up on and wear that red dress!' he demanded.

'Yes Alpha,' I said, knowing if I did this, he would pay me a visit tomorrow night. I couldn't have that now, could I?

'Oh, once you're done here, you're to cook for the entire pack each and every night that you are not away. Do I make myself clear?' he grinned, giving me the sense, he wasn't joking around.

'I was supposed to go out with Shay this evening,' I said, as his roar shook the room.

'Yes Alpha!' I spoke softly and quietly to avoid rattling him further. How on earth was I going to cook for so many people?

Surely the pack will know something is off if their Luna suddenly starts cooking every night.

'Unaided!' he added, before leaving the room.

I am not a wife or a Luna, I am a slave being punished for eternity.

After my day was finished an eager Shay rushed through my door, resisting the urge to jump up and down I watched as her foot tapped frantically.

'Can we go now? I have been waiting for hours!' she said, as her excitement radiated from her.

'I can't,' I said, avoiding eye contact.

'Why not?' she said, folding her arms together.

'I'm not allowed, I have to do dinner,' I replied.

'You have to what?' she said, laughing thinking I was joking, but my face remained the same.

'But we have cooks,' she laughed.

'Not anymore, it would seem they have been promoted,' I said, my eyes lowered to the ground, heavy and full of sadness.

'How can they be promoted above you?' she snapped.

'It's fine, I needed to learn new skills given the fact I cannot go out on patrol,' I said, changing the subject.

'Luna, that is beneath you,' she said.

'Nothing is beneath any of us, you will do well to remember that!' I snapped.

'Can I at least help you?' she said, as her eyebrows lowered, a sadness flashed in her eyes.

'I can't have help I have to do it alone, it would be best if you ask one of the girls to go shopping with you,' I said, holding back my emotions.

'But I wanted to go with you,' she said.

'Next time,' I said, filling her with hope and reassurance, even though I knew this was never going to happen.

My working day just doubled as I'm sure I would have to clean up after as well, working all day cooking then cleaning, then not sleeping. Some charmed life I lead aye. What changed? Why now do I no longer know who I am? Or what my life even means? Why is Luca being so cruel? So many questions I did not have the answers to.

Cooking dinner was absolute hell for a moment I thought cooking for so many each night would more than likely kill me off, a blissful reprieve I longed for.

It has been so long since I saw my family, my pack didn't even tell me where they had moved them, or if they were even okay, completely blocking me from them and them from me. Nothing but a distant memory, one I longed to relive.

# Chapter 13
## By night and by day

It was time for us to go about our duties it was a two-day trip to silver lake pack, unlike other packs my pack would send their Luna off to do business with other packs, as it was far better to sacrifice a Luna than it was to lose an Alpha, making you completely expendable, that feeling was bizarre. If you did not return who would care? Would it even matter? however they would do a decoy Luna that was something I suppose.

It has been over a year since I have seen my family missing them hurt my heart, never really fully healing when I left them, the pain sometimes was almost too much to tolerate. My life at the pack house was getting worse, knowing what I know about Luca was tearing me apart. I was quite gullible back then hanging off his every word, I was so sure he would be mine and mine alone forever. Stupid girl.

Walking towards the end of the drive the car pulled up beside me as I patiently waited a moment, Boid loaded my luggage into the boot. Going round to the side of the car I opened the door, seeing Luca inside the car made me burn with rage as he was not supposed to be there, Orion by his side as she looked at me with guilt. I didn't think twice when he did not open the door for me anymore, this was a life chosen for me, one I didn't want in the first place, sitting in front of him his face turns sour as he looked me up and down.

'I told you to wear the red dress!' Luca sighed, rolling his eyes at me. I looked down at my dress as I pushed off the dog hair that had accumulated from this damn pack. I sighed heavily adverting my gaze to avoid making a scene. 'I told you I didn't like that one!' he added, as I frowned at him, wondering why a dress got him so vexed.

'I'm sorry, would you like me to go and get changed Alpha?' I said smugly, knowing we didn't have time. Pulling away I flinched a little expecting a sudden burst of rage to come from him, but it didn't, he remained calm. Why? What has changed? Before we got together, he wasn't known for being cruel, but his hatred and anger filled the more he was in my presence.

Being mated to a human did us no favours, he tried to love me I will admit, in the beginning he was kind and gentle. All the time he didn't mark me he could pretend I was normal, well normal for them anyway. But I was not what he wanted, and I knew it, he promised me the world on a whim, broken promises to a broken girl. The mark on my neck proved I was his, a branded girl with nowhere to go, to leave would make me a rogue human and a target for anyone who would come across me.

We had been trying for a baby as he desired a pup, it was one of my duties as Luna to deliver an heir, one I wasn't sure I myself wanted, I was happy our encounters were only once in a blue moon, pressure from his father I'm sure. How I hated them so much!

The initial meeting went well, I knew something was off when he had other business to attend to, but I smiled sweetly and bowed before him to not raise any suspicion, wearing a scarf over my mark to not be recognised.

113

The lies I told; I was now use to. A lie use to be something I couldn't muster up easily but now, now I did it with ease, remorse was a thing of the past for me. Sadly, once the deal was done it was time to go home.

Returning home was quiet and rather icy, the warmth I once knew from my mate was long overshadowed by the fear of him, an heir was all he required of me to fulfil their pack legacy. I no longer cared as I knew the moon goddess would bless me when she saw fit to do so.

Finally, we made it home and I for one couldn't wait to get out of this damn car, taking my things to my room I unpacked them before going back downstairs.

It was my turn to rally the family, I shouted for them, but something was wrong, the south corner of the property was quiet, too quiet. Walking into the kitchen to a pack of wolves I once loved and cared for was tiring. However, I was unable to ask them to leave as they eat the fresh cookies I made this morning. The rest of the pack are supposed to be on patrol, so I will swap them out later for a break.

In my infinite wisdom I decided to go out and clear my head of all the turmoil that it was going through. Orion close behind me for my protection, she was a lovely girl with dark hair, standing tall at 5ft8 with a beautiful complexion like shimmering glass, her skin was flawless. My most trusted friend and biggest protector, I loved her like a sister.

We was walking along the bank smiling and laughing when something caught her attention. 'Annabeth!' she signalled me to wait, transforming into her wolf as she sniffed the air, before taking a fighting stance. Sniffing the air further her heckles raised and her growl became menacing. The tree's rustled above the fence and suddenly a rogue wolf climbed through the gap, slamming to the ground in front of her with its claws showing an teeth bearing. Getting down low It growls and snaps its jaws at us, Orion jumped in front of me for my protection. We paused for a moment awaiting the pack, but they didn't come. Looking at this wolf I noticed something was wrong with it, it smelt like a rogue as I tapped into Orion's senses, but it was big, too big. Usually, they are small due to being malnourished and weak, snapping again it lunges for Orion, bouncing over her she rolled on her back and kicked out, its jaw clamped shut as it missed me by inches as it propelled backwards. Lunging for her again, it clawed and snapped at her legs and neck, drool flicking with every bite, gripping hold of her it begins to rag her lifting her 6ft off the ground, tossing her to the side she slammed into a tree rendering her unconscious as if she weighed nothing, she laid limp and lifeless on the ground, I looked on in horror as it turned towards me.

'Orion!' I screamed, closing my eyes desperately trying to mind link my pack, but the link was closed. Shock and panic surged through my body as the wolf begins to slowly stalk towards me, dribble oozing from its jaws as it lowered itself closer to the ground and approached me.

'Luca,' I whispered, before the wolf attacked.

I turned to try and run as it's paw slammed across my back throwing me to the floor, feeling a sudden weight thrust upon me as it threw its weight down. Pinning me to the ground whilst biting my left shoulder, ripping, and clawing at my body as it tore into my back and sides running its razor-sharp claws down my spine, the pain was unimaginable. I felt him tear into my flesh latching onto my leg, it drags me backwards, the blood draining from my wounds and dropping on the grass around me.

I clawed out digging my frail nails into the ground only for them to snap beneath the earth as it continued its torture, dragging me back and forth my breathing becoming desperate. my eyes growing heavy as my screams filled the air, but still nobody came.

'Orion!' I screamed again, the intense pain setting in. The wolf threw me into the air and onto my back, as I collided with the cold damp earth, another swipe came causing blood to splatter from my mouth as bubbles filled my left lung, I was sure he had penetrated it. My breathing became harder as the bubbles got bigger, laying praying for death taking snatch breaths in and out as I laid helpless staring at the cloudless bright blue sky.

'I'm going to die!' was my first thought, a long overdue welcomed embrace. Looking up I stared death in the face as this wolf snarled back at me. I was done, my strength was waning, I had nothing left to give and nothing left to live for. Staring out I saw his paw rise for a final time as it separated revealing sharpened claws ready to strike. Closing my eyes I thought of my family, my thoughts took me back to a time where I was happiest and where I was free.

A swift breeze whooshed past me, opening my

blood-soaked eyes I saw Paddox and Shay standing before me Shay lunged for the wolf catching him off guard allowing Paddox to come up behind the wolf, bringing his jaws down against its neck as they crashed to the ground, the wolf screamed and screeched as it desperately tried to claw its way out. With one fowl swoop Paddox broke his neck and the screaming stopped, the wolf laid limp on the ground not moving. My consciousness dipped in and out, coming around I felt the warmth of my blood dripping down my arms and legs, my world went dark and that is how it stayed. For a number of day's at least.

Days later I finally awoke in the pack house infirmary, but Luca was nowhere to be seen.

'Luca!' I called out his name shamefully, that burning pain was there again but this time I knew what he was doing. Anger filled my eyes as the pain got worse, a feeling I knew all too well that I kept to myself. See I learnt from an ancient book I had to read, that when a wolf is unfaithful their mate can feel it, the pain starts off as a slight tingle but the more the betrayal continues the worse it gets. I doubled over in pain not because of my wounds, but because my mate is being an unfaithful git. Normally I would scream into my pillow but tonight I am whaling out-loud, clawing at my burning skin as the fire that engulfs my soul is excruciating.

'Annabeth, stop please!' I hear Paddox say to me, but I am unable, the pain is just too much.

It weakens my very essence as I feel he is near the end, enduring this kind of torture night after night is unheard of, that is why no one recognises it. Because when you mate you mate for life. Every time he is unfaithful it weakens me and breaks our bond, making me more of a target and unable to defend myself against threats.

'Doctor!' Paddox yells, as I scream in my bed unable to move unable to run. The doctor runs in to sedate me, but it was already too late the deed was done and so was I.

'Paddox?' I whispered.

'Yes Luna?' he said, gripping my hand.

'Where is Luca?' I asked, with the last breath I could muster, hating the fact I still needed him.

'I will go get him!' he said, gripping my hand a little tighter, he shot off as fast as his legs would take him.

Rolling over slightly my eyes filled as the tears streamed down my face.

'I left my family for this?' I thought, as my sobs got louder, the sedation finally started taking effect as my head became woozy. A little while later Luca entered the room.

'Stay here Paddox!' Luca said, as he came into the room.

'You sent for me!' he added, in an angry tone.

Looking upon his face I couldn't help but reach for him, but what held my hand back was not Luca, it was Blane, and his eyes were sad.

'We are sorry, please forgive us?' he pleaded, as he gripped my hand tightly.

'I love you,' I said to him, hoping he would say it back, but as soon as Blane went to speak he was pushed back out again.

Luca now stood before me, his eyes where angry and full of rage, he pulled back his hand in disgust as he wiped it on his trousers.

'Doctor!' he called, as the doctor re-entered the room.

'What is her damage?' he asked, so cold and so callus. After all this time all I wanted was this man to love me. Sad isn't it really.

'Alpha she has lacerations to sixty percent of her body, five broken ribs and a punctured lung,' he replied.

'Her prognosis?' he said, his eyes glared at me, before looking back at the doctor.

'Good, she will make a full recovery; however, she isn't healing as quickly as she should be,' he said.

'Probably because she is a human!' he said, in a vicious tone.

'No Alpha, she should be mostly healed by now given the fact she is mated, it makes her less human granted, but her healing should be nearly done but something is preventing it?' he said, quivering when he spoke.

Luca looked over at me and looked back at the doctor.

'She is a useless human, what do you expect!' he roared, making the doctor drop to his knees.

A rumble heard by all causing Paddox to enter the room, but as soon as the door opened Luca was gone, a swift breeze hit my face as my Alpha was gone. I turned onto my left side cradling my shoulders as I wrapped my arms around them, the bandages clung tightly to my skin as I winced in pain from my movements.

A hug I so desperately craved came from someone unexpected, as I laid sobbing reaching for breath as the tears flow freely down my chin, I felt an arm wrap around my core pulling me in, causing me to wince in pain but my muscles relaxed.

'I've got you!' Paddox whispered, as I sobbed some more, his grip tightened as he rested his head on my shoulder.

'I thought you don't do crying?' I said, causing him to laugh a little.

'I don't, but for you my Luna I will make an exception,' he said, hugging me tighter.

'Thank you Paddox, I don't know what I would do without you,' I said, crying some more into his arms.

'I've got you Luna, for as long as you need, okay?' he said, pecking my shoulder, gripping hold of him I hugged him back, I sighed in relief as I slowly sobbed myself to sleep.

# Chapter 14
## Only the bold are brave

A week went by, and my wounds had healed, the wounds on my arms and legs weren't deep enough to scar but my back, torso, and ribs were, the wounds healed but the fear remained. Why did my pack not come for us? Why was my link closed? Was this done on purpose? Knowing that sensor should have triggered was doing my head in, with many unanswered questions I feared would never be resolved.

Holding my head up high I resumed pack duties strolling through the corridors and looking upon the faces I had come to know and love. But not one of them helped me when I needed them the most, they had completely forsaken me and to tell you the truth it hurts.

Today was a day of meetings again but with the half-moon pack, a new treaty needed to be signed before war is waged upon us all. Getting out of the car I stretched my legs and it felt glorious, as I reached my arms above my head pulling upwards I had to remind myself to stay behind Orion. She was mighty and strong and ready for anything, I knew my days with Luca were numbered, since he was already cheating on me it gave me cause to do as I pleased. For tonight and for tonight only I will be having some fun, and no one was going to stand in my way. We was invited to the half-moon pack who were hosting a grand event, this was the feeling of freedom even if it was just for a night. No one knowing I was the Luna made things so much more exciting, as Orion was the one who had to do as she was told, me on the other hand I could do as I liked and that was what excited me the most.

Getting to the event we were shown to our rooms, Orion being the Luna meant she got the bigger room, I didn't mind though I was grateful for the time away from Luca.

'Luna, how are you feeling?' Orion asked.

'Who me? I'm fine, please don't worry about me. Let us just have fun for once,' I smiled excitedly.

'Well, it would seem I will have to leave the fun to you,' she smiled sweetly.

'Well then, I will have to have enough fun for the both of us,' I laughed.

'Yes it would certainly seem that way,' she replied.

'But one day all bets are off, agreed?' I nodded instantly, hoping one day that would come true.

After getting dressed we went downstairs, I was wearing a black slim fit dress that had a trail behind it and Orion was wearing an Emerald green dress with sparkles and lace sleeves.

'You look beautiful, Orion,' I said, proudly.

'Not as beautiful as you Lu... Annabeth,' she said, correcting herself quickly.

Going through the hall was magnificent, beautiful decorations lined the ceiling and balloons filled the room. Every pack member was at this event other than my cheating mate of course, too cowardly to do his own dirty work. After meeting and greeting the other pack members I quickly approached the bar, the first thing I was ordering was a Tequila slammer, I had never had one of these before but who cares right its only one night and I sure as hell am thirsty. After doing the first one I felt on top of the world, a heat surged through my core not knowing if I liked it or not was strange,

so, I did what anyone would do I had another and another until my tiny frame couldn't take anymore. Moving off of my stool I dragged myself across to the dance floor, dancing like no one was watching was like magic, as I allowed myself to be encased in the vibrations surrounding me without a care in the world, feeling the eyes of unmated males watching my every move, I had put on the perfume that blocks the scent of a mated woman gifted to me by my father-in-law. Thank you for that. It certainly prevented me from being noticed or worse captured. A couple of drinks later I began to stumble slightly, it was no secret as to how clumsy I was. I looked around for Orion but couldn't find her to begin with, until I caught a glimpse of her talking to someone realising rather soon after that I had too much to drink. I snuck off leaving Orion to entertain the other wolves, I walked around looking for my room, but every door looked the same, thinking I had found it I stormed in throwing my bag down and kicking off my heels, feeling the heat warming my stomach from all the alcohol I let out an almighty burp.

'I am so sexy,' I said, as I began taking off my dress, and launched it to my left. Bending down still in darkness I began looking for the mini fridge for food.

'How hard was it to find a damn fridge!' I thought, after finally locating it.

I took a step back slipping on a pair of shoes in the middle of my floor, thinking they were mine I picked them up and examined them.

'I don't remember having feet this big?' I said, letting out a belly laugh.

'Who's boats are these?' I scoffed, holding the shoes up, whilst lying on my back.

'Who are you?' I heard a rumble from behind me, nearly making me wet my pants. Launching myself to my feet my back straightens as I look around.

'Hello, are you a ghost?' I asked, feeling my way around the room, letting out another roar of laughter.

'No, who are you?' he replied.

'Hello, are you my conscience?' I burped again.

'No, I said who are you?' he replied, taking me by surprise.

The room was pitch black, so I was rendered blind, feeling around I tried to search for a light. I turned to try and head for the door, but I felt a sudden breath on my back making me shudder as it warmed me slightly, he whipped me around pushing me backwards with my back now pressed firmly against the door.

'I said, who are you?' he said, as his fist pounded against the door beside me, his other hand still trapping me in place, he let out a mighty growl and my body began to shake.

'Annabeth,' I whispered.

'Why are you in my room?' he said.

But in my drunken state I replied. 'Erm, no; I think you will find this is my room,' I said, trying to shush him with my fingers, hearing a faint snigger in response.

'No it's not, this is my room,' he laughed.

'Then how did I get in? exactly now kindly remove thyself from my room so I can get changed,' I said, trying to move past him.

'Oh you're already changed!' he whispered, in my left ear.

124

My intoxicated bubble ridden mind didn't register fully what was happening until suddenly it caught up.

'Oh lord!' I replied, trying to cover myself.

I was mortified to say the least, I could have died on the spot as my body began to tremble.

'What's the matter, are you okay?' he said, worried and slightly cautious.

Hearing genuine concern from a man was refreshing to say the least, and quite unexpected.

'I'm fine,' I said, trying to find my clothes.

His nose pressed against my neck as he took in my scent, I could feel myself leaning into his touch. I reached for my dress to try and cover what dignity I had left at this point, which by the way wasn't much. Leaning too far forward my lips accidently brushed his kissing him. Feeling his breath on my face sent shivers down my spine as he pulled me in closer towards him, his eyes were yellow and glowing in the dark.

'Beautiful,' I whispered, having never seen a wolf with those coloured eyes before.

His eyes filled with lust and desire, the fire that ignited between us was like nothing I had ever experienced, the sensation was empowering a feeling I was sure I would never experience again, so I relished in it fully making the most of it. Not knowing who this man was I felt it safe to slither away in the night, before leaving I looked back at him whilst he was asleep. I gathered up my stuff and returned peacefully to my room, with nothing but my memories of such a beautiful encounter. In that moment I hoped Luca felt every last bit of it, then he would have some kind of feeling as to what I've suffered for months.

The next morning after a long shower to wash off the scent that was overpowering mine, I met with Orion in the lobby of the hotel.

'Good night, was it?' Orion asked, with a smirk.

'What do you mean?' my eyes widened out of fear.

'You were wasted!' she laughed.

'Oh yeah that, well you know,' I said, lowering my head in shame, as we began to walk out of the hotel.

'We've all been there,' she said, shoving me playfully.

'I'm sure we have,' I said, shoving her back.

The journey home was silent, I unwound the window halfway to look upon the scenery, it was a beautiful summer's day, and the day was just getting started. Darkness soon clouded my head as I realised what I had done. What if he knew what I had done? What if he is waiting for me right now? What am I going to do? My mind went a hundred miles an hour, making the journey now seemed longer as dread filled my heart. Pulling up the drive we arrived home, Paddox comes to the car.

'Hi Luna, did you have a good trip?' he said.

My mind rested quickly, because if he had any inkling he would be waiting for me himself.

'It was fine thank you, Paddox,' I smiled, knowing full well he knew all along what Luca was up to.

'We are rather tired from our journey, where is Luca?' I asked, not really sure I want to know.

'He's been called away on business,' he replied.

'Business huh?' I replied, shaking my head.

'Yes Luna,' his eyes saddened as he spoke to me.

'Can I get you something?' he said, instantly as I took a step forward.

'No thank you, we just need to rest,' I replied.

He nodded and bowed as I walked away.

I had to find a way out of this life before my deceptions became a reality and my secrets revealed. Returning to my room completely alone with my thoughts, remembering every touch, every kiss, every motion was like bliss. I had to calm my thoughts before they got the better of me.

The next few days were long, too long in fact, I had a lot of paperwork and minutes to take from the meeting at half-moon pack for the packs records.

'Maybe I will leave some parts out,' I sniggered to myself, when my door bursts open, Luca comes rushing through.

'What's the matter, Alpha?' I said, pleased with myself and hoping on some level that he knew.

'The silver moon pack have retracted their agreement; I thought you had handled this!' he said, infuriated at me as his fist collided with my cheek, throwing me from my chair and on to the floor, followed by a kick to my rib cage as I let out a yelp.

'I'm sorry Alpha, I thought the deal was done,' I said, trying not to anger him more, my body too weak to fight back.

'You will go back, and you will fix this!' he growls, bringing me closer to the floor, as it rumbled through my chest. 'What good are you to me anyway, useless human!' he spat, kneeling down to my ears.

Now before those words would have floored me, but since I was already down here it didn't matter.

'Yes Alpha, right away,' I replied, holding my side fighting for breath.

Cowering as he leant back down to laugh in my face, I'm not sure what I ever did to be cursed with this life, but it must have been bad.

'You had better get to work,' he hissed.

I wait for him to take a step back to let me know it was okay to get up.

'Move!' he roared, as I rushed out of the room running through the pack house to find Orion.

Soon finding Orion in her room we set off right away without a moment to waste. With my heart still racing, my life still constantly felt like it was hanging in the balance. How do I escape this life.

# Chapter 15
## The treaty

The journey to silver lake pack was quiet, I sat with my feet up cradling my sides. All I knew was after a year and a half of this I have had enough, I left previously thinking the deal was closed, but it would appear some people questioned the alliance with my pack, they feared that Luca was too highly strung and a danger to them all.

'Orion, what exactly happened at the meeting?' I asked, knowing I left her and Luca too it.

'Well you know Luca came with us, well their elder was present and he implied that Luca was dangerous, a risk to their pack and their way of life,' she said.

'What did he do?' I said, my eyes widened in horror.

'He threatened the families,' she said, wincing a little.

'Show me!' I said, holding out my hand.

I may not have had many abilities but access to memories was something the moon goddess granted me. My eyes glaze as I looked into the past, the conversation blurring In and out getting closer and closer I heard Luca's growl, to see him sitting in a room full of Alphas.

'Is he totally mad?' I thought, watching as he threatened the founding members.

'It gets worse, Luna,' she said, whispering to me in her head.

'Show me!' I demanded.

As I entered deep into her subconscious mind, I could see as the rage filled the room as each Alpha stood their ground, each bowing out of their own agreement with my pack saying Luca is unfit to rule.

'Mark my words, if this treaty isn't signed it will be the death of you all,' Luca scowled, as he brought his hand down slamming it against the desk, making the other Alpha's puff out their chests with outrage.

How in the world did he think the deal should have been done? I was not present for this meeting Orion was, as she was my Decoy but because Luca was there I wasn't allowed in. Letting go of her hand I sat back closing my eyes whilst I tried to think of a way out of this, I brought my hands to my face pulling them across my brows as I tried to think of a solution. How Is he such an idiot?

'How in the world did he think the treaty would be signed under those circumstances?' I sighed.

'I don't know, I couldn't do anything either,' she said.

'No I know you couldn't, but how are we going to fix this?' I groaned a little in despair.

'I don't know, but we don't have long to figure it out either,' she said, as she pointed out the window beside me. Looking down at my watch I realised we had spent too much time in her memories that we was already here. I slumped in my seat closing my eyes again as they frantically move from side to side in search of a way out.

'Okay, here is what we are going to do,' I said, as her eyes flutter as she listens intently. 'We are going to say his anger was high because he had a sickness,' I added.

'We can't do that Annabeth, because that would make him and us a target,' she said, with a shrug.

Her words were true I couldn't make the pack pay for his mistakes; I pursed my lips in anger looking out the window I could see we were nearly there.

'Well then what do you suggest?' I said, in a panic.

She shrugged 'Tell them the truth?' she said.

130

'Fine you tell them he is just a ball of rage and see how that goes,' I said sarcastically.

'No we tell them he was merely having a bad day, that no threat was intended to offend them,' she responded.

Well it's not the worst idea but by the looks of things we are going to have to do a lot of kissing ass, as there was not one person in that room who didn't seem to want to tear him apart.

The door opened up on Orion's side, a hand extended out for her, and she took it. Putting on my scarf and my perfume before I too exit the vehicle, this was going to be an awfully long and very costly day.

Walking into the pack house all eyes were now on us, the fury coming from this pack was terrifying, we was shown to the office of Alpha Valencia who was an equally matched opponent, a strong pack member who was of course one of the founding families.

'Why have you returned!' he spoke loudly, for all to hear as he shuffled the paperwork Infront of him.

'It would appear there are questions about the treaty?' Orion answered, in her most polite voice.

'You were here the last time, where you not?' he demanded.

'Yes, Alpha Valencia,' she replied, with a bow.

'Then you are aware of what...' he stopped in his tracks as his attention was now fully on me, I lowered my head to the ground in fear.

Standing to his feet he walked over to me, sniffing the air around me as his nose brushed past my face.

'Oh god, he's going to eat me,' I said out-loud, making him laugh at me.

'Eat you, no thank you,' he replied, his playful attitude made me smile.

'Suit yourself,' I said, shrugging my shoulder.

'You remind me of someone I once knew, you smell like her too,' he said, placing his hand on my shoulder.

'Oh yeah, who's that then?' I enquired.

'It's not important, what is it you want my dear?' he said, his attention still on me, but his face softened.

'I wish for you to sign the treaty, but for a reduced term; let him prove he is not a threat,' I announced.

'So instead of the fixed ten years, you propose what exactly?' his eyes still scanning me.

'One year!' I said with confidence.

Orion's face drops as she looked over at me urging me to reconsider, but I was not going to listen, not this time.

'Are you sure?' he paused scanning me for a moment. 'Then so it shall be. One year to sort himself out and if he does not comply then the treaty is void, and your pack is on its own. Understood?' he added.

Orion moved forward trying to introject, but she was shut down instantly.

'Forgive me Luna, but I was not talking to you,' he said, giving her a quick glance, before looking back at me. 'Do we have a deal?' he added looking at me.

Now I realise you shouldn't really make a deal with the devil, but I already did once so what's one more going to make any difference.

'Deal!' I said, extending out my hand as he shook it.

'I like you, what is your name?' he said.

'My name is Annabeth, Alpha Valencia,' I bowed, watching him take in a deep breath as he walked back to his seat. 'Nice to meet you, until next time; Oh Annabeth, the next visit I will only deal with you, should you not be present I will not talk to anyone else. Do I make myself clear?' he said, I nod and bow before him. As we turned to leave the deal was done, but I think I'm going to be in trouble when I get home. The treaty I was returning with was nine years short, something I'm sure was going to be of great cost to me. I had to figure out a way out of this life before it was too late, after the treaty was finally readjusted and signed I saw someone familiar to me, someone I had only seen once but a long time ago.

'Jason?' I smiled, tilting my head to the side slightly.

'Well if it isn't the little firecracker! Are you here making waves?' he said sweetly, as his heavy build towered over me.

'Hello to you,' I said, as I watched him sniff the air around me, getting my perfume out I sprayed around my neck. His face turned to anger as realisation hit him.

'It's okay, Jason,' I said, as I tried to calm him.

'How could you let that animal mark you!' he asked, quickly pulling me to one side.

'I didn't have a choice; he is my mate!' I said, intuitively knowing I was being listened to.

'B-but' he stuttered.

'No Jason, I am happy with my mate; he is the love of my life my one true mate!' I said, my eyes wide as I signal him that we are being watched, that it would be wise for him to stop talking. I don't actually know much about the man who stood before me as I of course only met him once, or indeed whose pack he belongs too. I didn't care all I knew was I wanted out of this life altogether, and that was exactly what I was going to get.

# Chapter 16
## Fear and Loathing

It had been a month since the meeting at silver lake pack, it was a mistake to offer only one year to them that earned me another demotion. I was allowed to stay in my room, but my privileges revoked, I was now not allowed to use the water daily, if I wanted a shower I had to use the lake out the back. My luxuries were removed, not only did I now have my Luna duties, but I also had dinner service, cleaning service and laundry duty. That was my punishment, I was only allowed to leave the premises if it was for good reason other than that I was a prisoner.

I haven't seen Luca since the new treaty was signed, but I felt him torturing me day and night. Something was different though, as tonight I had a fluttering in my tummy. A lightly bubbling feeling of good fortune, that something in my life was going to change forever. What is this amazing feeling? And why can't I shake it?

Each high-ranking pack member is paid a monthly fee for their work, I have been transferring mine into my old account each month readying myself for the inevitable.

A little while had past and whilst cooking pack dinner I was heaving constantly, my breasts becoming sore and tender and food that use to smell divine to me now smells like a dumpster. I knew what this was, confirming my fears as I was already a week late for my monthly cycle, terrifying me knowing if he ever found out he would kill me for this. Looking up I saw Luca watching my every move as I plate up their food, I found myself continuously swallowing my saliva, holding back the sick that floated to the back of my throat pushing it back as the acid burnt my oesophagus. His eyes move towards me, I was about to call for the other pack members when I heard the dreaded words.

'Are you pregnant?' he asked, knowing full well we hadn't been together for a while.

'No, just a stomach bug,' I said, with a scowl.

Luca was becoming suspicious of me as the sickness was getting to much to bare, the saliva pooling into my mouth as a little warning before the retching starts again.

'We shall make an appointment with the pack doctor at once, can't have you making the pack sick!' he spat,

I nodded not sure how I would get out of this alive.


The next day the appointment was made, being watched closely meant I was trapped, my emotions were soaring as it was the same pack doctor I saw when I was attacked, I could see he felt bad for me getting up he bowed as I entered the room.

'Hello Luna,' he said, as he smiled at me.

'Please call me, Annabeth,' I said in annoyance.

'So Annabeth, what brings you in today?' he smiled.

'Well Alpha Luca wanted me to have a physical as I have been feeling sick lately,' I said, with a gulp.

'Could you be pregnant?' he asked, my eyes widened in horror. I knew I was, but I also knew it couldn't be his. Fear ran down my spine as I gripped tightly on the arms of the chair, searching around desperate for a way out.

'It's not possible doctor,' I said, as Paddox and Boid stood behind me, my eyes becoming desperate.

'We will take some bloods to be on the safe side,' he said, with a smile. Oh god that's it I'm done for!

'Or we could do a urine test now to clear things up?' Boid said, behind me as my heart sank.

'Of course, here please fill this up to the line,' he said. Maybe I am not pregnant, maybe this is just a sick joke my mind has concocted to mess with me. I reach out for the cup getting up I walk towards the bathroom, I stared at it trying to figure out how I was going to do this then it hit me. I would pee a little and fill the rest with water, surely that would dilute it enough to not be conclusive. After I filled the cup I walked back to the doctor, handing him my sample.

Taking out a strip he tests my urine. 'Hmm, the test is negative,' he said out-loud, as I sighed in relief.

'We should do the bloods just to be on the safe side,' the doctor announced.

Is he for real, just accept the damn results!

'Thank you doctor,' I smiled, as he raised my sleeve.

'Slight scratch!' he said, jabbing the needle into my arm. I always thought that was a bit of a joke, slight? I looked away, as I'm a big believer in my blood remaining in my veins and not in a pot.

'We will schedule an appointment for a couple of weeks' time,' he smiled as I nodded.

Getting up from my seat I turn to only see Paddox there, stupid Boid running to his master to tell him the good news. A true soldier and a total bastard.

Walking back to my office I ran through the internet searching for a family with those coloured eyes, as it would be important for me to know where I would be going as soon as I found a way out of this mess. I finally found what I was looking for, the Genai family. Given the fact there is only mention of a son I figured he was my best bet. God I sound like a hussy, which technically I am. I shared a beautiful encounter with a man I didn't know and now, well now I will have to share a lot more with him. Reaching for a pen I write his address down on a pad in front of me, Lycanthrope valley Ohio. I spent a little while longer thinking on how I was going to do it, even though I wanted nothing from him he deserved to know he had a child on the way, when suddenly I slowly thought of a cunning plan to get myself out of this world and onto freedom. Getting to my feet I called outside of the room, to see a fresh faced Paddox standing beside the doorway on guard duty.

'Paddox?' I said, as he stopped and looked at me.

'Please tell Luca, I need to go to the library!' I added.

'Why do you need to go there?' he said confused.

'I need to find a book on the local rules for planning,' I said. This was of course a brilliant idea, as we had put in plans for expansion, instead of going to him he opened up a channel for a private conversation.

'He has agreed, we must go before dinner,' he said.

Leaving the house the car was already waiting for us in the drive with the engine running, setting off I got my plans straight in my head of what I needed to do to achieve it. Pulling up to the library I got out in a hurry, Paddox didn't move.

'Are you not coming?' I said to him, as he shook his head.

'It's boring in there!' he huffed.

'Okay I will be about an hour?' I said, looking at him.

'Sure, I guess,' he shrugs, leaning back and pulling out his phone.

Slamming the door I rushed across the busy road; I had studied the doctors name and badge number by heart. I was looking for an official template, one that would make even

137

him believe me. Searching for the perfect one felt like it took forever, but then I finally found it, getting to work on my masterpiece immediately. Once I was done, I rejoiced in triumph with five minutes to spare.

It was time to go home. I tucked my letter into my inside pocket, as I went to leave the library Paddox bursts though the door making a ruckus.

'Shh!' the lady behind the desk said loudly.

'Paddox, chill out. I'm coming,' I whispered.

'It is time to go now, madam,' he instructed, pulling me towards the exit and out the door.

Again with the damn madam, I know this pack is aging me but seriously. I'm not that old!

Getting in the car I remained silent contemplating my next moves carefully, the pack link has been closed off too me and me to them for quite some time now, which meant I no longer had to worry about them being in my head. Before I knew it we was nearly back at the pack house, the burning feeling ran through my stomach like a hurricane. He is such a pig! The pain stopped as I got closer the pack obviously realising I was nearly home they must have warned him. This man has hurt me for the last damn time! Over the next few days, I will execute my plan beautifully and this life will be no more mine to bare. Getting into the pack house I walked to my office with my head still high as I fake smiled at everyone, I checked my pockets making sure my letter remained where I put it.

Opening my door I stepped inside walking towards my chair, I folded myself in half as I lowered myself down, tired from my day I reach for a window envelope placing the letter inside as I kicked my shoes off of my now burning feet.

I will wait a while longer before delivering the unwelcome news myself, as I had high hopes he would take it as I intended it to be taken. This Genius letter states that I am unable to have children, that it would be impossible for me to conceive a child.

The fear of the unknown repercussions of this letter terrified me, but at the same time, if he has a Luna that is unable to provide an heir this would be worse. Realising I also had dinner menus to plan made my head spin, too much of my life is ruled by this pack. But don't worry, my time is coming, and it couldn't come soon enough.

# Chapter 17
## Plan in motion

A week had passed, and it was finally time to deliver the news. I cunningly didn't address the letter to myself I addressed it to Luca. This would be a day to remember and a day to start my life over. I slipped it into the post on my way to cook breakfast, my frame was small, my strength dissolved nothing but a mere shell of my former self. I came to this pack under promises of forever, but all I could think of now was when I leave when will it be safe to contact my family. Where would I even find them? So many lost moments due to this god forsaken pack only to be used as a slave, working like a dog for dogs.

I was flipping pancakes in the kitchen when I heard a roar rumble through the house, giving me moments of pleasure soon overshadowed by fear. I was expecting a sudden rush to happen but to my surprise nothing came. Alpha Luca did not join us for breakfast instead Paddox come through the door, his expression was different.

'I'm sorry Luna, he said you can't have food again today,' Paddox whispered, as I laid the table.

The wolves began jumping on the food like it was survival of the fittest, even though there was enough food to feed them ten times over.

'That's okay Paddox, enjoy,' I said.

'It's not okay Annabeth, its damn right cruel,' he replied.

'Please Paddox, don't make a scene,' I said, as my eyes pleaded for him to stop.

'He can't starve you forever, I'm with Paddox it's barbaric!' Shay said, banging her hand on the counter.

'This is not a pack; packs take care of each other!' Orion yelled.

'Please sit and eat your breakfast, before it gets cold,' I instructed, neither one of them hungry anymore. Walking up behind them I lean down to ear level. 'Please eat, or he will punish you too,' I said.

As I took a step back, they both reach for their plates.

My clothes were taken away from me, so I was currently only allowed to wear my old ones, unless I was needed for business. Luckily for me as my ever-growing bump would have been noticed by now, if it weren't for Luca I probably would have gained a lot more weight by now too. I eat but only what I am given which isn't much.

Cleaning the plates of all the left-over food with Paddox there to watch my every move, I scrape the remaining food off the plates and into the bin.

'I'm so sorry, Luna,' Paddox said.

'Paddox, my name is Annabeth,' I said, as rage filled my head. Resuming my duties, I continue to clean off the plates as my stomach let off a loud grumble, I stared salivating at the scraps that remained untouched.

'Please eat something, I won't tell!' he pleaded.

'I can't, I am not allowed!' I said, as he takes a hold of my hand,

'Please, I just can't stand it!' he urged, picking up an apple from the counter and placing it under my nose.

My mouth filled as the apple got closer to me, I have now not eaten in four days, slapping the apple from his hand it flipped up into the air and down to the floor.

'Please Paddox, just don't! He will let me eat when he is ready,' I said.

Pushing past him once I am done in the kitchen, I go to the list left out for me on the side.

141

The floors were added today hopefully to be taken away tomorrow, I couldn't do much more of this it was back breaking, I was the only one to clean this horrible house.

'Annabeth, please let us help you, you will be done in no time,' Shay said, as Orion and Paddox also stood before me. My heart filled with love at the sheer sight of them all willing to get in trouble just for me.

'I can't let you do that,' I said sternly.

As I said this Paddox swiped the list from my hands.

'Paddox please, you will get me in trouble!' I pleaded.

'Lucky for you, you didn't ask,' he said, pausing for a moment. 'Is he joking? Annabeth, how have you been doing all of this yourself?' he asked angrily.

'I get it done eventually,' I replied, shrugging my shoulders.

He stood staring at me for a moment before passing the list around, after everyone was done he signalled the others to get to work as soon as he was sure Luca had left. They were right the housework was done in a flash leaving me just enough time to get a bath. Walking to my room I gather my things and head for the garden, you would think I would just be able to turn on the tap in my room, right? Wrong, Luca had the plumbing shut off to the bath rendering it useless, the tap was also capped off halfway, only allowing out a slight bit of water, just enough to brush your teeth with. I had a bar of soap to clean myself with, as all my other products had been taken confiscated for my disobedience. My blonde hair was muddy from the algae in the lake out back, getting undressed was a task it was 5degrees outside.

The bumps form on my arms as the hairs raise and stood on end, walking down the bank my feet touch the water, sending a shiver through me as my once fierce

142

nature diminished, I slowly rinse and wash my hair with the soap, my scalp clogged, my hair was dull and lifeless.

I attempt to dry myself off quickly to avoid the cold. Once fully dried I threw on some fresh clothes, running back into the house to get dinner ready before Alpha Luca comes home. He had been gone all day and I did wonder what he was doing, how did he not come straight to me? I felt a stray tear fall down my face, in anger I brushed it away resuming my cooking.

When I woke up the next morning it was barely dawn, getting up I went downstairs and preprepared the food it was business as usual. I was sure he got the letter. With those thoughts came Paddox and Boid walking through the kitchen with serious faces.

'Breakfast isn't ready yet boys,' I said innocently.

'I'm sorry Annabeth, but Alpha Luca requests an audience with you,' Paddox said.

'Oh, what for?' I replied, still mixing the eggs.

'Please come with us!' Boid snapped.

Feeling this was not really a request and more of an order I obliged, putting the eggs down I followed them. Walking down the hall I felt every pack members eyes on me as I continued to hold my head high, we reached the end of the corridor on the fifth floor. Boid knocked twice and the door opened.

'Come in, Annabeth,' an unfamiliar voice summoned.

I walked in to see Luca his father and two other men standing before me.

'Annabeth, we received some rather unsettling news,' Mr Grayson said.

'Oh, what was that?' I replied, thinking I know full well what he meant but wasn't sure, cautiously I remained still and very silent.

'Useless Human!' Luca muttered.

Well I had to hand it to him he certainly was consistent with his feelings towards me, given the fact he no longer feels the need to hide them anymore.

'We have gathered here today, to put an end to this union!' the man in white said to me.

He opened his brief case pulling out a black and white piece of cloth along with a blue vile. Oh lord they are going to kill me! His face was completely disgusted in my presents. Turns out everyone hates humans here.

'Annabeth, it has come to our attention of your certain situation; we reserve the right to terminate this relationship,' Mr Grayson said.

'What have I supposedly done?' I replied.

'Unable to fulfil you Luna duties, to their full extent as to your agreement,' he announced frowning at me.

Now I was fully aware of what was happening, barely containing my smile I agreed.

'Now child you will recite this, giving up your rights to this pack.' The man in white said handing me a piece of paper.

'And if I don't?' I enquired.

'We will have to use force,' Luca said, gleefully, with a twisted scowl.

I take in a deep breath as I hold the paper out in front of me, Luca holding out his right hand and I my left as he placed his over mine, the man in white wraps the cloth around our hands, his smile so wide and proud his lips seem to disappear as his face stretched to its maximum.

144

'Repeat after me if you please,' the man in white said clearing his throat.

'I Annabeth Taylor Fortman relinquish my rights to this pack, and in doing so reject my mate unbinding our love and unbinding our fate, I reject thee Luca Michael Grayson Jnr and free you from this bond,' I said, as my heart skipped a beat.

Hearing Luca recite the same words was torture, it was like he said them slowly to hurt me as much as he could. The man in white was unwrapping our bindings as the words are spoken, slowly peeling of each layer was like losing a layer of my skin.

Once the words finalised so were we, a small droplet of blood taken from both of our hands dropped into the blue vile. The blue vile was then poured onto my mark causing a searing pain to occur instantly, the pain of our bond breaking knocked the wind out of me, I clawed at my scar as the same venomous pain ravaged my body knocking me to the ground as I thrashed and screamed. The emptiness that followed was like a hollowed tree no feelings and no remorse for what he had done, tears of fear betrayal and sadness streamed down my cheeks. Knowing my life had been altered completely was freeing, but mixed with regret as my heart was now broken.

'The mark should fade in around three days; you are to leave with what you came here with, no more and no less. Understand?' he said, standing over me.

'Yes Mr Grayson,' I said, holding back my smile.

The pain was still bad, but it was now manageable, but believe me I have felt worse.

Standing to my feet I looked back at the man I once loved in pure disgust, but I was free and there wasn't a feeling in the world that could come close to this.

'It is time for you to go!' Luca said.

I was so angry that I hadn't noticed the girl standing beside him, that same beautiful blonde girl I saw him with once before. Draped over him clinging to his arm whilst she whispered in his ear, before this would have sent me spiralling but now.

'You can have him,' I said, walking straight past her.

'He is no longer yours to give!' she growled.

'Your car is waiting for you outside, leave this place and do not come back!' Luca said, holding his arm around his new trophy wife.

'Wouldn't dream of it!' I replied, gritting my teeth, and heading for the door.

My smug grin growing as I knew full well that no one could do my job as good as I have, they wouldn't even know where to start.

'Good luck!' I said, as I left the room.

As soon as I was out of that room I ran as fast as I could, not stopping for goodbyes and not bothering with my things. I had only been allowed to have some of my own things, the rest was taken from me, so I required nothing. I ran as fast as my legs would take me before they changed their mind, I was finally free.

'Luna!' Shay screamed, as I continued to run.

'Annabeth!' Orion cried.

'Where are you going?' Paddox yelled, as he started to try and chase me but to no avail.

I could hear the sounds of my heart breaking, I was shattered but I was saved, the girl I knew in this house was gone, a mere memory. I was sure I would forget with time; it was a new dawn and a new chance at life, that I was going to grip with both hands and embrace this day as if it were my last. I had however done my research, the only pack I knew of with yellow eyes was the Genai pack. I had some bright idea that I would go there, tell him and things would be great. What a bad idea that was.

# Chapter 18
## A rogue girl

Driving down the road I unwound my window allowing the cold breeze to encapsulate my face, my newfound freedom made this effortless wave of wind feel amazing. I had been driving for a little while leaning over I grabbed my phone, opening maps I typed in the coordinates to Lycanthrope valley. I briefly felt sorrow and guilt for leaving my friends behind, this soon gave me the drive I needed to strive for greatness. Driving on I headed further into the mountains as the Genai lived just west of Ohio, the journey was long and tedious. With my legs now hurting I decided to stop by a gas station for some refreshments. Approaching the cash machine, I typed in my pin and withdrew some funds, stepping back going into the diner I saw all the food they have to offer and my eyes were much bigger than my stomach. When I soon came to realise it was my little brother's birthday today. I wept a little.

'What can I get ya?' the lady asked, her face was soft and friendly.

'Can I get a chocolate milkshake and some eggs please?' I said, licking my lips.

'What kind of eggs?' she replied.

'Scrambled please,' I said, as I watched her write down my order and slap it on the counter for the chef.

Scanning over to the counter I noticed some cakes placed delicately on a stand, they looked delicious! Upon further investigation I came across my favourite desert, pie! So I also ordered some pies to go, might have been the cravings who knows.

'Can I have some blueberry pies as well please?' I said, licking my lips in ecstasy.

'Once you've got your pie you need to leave!' she said, coming back leaning over the counter as far as she could, giving me the ultimate warning.

'Rogues aren't allowed in here,' she said, looking to her left, her face grew worried, as she glanced back in my direction with sorrow in her eyes.

'I'm so sorry I didn't know,' I said, gathering up my things and heading for the door. Was I really a rogue now?

What am I going to do when I get to the Genai pack? Will they think the same of me? Not wanting any trouble, I leave without a fuss.

I start my car up cradling my stomach, giving comfort to my unborn child was the only thing I could do to sooth myself in an attempt to calm my nerves.

The night was long and cold, and that bitter air was fast approaching, my heater had given up the ghost and stopped working completely, bringing my hand out I slammed my palms into it in the hopes that it would miraculously fix my problem, noticing it didn't help I reached behind me as I pulled out my blanket. Too tired to carry on I pulled over into a nearby road, locking the doors I settled in for the night.

'We are going to see your father,' I said to myself.

'Let's hope tomorrow is a better day,' I added, as my eyes grew heavy, and I slowly drifted off to sleep. My dreams were tiring as my waking life was nowhere near as terrifying as my dream world, petrifying me to my core as my dreams slowed my escape down, allowing me to visualise every waking moment of my life with Luca.

It was barely dawn when I was awoken by a tapping on the window, snapping up dripping with sweat I opened my eyes as I squinted at the light blinding them.

'Excuse me madam, but you can't stay here, move along now please,' the officer said to me.

I looked down at my watch, it was only 6am. Gosh I was hoping for a bit more of a lay in than that!

'Okay I'm sorry officer; I am going,' I said, starting up my car, I hear a banging again.

'Where is it you're heading?' he said, as he peered through my window.

'Lycanthrope valley in Ohio, sir,' I replied, leaning back slightly.

'That's still quite the drive from here, half the journey will bring you to a little hotel. Try stopping there for a while,' he said, with a gentle smile.

'Sure officer, thank you,' I said, rolling up my windows.

I set off for the hotel and the journey was longer than he said it would be, finally I made it to the hotel pulling up the drive to see a sign that said reception.

The place was old and creepy, old-style cladding ran up the side of the building with missing tiles on the roof.

'So much for a hotel, it looks like its closed?' I thought, silently to myself.

When suddenly the lights turned on.

'Not creepy at all,' I said, sarcastically to myself, not wanting to go inside.

After sitting for a while I finally decided to get out my car, entering the hotel I scanned the entrance. This place needed some desperate renovating, as dust and cobwebs gathered on almost everything. I approached the front desk, it was old oak rotten and flaking, a woman was sat reading a book, the front of the book read a fairy-tale. Oh lord please do not tell me fairies are real as well? I don't think I could take any more surprises today.

With her glasses pulled down low she looked over them at me as I caught her attention, book in one hand and a cigarette in the other, the misty fog clouded my face as she exhaled blowing smoke at me. I coughed and spluttered at her, fanning the smoke away with my hand.

'Oh I'm sorry, how can I help you?' she said, revealing the rest of her face.

She looked tired and worn with giant bags under her eyes, with white and frail hair, her smile however was sincere making me smile back at her.

'I need a room for the night please?' I asked, as politely as I could.

'When are you due?' she said, pointing at my stomach.

'How did you know?' I replied.

'Are you hungry?' she asked politely.

Since leaving the house all I have eaten was some eggs, and a piece of pie, which I'm sure was old. So it was safe to say I was starving.

'Oh, no thank you,' I said, quickly to avoid looking desperate.

'Come now, let me show you to your room and I will make us some breakfast,' she said, standing to her feet etching me to follow her up the stairs.

'Is this woman going to murder me?' I said to myself, as she looked at me with softened eyes.

'Oh well, if I die then at least it wasn't at the hands of my previous mate!' I thought, as I began following her upstairs.

Having a lot of business to attend to today I was very sceptical of her intention, I had to change my name as I was quite sure my results would come in soon and my ex-mate would come looking for me, there was also the small matter of finding the Genai family.

I let her show me to my room, looking around there was actually a lot of rooms here but not all of them are fully functional. She walked slow as if every step she took was agony, a feeling of warmth washed over me when she spoke to me as if I had known her my entire life.

'Here is you're room, sorry it's not much,' she said, with a shrug.

'No, it's perfect thank you,' I said, looking around completely overwhelmed by my surroundings.

She nodded for me to carry on, inviting me downstairs after I was finished and I agreed, it was going to be so lovely having an actual bath rather than my old alternative. Turning on the tap to full heat I tested it with my hand as the water ran down my elbows, I placed some of the bubble bath provided on the side in the bath below me, there was even hair shampoo.

Oh lord it had been so long since I got to use hair shampoo, I wasted no time slowly undressing myself I got in the bath and fully submerging myself in the boiling water creating an uplifting feeling of pure ecstasy.

'Amazing!' I whispered.

After I was finished and positively wrinkled, I got out of the bath to a pair of cotton towels waiting for me folded neatly on the rail, one for my hair and one to wrap around me. They were so soft like a fluffy piece of heaven, walking over to the bed I sat on the corner and wept into my hands.

The bed wasn't the issue that was the only thing they didn't take from me, but my old room was bare. This one had a tv and some warmth to it, with paintings hanging on the walls it felt like home. I know it's hard to imagine being surrounded by people but feeling so utterly alone, no tv just the endless working day with little sleep to keep me saine. Hardly anyone was allowed to talk to me in the pack house, Shay, Orion and Paddox would try and talk to me, but wouldn't dare if Alpha Luca were around.

I finally got myself dressed and plucked up the courage to go downstairs, the lady had made beans on toast, it wasn't much but I was starved, my mouth watered just looking at it.

'What is your name?' she asked me.

'Annie,' I replied, I was so use to my brother calling me it, that it would be easy for me to respond to.

'Nice to meet you, Annie. My name is, Julia,' she said, extending her hand for me to shake.

'Nice to meet you Julia, do you live here alone?' I asked, wishing I hadn't.

'Yes I do sadly, it's okay though I like the quiet,' she said, half smiling at me, but her eyes averted.

'Well believe me when I say you can be around all the people in the world, yet feel so terribly alone,' I said, as my chin began to tremble.

'That my dear is why I live alone, no one can disappoint me,' she laughed, sitting awkwardly in her chair.

'Where is your family?' she asked.

'I don't have any,' I said.

Of course I lied but for the past couple of years I had no idea where my family were.

'Oh child, I am so sorry,' she said, with sad eyes.

'What brings you here?' she added, changing the conversation, as I reach down and stroke my belly.

'I'm looking for my child's father, he had yellow eyes that's all I know,' I said, averting my gaze shamefully.

Great now she probably thinks I'm some form of prostitute, what a way to start a conversation.

'I see, well I'm sure he will be pleased to see you,' she nods. Why was this lady so nice to me?

'I'm quite tired, is it okay if I go to sleep?' I said, with a fake yawn.

'Of course, I will see you in the morning,' she replied, taking my plate to the sink.

I had a lot to do tomorrow I had to meet with my contact to get my new papers, I made sure to pay in cash everywhere so that if anyone came looking for me they would have a job with a paperless trail. I did stop for gas, but I made sure it was a halfway point which could have taken me in four different directions. My mind unsettled as I thought of every possible outcome for the day ahead of me tomorrow. This world was bleak enough for me, being rejected again would destroy what was left of me. Laying on the bed my body emersed as I finally felt comforted, the burning pain from my neck still vexed me. What an ungrateful man, I gave up everything for him and in return he threw me away like rubbish!

After my deep thoughts slowly settled, I managed to finally drift off to sleep.

# Chapter 19
## Failure

The sun was shining through my window, bringing myself up to a seated position in bed I stretched out my arms with a satisfying yawn, that was the first free night of many where I awoke well rested for the time in a long time. I thought of how I would contact my family, but the danger was too great, knowing I had to wait a little longer was hard, but I accepted what would be would be. Getting up I go downstairs; Julia was sat at reception reading the newspaper.

'People still read those?' I thought, her eyes peering over them as the fresh ink wafted from it, a musty smell that was unmistakable.

'Hey Julia, I need to pay for last night,' I said, tapping the desk Infront of me.

'No payment necessary,' she said, with a wide grin.

'I must pay you, I can't stay here for nothing,' I said, whilst pulling out my purse.

'It was just nice to have the company dear,' she said, I looked at her not sure how to take that.

'Thank you, so very much,' I said, as I walked into the kitchen and began collecting ingredients.

'What are you doing?' she said, shouting at me from reception.

'Well if you won't accept my money, then maybe you will accept my breakfast?' I said, grinning at her as I mixed the eggs in a bowl.

'Okay fine,' she said.

Getting eggs together I cracked them into a bowl and began whisking like my life depended on it, luckily catering for two would be easy considering I had to previously cater to a whole pack.

After the food was cooked, I laid the food on the table and started to clean.

'What are you doing?' Julia asked.

'I am cleaning the kitchen,' I said, in confusion.

'Yes I see that but why? Eat your breakfast before it gets cold,' she said, urging me to sit.

It dawned on me that I was so used to cleaning and not eating, that I didn't realise I didn't have to do things in that order anymore. I sighed putting the pans on the side. Shocked was an understatement, I moved and took a seat beside her feeling as if I were doing something wrong the entire time. I ate my breakfast too quickly just so I could clean up. Burping as I go, the heartburn takes hold as

the acid rises and burns my throat, I try and push it back down, but it was too late. Clutching at my chest I hear.

'You ate that far too quickly,' she said, leaning over and pulling out some Rennie's for me to take.

'I know, I'm just not use to this,' I said.

'Well you leave the rest of that to me; will you be coming back later?' she enquired.

I wanted to say for sure that I was, as this was the homeliest I had felt in a while.

'I will be back yes, but for how long I'm just not sure,' I said, as she nodded rising to her feet.

'Well then, you had best be going, I will see you later,' she smiled, tapping me on the shoulders.

Getting up I wiped my face and headed out for the day, today was going to be an awfully big adventure. One I wasn't sure I was completely ready for.

I had to go into Ohio town first, I secretly met a lady on one of our pack meetings and arranged for new papers to be done. After driving for what felt like five minutes I made it into Ohio, I was to meet my contact at the smiling café, what a name that was.

Pulling up outside I got out of my car making sure to lock it behind me, this was not a neighbourhood to be too trusting in. I walked towards the café reaching for the door I entered as the bell rings twice. The brown envelope with Annie written on it was laid out on the bar, I was expecting to see someone, but there was only the bar man stood there, the rest of the café was empty. Moving over I took a seat on one of the stools by the bar, I had no idea why this was even called a café as it was more of a bar than a café. Looking over in horror as

the bartender was busy drying glasses, leaning towards me he pushed the envelope forward.

'Can I get you a drink?' his low monotoned voice sent shivers down my spine.

'No thank you,' I responded, whilst taking the envelope. I waited a while to be told that I could leave, that really was an annoying habit I would have to break free from. He nodded his head towards the door, and I got up and left, running to my car I unlocked it and carried on to my next destination locking myself inside.

Driving for a while I started to have doubts, as the closer I got to my destination the grubbier I felt, looking down at my clothes I looked like a poor person as I had no time to stop and shop. Not knowing where I was going my phone's sat nav kept dipping in and out, I slapped it repeatedly to get it to work. You know the saying if in doubt give it a clout, this worked for a time until finally my phone died altogether. Looking to my left I saw the sign that said welcome to Lycanthrope valley, but I couldn't see anything else, no entrance no nothing finally giving up hope I cursed.

'Great, now what?' I said, slamming my hands on the steering wheel in frustration.

Bringing my eyes back onto the road I saw a lady running, pushing my foot down I sped up a little to try and catch her but that only made her run faster.

'Wait!' I shouted, desperate for help.

She slammed into the ground attempting to get away from me.

'Even better, now I look like a stalker or worse a murderer!' I thought, slamming my foot on my accelerator, I manged to get in front of her unwinding my window quickly before she passed.

'Excuse me, Miss?' I said, as she stopped quickly.

'Jesus Christ lady,' she said, gasping for breath.

'Nope the name is, Annie,' I said, smiling at her.

'Oh yeah, you're so funny,' she said, breathing heavy.

'Sorry can I ask you a question?' I said.

'Oh are you trying to give me a heart attack?' she said, her breathing now heavy, as she steadied herself.

'I am so sorry, I'm looking for the Genai family home, have you heard of it?' I asked, shielding my eyes from the sun.

'Have I heard of it, are you joking?' she scoffed.

'No, I'm being serious,' I sighed, rolling my eyes at her.

'Sure okay, go down this road make a left and follow the road up the hill until you reach the gate, believe me you can't miss it,' she said, continuing to run on the spot.

'Thank you so much, can I give you a lift?' I asked, with gratitude.

'No thank you, you've scared me enough for one day,' she said, with a slight attitude. Understandably.

I laughed a little as I apologised to her over and over again, couldn't really blame her for having the hump I did stalk her for half a mile. Giving her a final wave, I pulled back onto the road and did as she said, I followed the path round as it winded in a half circle, finally the trees began to slow revealing a giant wall behind it, opening my eyes further I slowly began approaching the gate.

'Can we help you?' it said, as I heard a voice coming out of the little radio beside me before I had a chance to ring it.

'I'm here to see, Mr Genai,' I replied confidently.

'Do you have an appointment?' he asked.

'Yes I do, it's to do with the Grayson pack,' I said.

I lied it had nothing to do with them, but I needed to get inside. I wasn't greeted by who I thought I would be, I get out of my car and there stood before me was a bunch of Omegas, I knew an Omega when I saw one, little to no power and an ego you couldn't mistake.

'Your name?' he smirked, folding his arms at me.

'My name is, Annie,' I replied.

'What do you want?' he snapped, looking at me up and down, as if I was a lowly peasant.

'I'm here to see your boss,' I frowned.

'For what reason?' he said, narrowing his eyes at me.

How was I going to put this? he's my baby daddy, no maybe not like that. I paused for a good few moments before answering.

'I'm carrying his child,' I replied, to which a bunch of laughter was thrown back at me.

'Yeah you and every other rogue whore!' they replied.

'I am not a rogue!' I said, in a disappointed tone.

159

The biggest one got closer to me in an attempt to frighten me, but little did he know I've fought my fair share of demons, so he was like a little kitty compared to them, his name was Mal that's what they all kept calling him anyway.

'You smell like a rogue?' he said, sniffing my hair.

'Well, I'm not one,' I snapped, pushing him away.

'Ohh this one has fire, get out,' he spat, with a darkened stare.

'What do you mean, I need to see Mr Genai!' I said, as the desperation showed in my voice.

'Yeah, you and everyone else,' he said, glaring at me.

'I will remember you, mark my words,' I said, as the other Omega's man handled me to my car.

Whipping myself around I managed to sucker punch one of them in the gut, I was forced into my car kicking and screaming, turning myself around as they threw the door closed behind me. Situating myself fully I slammed my foot in reverse, I drove backwards out the gates watching as they slowly closed behind me. Getting out of my car I slam my foot into the steel gate, making me wince a little in pain. A rumble occurred through the sky, as the heavens opened and the rain began to pour, I stood helplessly as droplets of water hit my face and cheeks.

Getting back into my car I didn't realise I had left the window open, so not only was I wet but now so was the inside of my car. I had failed my child. I fully intend in that case to be everything my child needs. I will be their mother, father, auntie, and uncle my love for them will mean they do not need anyone else. I return back to the hotel in defeat as my moistened face slowly turned to anger, at the thoughts of another person not wanting me, not wanting us.

'How did it go?' Julia asked.

'He wouldn't even give me the time of day!' I replied deflated.

'Oh that is so unlike him, I'm so sorry,' she said, as her eyes saddened for me.

'That's okay, we don't need them anyway!' I replied.

I was so sure of these words, that the fire in me ignited as I was now determined more than ever to make our life great, I was going to let nothing, and no one stand in our way.

# Chapter 20
## Whistle while we worked

A couple of months went by, and my belly was getting big, my bump was still small, but my ankles were certainly feeling it. Walking down to reception I attempt to pay my bill again, but Julia would never accept, it was a daily occurrence I insisted on. So, I decided I would work for it, no one ever came but the least I could do was try and help this ruin of a hotel to become more habitable.

'Julia, can I ask you something?' I said hesitantly.

'Of course, what's the matter?' she said.

'Having the baby on the way means I can't stay here forever, but would you consider maybe just a while? At least until I find somewhere else?' I said, twiddling my thumbs patiently awaiting a response.

'I would love that!' she replied.

'Well, that settles that then,' I said joyfully.

I must admit I was growing very fond of her, I'm not sure what I would do without her sometimes.

She is like an angel sent to guide me on my path, if you believe in that sort of thing that is.

I went out back to see the rest of the hotel, I had never been out here before and it was much larger than I expected. From what I could see the back was all overgrown and very unkept, I'm not even sure what is actually back here other than weeds and possibly the odd grass snake, I looked a little more and find a building to the side of the property, it was very big in stature.

'We could do something with this place,' I said, running back into the hotel.

Without saying a word I grabbed a pen and some paper from Julia at reception, I ran back through and out the back prompting her to follow me. Using the paper and a pen I traced a rough outline of the property.

'That's it!' I said loudly.

'What is it?' she enquired.

'We could transform this place Julia, into a fine establishment where people would be dying and queuing up to come!' I said, as I paused for a moment.

'I have some savings that would get us started, if you wanted to that is?' I hesitated, thinking what if she liked the hotel the way it was, that maybe I was stepping on her toes. I search her face for any type of clue as to what she was thinking when.

'I don't need your money I have my own, we can use that?' she responded, as my smile grew.

'I think that's a fantastic idea Julia, we can really make something of this place. I will go into town tomorrow and hire some builders,' I said, giving her a big hug.

'We could start doing it ourselves, some of these rooms need some dusting before anyone comes,' she said, causing me to laugh as dusting is an understatement, but I agreed. We got to work immediately. This wasn't going to happen overnight, but it certainly was a step in the right direction.

After working for what felt like hours I began to sweat, I had never done manual labour before, cleaning and cooking was one thing, but this was different, I have to admit I wasn't enjoying it, but the sheer thought of what it could look like kept me going.

Peeling back the old carpets we discovered old oak flooring below, deciding we would sand these back and stain them along with the overhead beams trying to keep the architecture the same.

'Would you like some home-made lemonade?' Julia said, I must admit it was stifling in this room.

'Sure, thank you Julia,' I said, licking my lips, as I poured the lemonade down my gullet without taking a breath.

'Hmm thirsty was you, luckily I brought more,' she said, as she filled my glass to the top again.

'Thank you, tomorrow will be a great day,' I said.

'Yes well, don't be surprised if not everyone is willing to help us,' she said, making my head tilt to the side, wondering exactly what she meant by that.

'Why wouldn't people want to help us?' I asked.

'You'll see,' she said, reaching for me she touched my shoulder, nodded, and left the room.

Growing tired and weiry I decided to leave the rest for the day, going downstairs I made dinner for us both. Before sitting down Julia told me a story, it was the story of a foolish woman who fell in love with a man she couldn't have, he use to visit her but whenever he left, her heart broke a little more each time. Looking at her I placed my hand over hers, I couldn't help but relate to some of her story, she must have really loved him.

'Thank you for sharing, that was a truly inspiring story,' I said, secretly wondering who it was about.

Letting it go I decided to walk back to my room, the moral of that story is no man can be trusted, and tomorrow I would apparently have my work cut out for me for reasons I was unsure of.

Waking up I felt something tapping on my head, opening my eyes I wipe it off with my hand. Squinting up at the ceiling the dripping was coming from there, like a leaky tap only bigger and dripping onto my brain. Gosh it was annoying, nothing like a little water boarding to get the day moving. Getting up I decided to skip breakfast, rushing out of the hotel I barely had time to get myself a coffee.

'Bye Julia!' I shouted, but with no response.

Leaving in a hurry I got in my car and drove to town, of course I didn't know anyone in town so this was going to be interesting, the last town I lived in didn't even want to hire new people let alone help them, but this time I was paying them not asking for a job, so I was convinced this would be different. I could not have been more wrong.

As the day was going on I grew increasingly impatient, this town had every trick in the book to avoid outsiders, I had about given up hope when I came across this little store just to the side of town. I gathered up my courage but will admit I was raging at this point, getting out my car with balled up fists I was coming for them and was not accepting a no for an answer.

'Hello miss, how can we help you?' he smiled.

'Alright cut the crap, my auntie owns the Lakeview hotel wishing to renovate it. Will you help us or not, I don't have time to waste!' I shouted, wiggling my tiny fingers in this man's face.

'Hello to you too,' he laughed, making my blood boil.

'Will you? or won't you?' I said, with a slight stamp of my foot. He looked down at my little size four feet, raising one eyebrow as he looked back up to my eyes.

'You can't be serious?' he giggled.

'Deadly!' I said, scrunching my face and moving towards him, causing a sudden shift in his stance.

'Okay fine, we will work for no less than £12 an hour, got it?' his smirk widened.

'I heard £11.00?' I said, tutting at him.

'Better get those ears checked then, £11.50 and that's final,' he replied.

'Deal!' I said, shaking his hand.

'Just so you know id of done it for £12,' I replied. 'Just so you know madam, we would have worked for £11.00,' he smiled, chuckling a little. 'Go inside with Pete over there, and he will get your information,' he added.

'Okay do you need the plans?' I asked.

'Well yes, that would be helpful otherwise how do we know what we are doing?' he laughed again.

I think I'm going to get sick of that laugh but equally I'm grateful for the help.

After giving them the information I went on my way, racing home I drove onto the drive, I ran to Julia who was standing in the front porch.

'What's wrong?' I asked as I checked her over.

'I'm fine, what happened in town, or don't I really want to know?' she said, pulling her lips together.

'Well it was pretty much as you said, but I managed to get a firm to help, they are not your average company and they look a little rough around the edges, but it was the best we could do,' I said, half smiling from exhaustion.

'Fine, but you have to watch them,' she said.

Ahh great why do I always get lumped with the slump! That was what we called it if the other didn't want to participate.

'Why do I get lumped...' I said, before being interrupted.

'With the slump?' she said, finishing my sentence.

I hated it when she did that, but equally I loved her all the same. This was going to be a hard couple of months.

# Chapter 21
## Lakeview at your service

A couple of months went by, and I was feeling like I surely was ready to drop, my body expanded like a balloon; I didn't care weren't like I had anyone to impress these days anyway. The pregnancy glow was in full bloom, not a mark and not a blemish, I however felt sick as a dog and as angry as a predator ready to pounce. Getting myself together I walked out the back, the house was coming on beautifully, now fully able to see the garden space it was being transformed into a playground, to go with our new restaurant where anyone was welcome.

'Uh oh, quick run!' I heard Pete say sarcastically.

'I am in no mood Pete! Do you really want to push it?' I said, balling my fist up at him.

'Erm no, ma'am,' he said sarcastically.

'Oh he's asking for it!' I thought, digging my heels into the ground.

'Don't call me, ma'am!' I said, looking at him with a cold blank expression.

'Touchy, maybe buying some new clothes would make you feel better?' he said, looking me up and down.

'Listen here you, I will not hesitate to bury you under the bloody concrete, got it?' I snapped.

'Hmm yes, loud and clear,' he smirked.

Nodding at him I turned around and began to leave, looking down finally I could see what he meant, I think in his own way he was trying to help me realise I needed some new clothes. Trying to squeeze into these was turning out to be not an option anymore, as my stomach protruded out the bottom of them.

'Annie just take a moment, look around, or down at least?' he said, only adding to my annoyance and clear irritability.

'Buzz off Pete!' I said, thinking that would show him. I gazed down at my round belly trying to remember what my feet even looked like, I was so big now that I couldn't actually see them. My thoughts trailed off as I heard something out the front, barging past Pete I walked to the front of the house to see someone coming up the drive, it was a young girl, I couldn't help but approach her.

'Hello can I help you?' I said.

Noticing she was crying carrying her things in her hand, thrown into bags as if she had either run away or been thrown away one or the other.

'I'm looking for somewhere to stay, a police officer said you might be able to help me,' she said, whilst wiping her nose with her sleeve.

'Okay, what is your name?' I asked.

'My name is, Ava. Please I don't have much, but I am willing to work,' she begged.

I nodded bringing her inside leading her towards reception, as I put my arm around her cradling her shoulders she flinched, making me remove it quickly.

'Julia, this is Ava. She needs somewhere to stay; can we help her?' I said, watching Ava hunch over.

'Please I promise I won't be any bother, I can clean and work whatever hours needed,' she said, with wide eyes.

'Relax dear child you may stay as long as you need. Annie will show you to a room, then you can come down and have some lunch. How does that sound?' Julia said, her smile was soft and gentle.

'That sounds amazing, I'm so hungry,' she said, rubbing her sides and stomach.

This poor girl reminds me of me before I got here, desperate for a meal and would do anything for one. How can people be so cruel?

Showing her upstairs, I couldn't help but be proud of all we have accomplished in just a few months, this feeling was shortly overshadowed by the fear in her eyes when I dropped her room keys, I was sure more than ever now that she had been mistreated and in the worst possible way.

'It's okay you're safe now, please don't be afraid. Go in and have a nice hot bath and we will see you downstairs, Okay?' I said, as I offered her reassurance.

'Okay, thank you,' she replied.

Turning I left her to relax as she took her things inside and closed the door. I couldn't help but wonder what had happened to this poor girl to make her flinch constantly, something I'm sure I would learn when she is ready to tell me.

We waited downstairs for her for what felt like hours, wanting to know the answers to the questions that crossed our minds but not our lips. A gentle footstep descended the stairs, the constant turning up and down the stairs as she was deliberating as to whether she wanted to join us, I went to stand but Julia stopped me patting my hands to make me sit down.

'She will come when she Is ready,' she said, stroking my hand.

Suddenly a figure appeared in the doorway, it was Pete.

'Well no wonder she wanted to go back upstairs, its flipping stinky Pete!' I said loudly.

'I know you're pregnant so I will let that one go,' he sneered, giving me the finger.

'Being pregnant has nothing to do with it, you really do smell you know,' I said, holding my nose.

'Well you're just petty and pregnant!' he replied.

'Yeah good one Pete, try again you idiot!' I laughed.

'Annie, what's gotten into you?' Julia said.

'Hormones,' I said, as I shamefully looked down at the floor. Pete insisted he had to show Julia the garden, pulling Julia away Pete looked back poking his tongue out, he was like my brother if my brother was all grown and super annoying. I hadn't dared to think of my family in so long that I wonder what they are doing now.

Just hours after I moved in Luca had my family shipped out, he removed my phone and replaced it with a new one leaving no direct ties to my old life. My father of course didn't know where I had moved to as I was not allowed to tell him, oh the anguish and turmoil it caused me as I often sat thinking of what my brother looked like now.

Suddenly there was an explosion coming from downstairs, the stupid idiots had gone through one of the main water pipes, water gushed propelling the sink taps upwards, thank God no one was in there they could have lost an eye. I get to work to help them isolate the water mains when I came across something most peculiar, something I hadn't noticed before due to the overgrown weeds, I hadn't noticed the houses beauty before because it was overshadowed by weeds. It was a tiny little cottage most beautiful looking from the outside, off-white shutters with little windows, vine weeds had travelled up the door frame like a barrier. Whilst I stood daydreaming about this house my thoughts disrupted.

'Pete, what are we going to do?' I yelled.

'What do you mean we?' he scoffed.

'Sorry I meant you, you idiot!' I said, slapping his arm.

'Ere stick your finger in it!' he said, with a smile.

I glared at him as the ice-cold water ran down my back, drenching me from head to toe.

'Relax, we're on it,' he said, grabbing his tools.

'Can't you be on it quicker, the garden and the bathroom is flooding,' I said, attempting to clean.

'Nearly there, ah there you are that's better,' he said.

Clearly he is deluded, as the garden now looks like a swamp. Why did we employ this idiot?

'Clearly you have no idea what you're doing!' I screeched.

'Look don't lose your blob, it's the price of plumbing,' he replied, with a strained expression.

'Don't make me re-arrange your plumbing!' I snapped, rolling up my sleeves.

'I hope that baby comes soon, you're becoming a grouch,' he said, I stood looking at him amazed.

Was I really becoming a grouch? Maybe I was but I certainly was not going to accept this from a man.

'You are wrong!' I said, 'Oh yeah wait ago, I really showed him,' I thought.

It was quite laughable actually; out of all the things I could have said I chose those words. Pathetic.

A few more months had passed, and the hotel was nearly ready, spick and span as I like to say. That was until Pete knocked over a bucket of oil completely spoiling the new decor.

'Are you joking!' I said, pursing my lips in anger.

'What I didn't mean too!' he said, trying to help clean the mess he had just made.

'Pete, you've ruined it!' I screamed.

'Oh, relax it's not that bad, I will get you a new rug,' he said, reaching for me.

'You total git, you can't buy another one of these it's one of a kind,' I replied, moving towards him.

I was about to rearrange his features, when I felt a sudden rush of water run down my leg.

'Eww did you just pee?' he said, looking at me confused, trying not to laugh.

'Erm, I don't know?' I said, as we laughed together.

My stomach began to twist and bubble, and my laughter slowed as the cramping started.

'Erm Pete, I think the baby is coming,' I said, as calmly as I could.

'The baby is coming, oh that's nice,' he said, smiling at me, when reality hit him. 'Oh no, the baby is coming!' he added, as he began to yell loudly. I think even Jesus could hear him; he began slowly descending into panic as he scrambled to the house still screaming. Holding out my hand I assumed he would take me with him, but instead he ran straight past me.

'Pete?' I yelled, as he raced back out, gripping my arm rushing me through the back door.

'You're not having that baby near me, I don't want to see nothing come out of there!' he said, pointing to my vagina. The panic set in as he began to scream louder like a girl, I would have laughed had I not of been in pain.

'Julia!, come quickly!' he said, listening intently.

Julia did not answer, and he began running around like a crazy person trying to collect my things.

'Julia! Baby! Julia save me, somebody save me!' he pleaded, crying a little.

Unable to wait I took him by the collar dragging him towards me, I snarled in his face with my nostrils flaring and my eyes now sinister, narrowing my eyes at him and gritting my teeth.

'If you don't take me to the damn hospital, I'm going to kill you. I will bury you so far in the ground that the earth's core is going to burn your ass!' I said, shoving him backwards, but still holding his collar.

'Okay I'm going to get my keys,' he said, patting my hands making me release him.

'Yeah you do that!' I said, with a crazed look.

The drive to the hospital was awful, pushing me towards the car he herded me like cattle, not waiting for me to be fully seated, before screeching off down the road and hitting every bump on the way over. The labour was horrendous like nothing I had ever felt before, this was not a walk in the park and all the damn books lied to me. Not to mention the after birth looked like a war zone that they don't inform you by the way that you also have to push this out afterwards, it's just a giant blob of nastiness. But even with all of that going on I couldn't help but think he was perfect, his little toes and tiny hands.

The miracle of life really is a funny thing, I guess love at first sight really does exist. I couldn't tell if I was hot or getting hot because of this giant nappy they stuck me in. There is nothing graceful about giving birth and you're not even bothered when your vagina is hanging out and everyone wants to look at your cervix. Looking back down at my baby, I gazed lovingly at him as I cupped his little cheeks.

174

'Hey baby, I'm your mummy,' I said, in awe of him. Cleaning him up they checked his throat was clear before bringing him back to me and placing him on my bare skin.

'I'm never going to let anything happen to you, I will love you for an eternity,' I said, as I cradled my son.

I looked up to see Julia, Ava and Pete come through the door. The nurses here were not friendly, I am considered a rogue wherever I go, that's fine I didn't care anymore.

'Hey crazy lady!' Pete waved.

'What's his name?' Julia asked.

'Ronan,' I replied, with a smile.

'Why Ronan?' Pete asked.

'Pete mind your business!' Ava snapped.

'Because it means little wolf,' Julia replied, smiling from ear to ear as she looked on at us.

I search my memories to see how she knew this but in the end only one thought remained, my baby boy was here, and he was completely healthy.

'You're going to make an amazing mother,' Pete said to me almost making me cry, damn that man not a brother by blood but I wouldn't change him for the world. Maybe he was right, I did just have to have the baby after all. Or I will just kill him later considering he made me feel like he was herding sheep into his damn jeep. All I know now is I now have a tiny human that depends on me, and that scared the hell out of me.

# Chapter 22
# Home sweet home

It had been six years since we'd opened the hotel officially to the public, in the beginning no one came. It was hard to watch all our hard work going to waste but eventually word got out and business was booming.

My boy was thriving in everything he was doing, carefree and highly intelligent, unlike his mother that is.

We even had to take on more staff to cope with the workload their names were, Olivia, Emma, Echo, Ava, and Millie and that was just the waiting staff let alone the kitchen staff it was hard to keep up sometimes. Echo was the fieriest out of all the staff she was a no-nonsense kind of girl, quite handy with a bat seen as she had quite the swing. She would quite literally either start an argument or a fight in any way she could, she is currently in anger management, and I have to say it's not working. We was expecting a large party to arrive tomorrow, the preparations are underway, but we are slightly short staffed which meant I had to cover the nightclub with Echo, not that I minded so much as I knew she would take out the rubbish. Poor Ava would also be joining us, if I can get through this evening then I can get through tomorrow.

Getting up I go over and look in the mirror, gosh I was looking half dead I thought reaching for my eyes pulling on my eye bags. Dragging myself from my reflection I moved over to the bathroom as I ran myself a bath, getting it to my preferred temperature I started getting changed when a half-naked Ronan came running towards me taking his clothes off as he jumped in my bath.

'Hmm so much for mummy's bath,' I laughed.

'Mummy I was dirty!' he said, looking at his hands.

'Where was you dirty, you had a bath this morning,' I said, raising an eyebrow at him.

'I dirty, look!' he said, pointing to the small piece of pen on his hand.

'Baby you could have washed your hands,' I sighed.

'No I'm dirty!' he said, with a frown.

He was so particular about everything I wondered why he was so obsessive.

'Okay but the next ones mine,' I grinned.

When he was finally all wrinkled up and couldn't take it anymore due to the uneven patterns on his fingers, I helped him out, leaning over I threw a giant towel around his small frame.

'Can we go for ice-cream?' he asked politely, drying his face from the bubbles.

'I can't sweetie, I have to work,' I said.

'You always have to work!' he said, stomping his feet. Those words struck me down where I stood, he was right I did work a lot, but I wanted to give him a life and a great one at that.

'I know sweetie, we can get ice-cream tomorrow,' I said, in hopes that he wasn't angry with me.

'Promise?' he said, holding out his little pinkie, urging me to make the ultimate unbreakable promise.

'I promise,' I said, as I latched onto it, praying he stays this young forever.

'Now grandma Julia should be downstairs, go see if she's made you anything,' I said, as he looked up at me with those beautiful yellow eyes. His toothy grin melting my heart, as he rushed out of the room with his favourite dinosaur in tow. Not having time to run another bath I jumped in this one, putting in a little hot water to make the temperature bearable. Climbing out I wrap the towel

177

around me as I dry off., picking out underwear as I got myself dressed. The uniform was simple to work in the bar you could just be yourself, because if you have to deal with drunken fools then you might as well be comfortable. I chose a black top with black trousers and of course my pink converses. Putting on my favourite perfume, Calvin Klein eternity and make up to cover my sins. Away I went with a slight drag in my step, I hated covering the night club, but we all had to do it.

I walk downstairs to see Ronan making Julia cut his sandwich into equal squares putting equal amounts of everything on his plate, it really wasn't worth the tantrum that would follow if you didn't comply.

'Okay baby, mummy has to go to work now,' I said, pulling at his little cheeks.

'Mum!' he said in a huff, but that sadly only made him look cuter with his scrunched up little nose.

'What do we always remember?' I said, as his attention is no longer on me but on his dinner.

'Ronan, what do we always say?' I added.

'Pete's feet stink?' he said, peering over his juice cup. Oh lord, I should remember to keep my thoughts from my child, as he will get me in trouble one day, however he wasn't wrong Pete's feet do stink.

'No and if Pete should ask, we never say such things, Okay?' I said, staring at him waiting for a response.

'Mummy, that would be a lie,' he said, scanning me for my response.

'Oh, he got me there,' I thought, side eyeing him.

'Well maybe just keep it to yourself then,' I said, as Pete walks through the door.

'Keep what to yourself?' he said.

178

'Mummy said not to tell you your feet stink!' he said, bouncing slightly. little traitor, I could have died.

'My feet don't stink, look I will prove it!' he said, pulling off his shoe and sniffing it. 'Hmm okay maybe just a little,' he laughed, as his face greyed.

'Maybe just a lot,' Ronan said, causing Pete to chase him around the kitchen.

'Come here you!' Pete said, playfully as he nearly cornered him.

'Can't get me stinky Pete!' Ronan yelled.

'Wanna bet?' Pete announced, getting ready to pounce.

'Right I'm off, I will see you all later,' I said, leaving the hotel.

I slowly made my way to work taking in what little fresh air I could. Arriving I noticed Echo was already making waves. 'Oi if your gonna touch the staff then get out of here, you absolute vermin!' she said, yelling across the bar at a group of men.

'It's going to be a long night,' I thought, as I began to re-stock the bar ready for the evening. Someone save me.

The night was alive, business was good, a fight broke out in the middle of the dancefloor causing me and Echo to go to work, throwing herself over the bar she lunges into the crowd. I begin joining her, but something distracted me, looking back seeing she had things under control as she goes down swinging with a little Ava trying to defuse the situation. Moving forward I caught the scent of something very aromatic and enticing coming from the corner of the club, it smelt like sugar plum pie, and candy apples. I followed the amazing scent knowing it was my birthday soon, thinking the girls had made me some form of cake, my mouth dripping thinking it had to be coming from out the back, how the scent was so strong was of no concern of mine I just knew I had to have it. Getting closer I walked out back to find I could no longer smell it. Maybe my nose is playing tricks on me? Coming back out I walk past the corner of the club again; a smashing of a glass causes my head to whip round. I see a man staring back at me with a masquerade mask covering the top half of his face.

'Mate!' he yelled, standing to his feet.

Oh no, not again. I ran to the back exit leaping down the fire escape running down the road, I didn't stop to find out who the man was I just knew I had to keep running, my sides like fire and my breathing laboured. I ran all the way home thinking it was either a dream or an unbelievably bad joke, surely the moon goddess wouldn't do this to me again.

Later that night I could see something was on Ronan's mind, as he twiddled his little thumbs around and around dying to say something to me.

'Mummy?' he asked.

'Oh finally, I thought you was going to explode,' I said, tickling his petite belly.

'Mummy I was talking to nanny Julia, she showed me this picture. Is that my daddy?' he asked casually, as if he had known him his whole life. I thought for a moment, realising I couldn't lie to him I exhaled loudly.

'Yes baby, that's your father,' I said reluctantly, before he could say anymore on the matter I cut him off.

'We will talk more about it tomorrow,' I added.

'When we go for ice-cream?' he said.

Oh shoot I had forgotten about that; I was not going to break my promise, but it was not a discussion I wanted to have. I panicked a little before answering him.

'Maybe not at ice-cream, maybe tomorrow evening?' I said, his eyes rolled until he agreed.

I was more than sure that someone would have been looking for me by now from my old pack, due to my deception but what I didn't know was just how close they really were.

After ice-cream I took Ronan to nursery, he was too young for nursery now, but I hadn't actually figured out a school for him yet, as no one would take him due to his rogue mother. I hated being called a rogue, given the fact I wasn't even a wolf made me angry.

Leaving the nursery, I had a couple of errands to run before my busy shift started. On my walk to the bank, I saw the same man again from last night, he was getting in a car. I turned on my heels and began sprinting to the nursery, to pick up my son only to find he wasn't there.

'Tina, where is Ronan?' I said, as she looks at me blankly.

'Where is my son!' I screamed, getting closer to her face.

'I don't know, he was here not too long ago,' she said, as she searched the classroom.

My mind racing as my stomach began dancing, searching the nursery I begin to tear it apart as the feeling of loss washed over me.

'Where is my boy! show me the cameras,' I ordered. As Tina grabbed her keys moving towards the security office, loading the footage I watch in horror as my son had walked out the front gates, no one watching him, and no one had stopped him.

'If anything happens to my boy, I am holding this place personally responsible,' I said, as I screamed in her face once more. I paced up and down, frantically bringing my hands to my forehead as I run them through my hair, unsure of what to do or where to go my stomach pitted and rolled as my mind raced.

'Call the police!' I demanded, as she scurried away into the back office. Moments later she returned.

'The police have been called, they are on their way,' she said, as my colour drained as thinking of every possible outcome and none of them were good.

I sit unable to move my baby was gone, I swore to protect him, my emotions wild and my temper raging. How could I let this happen? The big meeting was in a couple of hours, but I didn't care. With my heart now pounding and my head splitting, I sat on a chair shaking uncontrollably while a man asked me questions for a full hour.

'Ma'am has your son ever run away before. Did you have an argument with him? Where is the boy's father?' he asked, with judgmental eyes.

'No, no, and he doesn't have one,' I replied, begging him to go out and find my son.

'Ma'am, officers are currently looking for your boy. Do you have a recent picture of him?' he asked.

When he asked me this it made me feel sick, picking my bag up from beside me I scrambled through looking for my purse, I pulled out a recent picture of him and handed it over to the officer. Worry filled my heart as I waited as patiently as I could for any news, an hour went by, and I sat tapping my foot until the numbness took over.

Unable to take it anymore I spring to my feet grabbing my bag and heading for the door, a car pulls up outside and Ronan jumps out, falling to my knees I hold my arms open for him, he rushes to me, and I bring him into a bone crushing hug.

'Where were you?' I said, checking him over.

'Don't you ever do that to mummy again, why did you leave?' I said, as my voice breaks and my eyes stream.

'I went to find daddy, but I saw this nice man who brought me here,' he said smiling.

'Baby, what nice man?' I asked, looking past him.

'I don't know,' he replied.

'What do you mean you don't ever get in a car with strangers, you could have been hurt or worse taken! Promise you will never do that again?' I said, holding my breath to prevent me from exploding.

'I promise,' he said, with sorrow-filled eyes.

'Okay stay here for a moment whilst I go and speak to the officers,' I said, ushering him back into the nursery.

'Sir I am so, so very sorry,' I said, trying to explain.

'Ma'am, do you realise it is a crime to report a child missing when they are with your friends,' he frowned.

'Excuse me?' I said loudly.

'Your son quite clearly knew the person,' he snapped.

'No, he said he didn't know the person!' I replied, not understanding what was happening.

'Ma'am settle down!' he said, as he placed his hand on his holster. Realising this could be dangerous I stepped back in defeat, lowering my gaze I agreed as he went to walk away, I heard 'Bloody rogues!' I bite my cheek so hard I felt the blood pour into my mouth, shaking it off I go in collect Ronan and take him with me to work.

'Mummy I don't want to work, I too little,' he said, showing me his height with his fingers.

'Well if you weren't a little escape artist you wouldn't have too, plus Grandma Julia isn't home right now so you will just have to stay here with me,' I said, trying to calm myself.

'Mummy please!' he said, stomping his foot at me.

'What if mummy gets you some lunch?' I said, trying to distract him, after hearing his little stomach grumble. He nods, realising I didn't have the time I called for Olivia, instructing her to ask the chef to make Ronan some food.

'Olivia, can you make him lunch, also take him with you for a second,' I pleaded.

Holding out her hand he charged her, I watched as she lifted him off his feet placing him on her right hip as she bounced away with him.

Turning I go over the seating arrangements with Echo, as we fight to make everything perfect.

'When they arrive please seat them, I need a minute,' I said.

After this morning's antics who could blame me. Walking down the hall I arrive at my office, quietly closing the door behind me I exhale loudly leaning up against the door from exhaustion.

'There here!' I hear Echo shout down the halls. Honestly could she be more obvious? Listening on all was silent as I hear the doors open.

'Right this way,' Echo said.

At this point I am just grateful she sounded nice for once, one of them must be cute, a little laughter escaped my mouth bringing my hands up I shush myself. Taking in another deep breath I walk out of my office and down the hall, to see Ronan playing with a man. Unable to see his face as his back was facing me, he stands lifting Ronan off his feet he inhales his scent and slowly ruffled his hair.

'Ronan?' I shout as I call him to me, the man stands to face me holding my boy, his eyes fixated on me with piercing yellow eyes.

'Oh no!' I whispered, looking to his left, to see Jason standing closely beside him.

'Annabeth?' Jason said.

184

'Mummy that's the man who brought me home,' he said, pointing at Jason excitedly.

The man walked towards me angrily, Jason not far behind.

'We need to talk, now!' his voice almost sinister, I try to pull Ronan from him, but his grip tightened. Reluctantly he placed him down putting one hand on his head but staring at me, I bend down looking him in the eyes.

'You need to go with Olivia, right now!' I said, as he nods and walks away. I feel a hand wrap around my wrist as he drags me towards my office, pushing me inside and slamming the door behind us, his yellow eyes turned to darkness as his eyes locked with mine.

'Who are you?' he said, abruptly.

'Annie,' I replied.

'Who are you really,' he said, sniffing the air around me.

'Erm, I think you'll find this is my office and my establishment, who are you to ask me who I am,' I snap, as I shoot a glare at him, his face softened slightly.

'Is he mine?' he said, as his fists ball up waiting patiently for my answer. Growing impatient leaping forward he pushes me against the door.

'Is he mine? Answer me!' he said, slamming his fist into the door frame beside me, causing my head and my stomach to bubble with rage.

'So what if he is?' I said, trying to shove him backwards, he looks on at me in shock.

'He's mine!' he said, he goes to push me away, but suddenly I smelt sugar plumb pie and candy apples. His scent was intoxicating, he buried his head into my neck pausing for a moment before running his nose up to my ear he whispers.

'Mate,' his breathing turning heavy.

185

'Oh no buster, I do not need, nor do I want a mate!' I insisted, trying to shove him aside.

'I am not your mate, now tell me your name so I can reject you and get it over with!' I asked, his eyes saddened as he looked at me heartbroken.

'Tell me your name?' I said, as he shook his head at me, I almost felt bad for him.

'Tell me dammit!' I said, as I slammed my fists into his chest repeatedly.

'I remember,' he said, with his eyes focused on me.

'You remember what?' I said, still yelling at him.

'Annabeth, you were the girl at the party?' he responded, no one had called me by my forename in years until today, my eyes filled slightly as I blinked the tears away.

'So you know my name and what?' I said.

Not responding his eyes glaze over for a second, blinking twice his eyes return to me full of lust and promises that I was sure he would not keep.

'That's my son, why didn't you tell me!' he said, yelling again in anger, letting out a loud growl, this time I coward remembering in that moment what a growl like that meant, a growl I had long forgotten.

'I'm sorry,' he said, after I flinched.

'How old is he?' his voice croaked at the mention of him.

'He's six, what do you care anyway; I tried to tell you, in fact I came to you, and I was sent away!' I sniped.

'You were what!' his face boils as the red touched his ears, his eyes glazed again as Jason rushed into my office.

'Who told my mate to leave?' he roared at Jason.

'Your mate?' Jason said, as his eyes bulged while looked at me.

186

'Annabeth, I knew there was a reason I felt warmed to you,' he said, turning to me.

'Back to me idiot, find out who it was!' he snapped, I reach for him to calm him, frightened at what he might do.

'It doesn't matter I don't want to be mated to a wolf; I want to be left alone!' I said, as his arm reached for me.

'Please Annabeth, can we just try I want to get to know my son,' he said, retracting his hand.

'You want to get to know your son huh, I've known who you was for years, you've known him for five seconds,' I huffed in annoyance.

'Please don't reject me, give me time,' he said, his eyes looking scared as he watched me closely.

'Fine I won't reject you, yet!' I said, as he lets out a sigh of relief.

'What's his name?' he enquired, wanting to know more about him.

'His name is Ronan Ethan Thomas Genai,' I announced. His eyes flicker as the tears formed, his wolf I'm sure pushed them away again.

'You gave him my name?' he asked, in disbelief.

'I gave him some of your name!' I snap, folding my arms across my body.

'Sir, might I make a suggestion?' Jason asked.

'Yes what is it, Jason?' he said, with softened features.

'Maybe you should both live together for a couple of weeks?' he said, with a smirk.

'Oh this is such a horrible idea,' I thought, looking back and forth at their faces.

'What a wonderful idea Jason,' he said joyfully.

'No, it isn't,' I glared, crossing my arms aggressively.

187

'Here us out, if you give him three weeks and you still feel strongly about this, then you can reject him,' he said, an evil glance came from him, as he moved towards Jason.

'Then you will leave me alone?' I said.

Turning his head and crunching his knuckles his lips curling inwards, he agreed and that was all the motivation I needed.

'No mark!' I said, as the burning memory remained, the feeling of flames as it etched off my soul.

'What? Absolutely not!' he said, just like a wolf to want to claim someone.

'I am no ones, I will not be claimed by anyone,' I said, firmly and I meant it.

'I will not mark you, until you ask me to,' he said. Silly man that would happen to be never then.

'Agreed!' I said, extending out my hand for him to shake it.

'Gather your things,' he instructed.

'I don't think so, if you want to stay with us then you stay here!' I said.

'Here?' they say in unison.

'Yes here you made your demands, now I'm making mine. No mark and we stay here!' I said, pushing the issue further.

They both take a moment as they clearly mind linked right in front of me discussing at great length their current situation.

'Rude much?' I said, knocking them from their trance.

'Fine we will stay here. Just one thing I know your last name, but I need to know your first name?' I said.

'Phoenix,' he replied, I nodded in reply, but my head was screaming, oh crap that's actually a beautiful name.

'Right I invite you to stay Phoenix,' I said, with a shiver. Oh my word even his name gave me goosebumps, a butterfly effect that pranced around my stomach filling me with pure joy. I looked over at a very lost Jason.

'What about me?' Jason asked.
'You, well you will have to rent a room,' I replied, with a giggle.

'That's not fair,' he said, with his mouth wide open.

'All is fair in love and war. Close your mouth Jason, you will catch something,' I laughed, feeling incredibly pleased with myself.

Once we were all in agreement it was safe to say it was going to be an eventful couple of weeks, he will be begging me for my rejection after what I'm going to put him through.

'Hello Phoenix Genai, and goodbye!' I thought, as my sniggering attracted attention. This was a situation I found myself eager to get out of as fast as I could, a man will not claim me again. This means this was going to be my most trying task yet, one I was sure I wouldn't be failing at.

# Chapter 23
## A long way back

Phoenix walked towards me with his hand out ready to shake, bringing his elbow back nocking the vase off the desk full of ice-cold water, as it poured down my leg, I let out a scream.

'Oi!' Echo said, running through the door wielding a bat bringing it down on Jason's head, it was like watching a baby play whack a mole, only harder and with more passion. I, Phoenix, and a confused Ava let out a belly laugh.

'Annabeth, call her off!' Jason yelped, in pain as
Echo continued with her beat down.

'Sir, my name is Annie!' I laughed.

Echo continues to rain down on him, visual lumps appear where she bashed him over the head.

'Annie!' he yelped, with every clobber that connected.

'Echo that's enough,' I shouted, catching her attention, before bringing her bat down one final time.

'Ouch! That hurt!' Jason said, rubbing the lumps on his head, with a pained expression.

'Jason, this is Echo,' I scoffed, as I introduced them.

'Hmm yeah charmed I'm sure,' he replied, continuing to rub the mind field of lumps on his head.

'Keep your hands where I can see them!' Echo insisted, pointing the bat towards him.

'Hmm feisty isn't she?' he said, staring at her.

His fixation on her every move was intriguing to say the least, and I think I know why.

'Oh you have no idea; shall we go and get you both settled in?' I said.

'Annie, can I see Ronan?' Phoenix asked, and sadly I couldn't refuse.

'Okay, we need to set down some ground rules!' I said, causing him to look over at me confused.

'Firstly, even if we don't work out you can't just drop him, he is your son, you will be there for him, got it? Secondly, we will not be sharing a bed, you can have the floor,' I said, furrowing my brows at him.

'The floor?' he said frowning.

'Yes the floor, got a problem with that?' I tutted.

'No!' he sighs, averting his gaze.

'Thirdly, you will take him to school and pick him up, make him dinner, and do the washing,' I said.

'Fine I have some rules of my own!' he said.

Looking on at him I tilted my head to the side, folding my arms together I listened closely, I'm dying to know what they are.

'Number one, you will give me a fair shot. Number two, you will also spend time with me. Number three, you will hold my hand in public at all times, got it?' he said, proudly.

Ohh that last one got my back up. What a weird request.

'Fine!' I mumbled.

After we had figured out the rules I showed them to the house, getting closer to the house Julia was waiting outside for me.

'We're so glad you're home!' she said excitedly, holding her breath when Phoenix walked up behind me.

'Come quickly,' she said, as her excitement was barely contained.

Julia had been so good to us she was there when no one else was, when no one wanted us she was my angel and shining light, lighting the way to my victory.

'Pete, what are you doing here?' I asked.

'Well, I'm family am I not?' he grinned.

Of course he was right, we are a dysfunctional family but none the less we are family.

'Come child, come with us,' Julia said, pulling on my arm, walking me through the hotel and out to the garden. What I then saw astonished even me, it was the little cottage I loved so much with a red bow draping from the front door, I gasped at it jumping slightly on the spot.

'Julia, what is this?' I said, in amazement.

'Well, this is your new home,' she replied.

'I helped!' Pete added, incredibly pleased with himself.

'Well that's good, seen as Phoenix will be living with us for the time being,' I said, blushing slightly.

Shock formed on all of their faces apart from Julia's she seemed excited, which was weird, but I had enough to worry about like how to get rid of him.

'Thank you all so much,' I announced, looking towards a quiet Ava in the corner, the rest of the girls at work in the restaurant.

Days have passed and I had literally tried everything to get this stubborn man to leave me, what the hell does he want! I have tried trapping him in the bathroom, turning off the heating, cutting off the water supply, showing him my OCD son, guess we know where he inherited that from, as I watch his father cut everything into even squares and placing them in the middle of the plate.

'Daddies like me mummy!' Ronan said, trying to contain his excitement. As I watched on, he was even putting equal amounts of ice into his drinks.

What the hell, why won't he leave me!

The next couple of days where harder than I thought they would be, coming home every day watching Phoenix be a father to Ronan was warming, it was seemingly something I didn't know I craved.

'Erm Annie, I need to ask a favour?' he asked, as a knock on the door distracts me.

'Hey Annie, did you forget it's girls' night?' Echo said, peering around the door.

Looking over at the calendar on the fridge I had forgotten we had planned a night out ages ago.

'You girls go over to the bar, I will join you shortly,' I said, quickly scanning what they are wearing, so I don't go over dressed.

'Be quick!' Echo said, shooting a final glare at Phoenix, she closed the door behind her.

'She really doesn't like me, does she?' Phoenix said.

'Nope can you look after Ronan tonight?' I asked.

'Uh yeah, what about my favour?' he said smiling, his boyish charm had me intrigued.

'And what favour might that be?' I said, fluttering my eyelashes, before kicking myself for flirting with him.

'I have an important meeting coming up, can I use here for it?' he pleaded.

'What sort of meeting?' I said.

'Relax it's a business meeting with another pack,' he replied.

'Oh really, do I know them?' I enquired.

'They are from the dark moon pack,' he said, as my vocal cords tightened, struggling for breath, I leant against the wall for support.

'Annie, what's wrong?' he asked.

My eyes flicker as the room began spinning, unable to keep my balance I fell to the floor. Eventually waking up, I saw Phoenix standing above me with worry in his eyes.

'Annie, Annabeth? wake up!' he said, shaking my shoulders.

'Sorry, I don't know what came over me!' I said, with a cough.

'Who are the Grayson's to you?' he said, as I sighed looking away.

'Annie, who are they to you?' he demanded, his voice was strained, with a growing look of concern on his face.

'There is something you don't know, I was once mated to a wolf,' I said, with guilt.

'You were mated to a Grayson?' he asked.

'Yes the relationship wasn't exactly a good one. Luca was my mate, but I had to get away. Having that mark melted off of my flesh, is the reason I don't want another one,' I said, as he reached for me, his hand caressed my skin.

'I would never hurt you!' he replied, and for a second I believed him.

'I've heard that before!' I replied angrily.

'I mean it, or may the moon goddess strike me down,' he said.

I sat for a second finding myself smiling at his candour, leaning into his touch as it was like a drug to me.

'What are you going to do about the meeting?' I asked, with hesitation.

'Going to have it here,' he said smiling.

'What do you mean,' I frowned.

'I'm going to show him you're my girl,' he said, again with the my. Is he stupid?

194

'You don't understand!' I said, sighing I decided to come clean, 'You see he was unfaithful to me for a while, when I couldn't give him an heir he got abusive; then I met you, falling pregnant straight away I had to make it look like I wasn't able to have children. I couldn't see my family, as he had sent them away. My little brother would be ten years old now,' I said.

My eyes begin to moisten as I hadn't mentioned my family to anyone other than Julia before.

'You couldn't see your family?' he said, taking a seat beside me.

'I don't even know where they are anymore,' I said, as the tears begin to stream.

Leaning towards me he pulled me into a hug, and I caught his scent, unable to control myself I reach for a kiss, this kiss was different, when Luca would kiss me, I could feel his disdain for me, but when Phoenix kissed me, I felt like the only girl in the world. If he weren't holding my arms, I was sure I would float away.

'Magic,' I said, as his smile bursts with joy.

'Fine we will have it here,' I huffed.

'Wait what the hell am I saying? Stupid mate luring bond!' I thought, as I cursed the bond further.

'The plans have changed, and they will not know what has hit them,' he said, rubbing his hands together.

'Daddy, you are staying with me tonight?' Luca said, with glistening eyes.

'Yes son I am, were going to have some fun,' he said, making Luca run in the opposite direction.

A couple of moments later Ronan returned, bringing with him a harry potter Lego house I brought him.

'Can we do this?' he said, shoving the box under his dad's chin, clipping his jaw, and shutting it with a chomp.

195

'Sorry daddy!' he said quickly.

'It's okay buddy, I'm not hurt,' Phoenix said, rubbing his chin better.

'So, we can still play?' he said, wiggling and stamping slightly.

'Of course go and set it up, I'll finish dinner then we can play okay?' he said, redirecting him into the lounge.

'Yayyy!' he said, throwing the box on the floor, tearing it apart to expose the pieces.

'Okay good luck with that, that thing has 100,000 pieces,' I said, as I turn to walk away.

'How many?' his eyes widened with shock.

'Bye!' I said, laughing as I walked away.

Grabbing my clothes from my room I walk into the bathroom, I undress to take a much-needed shower. Leaving the shower running I jump out, rushing to my room to get my favourite shampoo that I left on my dresser, returning down the hallway I hear sniggering coming from the kitchen. Looking on closely I see Phoenix and Ronan messing with the taps in hopes of changing my showers temperature, giving me a bright idea. I walk back to the bathroom giving it a second I wait for the laughter as I begin to scream, noticing I didn't get a reaction I climbed back into the shower, turning around I nock the shampoo bottle onto the floor of the bath, scaring myself slightly I move backwards standing on it and launching me out of the bath with a bang. I groan as the door opens, laying on the floor with my legs in the air in a daze I look up to a beautiful face.

'Annie, are you okay?' he said.

Searching his face I noticed his cheeks were flushed red, his eyes dilated, as he was looking me up and down. What am I a piece of meat?

'I'm, I'm okay,' I respond, before his eyes lower.

'What!' I snapped, before looking down and noticing I was completely naked, his blushed cheeks turned to lust in an instant before turning to rage.

'Who did that to you?' he roared, looking at me.

'It was a long time ago' I said, trying to hide myself.

'The Grayson's!' he roared again, as I pulled a towel over me to hide my scars.

'See this is what I was afraid of, you would take one look at me and be disgusted!' I said, blinking away the tears, trying to pull myself together.

'Darling you are my heart and soul, and you are perfect,' he said, kneeling down before me, cupping my cheek. Yeah that will do it the uncontrollable ugly crying started, but this time I was unable to stop it.

'It was a long time ago, the pack house wasn't patrolled, and a rogue got in, I called for my pack, but no one came, my link was blocked somehow. I was attacked and severely injured, but that's all in the past!' I said, brushing it off.

'That whole pack is going to pay,' he vowed.

'I don't want that, I just want to be alone,' I wined.

'Okay, you need to go and get ready, I have a Lego house to build; can I call for help?' he asked quickly.

'Sure,' I said, as I watched his eyes glaze over.

Leaving him I go to get changed, once I was done I came back into the front room, just in time for Jason to enter.

'Wow hot Mumma!' Jason said, earning him a warning growl from Phoenix.

'You look beautiful, Annie,' Phoenix added, giving me a fluttering tummy.

'Okay he needs to be in bed by 9pm, got it?' they nod as they all waved me off.

Grabbing my bag from the arm of the sofa I looked back to see Jason making a mess, throwing important pieces from the box. My boys were consulting the manual, yeah you heard me, my boys.

'Have fun,' I said, leaving quietly, as I closed the door behind me.

Going out with the girls was fun but I couldn't help but think someone was watching me, the whole night gave me the creeps, the constant feeling of being watched clouded my judgment and ruined my night.

I had a sudden urge to just go home, grabbing my bag I said goodnight to the girls before leaving the club in a hurry, I decided to walk home as I was just minutes away. Footsteps came up from behind me, as a hand grabbed my right shoulder propelling me into the wall at speed, hearing my rib break I double over in pain as an arm reached under my throat pinning me to the wall.

'Hello, Annabeth!' I hear a snake like voice grumble, as I struggle for breath.

'Boid!' I replied, choking trying to suck in oxygen.

'Luca, want's a word with you!' he hissed.

'Or maybe I will just kill you and get it over with!' he said, slamming his fist into my gut, as I gasp out-loud.

'What does he want?' I replied, still struggling for freedom.

Looking on at him refusing to show him any kind of fear, when suddenly I hear yelling coming from the street to only receive two final blows to the face.

'You will find out!' he replied.

'Oi, get off of her!' Echo said, as she rushes towards me, without fear or hesitation.

'We will be seeing you soon!' he said, with a devilish smile. His face pulled away from me vanishing into the darkness that surrounded us, a final leap as he escaped over the fence. I cough loudly, as my body readjusts.

'Annie are you okay?' she said.

'I just want to go home,' I replied, clamping onto my side, wrapping my other arm around her, whilst leaning for support. Why now after all this time? Something is not right here.

'Annie, are you sure you don't want me to stay? I am handy with a bat you know,' she joked.

'Yes I had noticed, no it's fine Echo don't worry,' I laughed, holding my sides.

'Okay if you need me then you call me, okay?' she urged. 'Okay, I promise,' I whispered.

Getting home Ronan was asleep in his bed and Phoenix was nowhere to be seen, knowing my son was okay was more than enough for me, I walked into my room clutching my sides still struggling to breathe, taking off my coat I let out a little yelp. A gust of wind brushed past me, and standing in front of me was Phoenix.

'What happened to you!' he said, pulling on me.

'Annabeth, what the hell happened?' his voice growing louder.

He brought me closer to him wrapping my arms around him he lifts me off my feet, his touch sent a chill down my spine and a tingling up my arms, laying on the bed brought me back to when I was attacked by a wolf, my body was shaking as I begin to whale.

'You can leave now,' I whisper, crying into my pillow. Lifting my chin he kissed my face, wrapping his arm around me making me wince.

'Oh I'm so sorry, I didn't mean to hurt you,' he said, but in that moment I didn't care.

'It's okay,' I replied, pulling him closer to me, his breath on my neck was soothing.

Pulling away he goes to leave me, 'Please stay,' I asked. As his arm wrapped around me again, a feeling of appreciation washed over me, that safe feeling he gave me was like no other. Soon after we peacefully drifted off to sleep arm in arm and sleeping never felt so good.

# Chapter 24
# The meeting

I awoke the next morning unable to breathe as the visible bruising ran up my right sides. Opening my eyes to see a worried Phoenix hanging over me, his warm breath touching my face and warming my heart.

'Mummy, Daddy!' in barged Ronan as I shield my body from his jump.

'Come here you,' Phoenix said, catching him in mid-air, as he aeroplanes him out the bedroom door.

'I can fly daddy!' Ronan screamed.

Turning on my side I dragged myself out of bed, that feeling I swore I would never feel again was back with vengeance. I walk slow cradling my side steadying myself with my other hand on the edge of the bed.

'How could I let this happen?' I whisper down the corridor. Then I saw them down the corridor, I stood looking upon the face I swore I would never accept, but something has changed, one final gaze at Phoenix was like receiving a bolt of lightning designed to kick start my heart. His voice echoing like a sweet Symphony around my head, I stood in the doorway watching him count Ronan's little toes, making sure he hasn't lost any. Was this man truly my happy ever after? Maybe I should give him a chance. Looking over at me his infectious smile gripped me, holding our gaze until it was time for them to leave.

The days were passing quicker than I would have liked, days becoming nights and nights becoming days.

My anxiety finally at its peak as the meet was tomorrow, going to bed Phoenix attempted to sleep on the floor, grabbing his pillow he placed it next to my bed as he sighed heavily, I smiled rolling my eyes at him, I open the covers beside me tapping on the mattress and without hesitation he springs up and leaped into bed.

'No funny business!' I said, he nods frantically moving around constantly to get comfy.

'Will you lay still!' I yelled, feeling his whole-body tense.

'I'm sorry, relax I will not chuck you out again,' I said, with a soothing tone.

With those words he settled falling straight to sleep, I often envied a man for this; wouldn't it be lovely to not have a care in the world to just drift off to sleep. Well I guess tomorrow will be a better day.

Waking up all refreshed the next morning to the sun shining was fantastic, today was going to be great.

'Woah, good morning,' I said, looking at his tired red eyes staring back at me.

'Did you get a good night sleep?' I asked, as he quickly shook his head.

'What's wrong?' I said, as the feeling of concern for his wellbeing, put me on edge.

'Well I would have slept fine, if you didn't snore like Darth Vader!' he smirked.

Okay that feeling of concern didn't last long.

'I do not snore!' I replied, slightly embarrassed.

'Yeah you do, it was like sleeping next to the grim reaper!' he said, making me ugly laugh.

As I pulled the covers over my face a slight snort escaping my lips, only making us laugh more, sadness soon graced my face as I recalled what day it was.

'What are we going to do about today?' I enquired. Knowing the Genai pack where the most feared and powerful pack around, I still couldn't help but think if they could get me here, they could get me anywhere, a lump swelled in my throat, and I begin getting ready for the day. I moved quickly to the kitchen.

'Phoenix?' I whispered, catching his attention.

'Yes love?' he replied, making my heart skip a beat.

'What are we going to do about the meeting today?' I said, lowering my gaze, hearing his footsteps get closer to me as he reached for my arms, sending tingles through my body trailing back down to his touch.

'Do you trust me?' he asked so easily.

'Yes,' I said, without a second thought.

This time however, I fully believed those words.

'I won't let anything hurt you again!' he said.

Those words sent a spark through my chest, I agreed in response unable to believe his comforting words.


The morning was long and tedious, waiting was like waiting for the rain in a drought.

Suddenly the rest of the Genai pack joined us, I hadn't met most of them yet other than a couple of Omega's, one in particular was marked to memory. Walking in one by one I spotted him.

'Mal,' I thought, his name burnt in my brain.

Fire ignited in my stomach; with clenched fists I go to approach him when the dark moon pack approached the entrance. Backing away slowly I walked down the hall returning to my office in silence, it would seem sifting through paperwork was the only way to calm my nerves.

Echo enters the room.

'Phoenix is asking for you,' she said, with a smile. Relief filled my body instantly putting me at ease, getting up I follow her out, my delight soon shattered as the pack remained seated at the table. Still unaware of my presence inhaling deeply I approach Phoenix, coming to his side, holding his arm open he reached for me pulling me in. Holding his lips to my ear he whispers, 'I'm sorry!' and my heart sank. But what was to follow would shock even me.

Pulling my head to the side he opened his mouth, with his teeth now baring he bit down hard on my neck, my eyes widened as my heart raced, blood streamed from my neck and down my top, the warm trail of heated blood was oddly uplifting.

The feeling was different this time, I was half expecting a sudden bout of pain to rush over me but all I felt was desire mixed with his scent. This feeling pulled me closer to him, my body was feeling weird like it was no longer just mine, I began glowing like a star in the

moonlight causing a glare to arise blinding them all.

A burst of wind jutted out from us hitting the Packs where they sat, a coursing constant wave of power. Phoenix retracted his teeth, letting go he sealed my bite with a lick and finally revealing my face.

'What is the meaning of this!' Luca snapped.

'Oh I'm sorry, this is Annie. My mate,' he announced.

The look of shock on my face diminished as I stayed by Phoenix's side, I must admit I was angry but the look on Luca's face was so worth it.

'What?' he said, balling up his fists.

'You heard me!' Phoenix smirks.

'No, she is my mate!' he yelled.

'Was your mate!' Phoenix added, causing Luca to lunge for him.

My reactions where different as my power increased, watching Luca moving towards me in slow motion, the wind hitting me long before he did, pushing Phoenix to the side I grab Luca by his neck throwing him over my head and slamming him into the ground. The look of horror on the faces before me was priceless, Luca got up from the floor stumbling to his feet.

'You bitch!' he said, lunging for me again, this time I nock him into the table behind me, propelling him as he plummeted to the floor. His clothes begin to stretch and tare as his wolf Blane appeared, sorrow in his eyes as he looked at me soon fuelled by rage as he stared at my neck. Phoenix began to change also, I must admit his wolf was sexy, he was a white wolf with silver ears and tail and bright yellow glistening eyes. Hearing a voice in my head for a second, I thought it was myself talking to myself. Am I going crazy?

'Hello Annabeth,' the voice said.

'Who said that?' I replied, pinching my ears.

Okay its official I'm going nuts, I know I talk to myself, but I've never actually replied to myself before.

Mum always said talking to yourself is normal but if you start talking back, well that's when you need to worry.

'Am I going nuts? Is this me?' I thought to myself.

'My name is Elsie, and I am your wolf. No you are not crazy, also why would you be talking to you? I am so sorry,' she whispers, with sorrow.

'For what?' I said, entertaining my messed-up head.

'For all the pain and suffering you have endured for years,' she said.

'It's okay, there is nothing that can be done about it now,' I said, looking at the door, fairly sure some kind of medical unit will be coming for me.

'You are not crazy! Will you shut up and listen,' she snapped, as her breathing increased.

'But Elsie, how is it I have a wolf? I am not a wolf myself?' I asked.

'Oh but you are now, see when our mate bite you the moon goddess saw fit to bless you with a wolf; not just any wolf, an Alpha blood wolf, so we would be Alpha's in our own right,' she giggled slightly.

'Wow that is amazing, I'm so looking forward to getting to know you better,' I said, still unsure.

'And I you,' she said, her voice soft and sweet.

'Hey Elsie, do you wanna come out and play?' I said, not fully believing I had a wolf.

'Of course but I must warn you, this is going to hurt,' she said, shifting our hand slightly giving me a taste.

'Wait what?' I asked worried, as a ripple washed over my body and my skin began to quiver.

Slowly rising to the surface turning into little bumps, my body began shifting back and forth from human form to animal form, my bones readjusting snapping and breaking as my skeletal structure completely changed. The pain was like nothing I had ever felt before my screams echoed in our ears, I clawed at my skin thrashing around as I attempted to stop the change.

'Let it all go Annabeth, become one with me, forget the pain, forget the people, just focus on me,' she said, not listening I tried to avoid my fate.

'Annabeth, you have to let go. You will doom us both!' she screamed.

'How do I do that?' I said, still wailing in pain.

'Listen to my voice, come to me. You must let me in!' she urged.

'Okay,' I replied, finally letting go, I clawed and thrashed some more before going silent for a moment. When I was finished, I stood tall and proud, Elsie shaking her fur as jaws dropped all around me.

My wolf was bigger and stronger than the both of them, I couldn't see what Elsie looked like, but I could at least see what colour we were, I have never seen a wolf coloured like this, we are a Navy blue with black socks white toes and big paws. I so looked forward to seeing what the rest of us looked like.

Our teeth bared claws showing we take a fighting stance, we stepped Infront of Phoenix,

'Stop now!' we projected outwards.

'Erm did she just do what I think she did?' Jason shouted, as all the pack members looked at each other.

'Mr Grayson!' we said turning to him.

'Tell your son to stand down, before I rip him apart!' we ordered, leaning forward towering over him.

'Get out!' Elsie growled, sending him lower to the floor. 'Now!' she roared, making him shift back immediately.

'How did she do that?' Mr Grayson asked the pack.

'I believe she told you to leave!' Jason insisted, folding his arms together looking at them.

'This isn't over!' Luca said, before turning and leaving the restaurant, with everyone else following closely behind him.

Turning back, I realised I had no clothes on, I lowered myself to the floor as Jason rushed to my aid throwing his suit jacket over me, putting it on I went to stand to my feet stumbling backwards I reached for my head before the world went dark.

# Chapter 25
## Training day

Waking up in a haze I didn't recognise my surroundings, beginning to freak out the door opened to Jason rushing through it.

'Calm down Annie, you're okay,' he said, in a reassuring tone.

'Where are they and where am I!' I shouted.

'They are all fine, and you are at the pack house,' he replied.

'How long was I out?' I said.

'Two days,' he replied.

'Are you joking?' I snapped, trying to stand.

'We are okay,' Elsie said, instantly soothing me.

'Where is Phoenix?' I shouted.

'He has gone to get the only wolf we have seen with your specific abilities,' he said, I sighed attempting to get up.

'Take your time, Ronan is playing with the other pups and Phoenix will return shortly,' he said, as he walked to me.

Finally getting to my feet I walk slowly towards the mirror, my reflection staring back at me altered, youthful and glowing like the last six-years didn't happen.

'Wow!' I thought to myself.

'I know, we're hot!' Elsie said, in the back of my head.

'Elsie we are not hot, we have scars!' I said.

'Oh yeah about those, when you became a wolf, your scars faded,' she said howling.

'They're gone?' I said, reaching for my shirt as I exposed my back and stomach in front of the mirror, to find not a mark on me, every blemish every line was gone.

'Oh my god!' I said, with wide eyes, as a sudden burst of energy flowed through me.

'Weird talking to your wolf huh?' Jason whispered.

'Where is my family Jason, where is Julia?' I enquired.

'Julia couldn't come, but Pete, Echo, Ava and Olivia are outside,' he said, pointing towards the door.

'They're all here?' I said, as I glanced over.

'Yes well them and your pack,' he said.

I frown as I realised I'm a marked woman again, I reached for my brand but again this time it felt different.

'Will I have to live here now?' I said, picking at the skin of my fingers for comfort.

'Don't do that!' Elsie snapped, forcing my hands down by my sides, Jason stood nodding at me.

'Okay Jason, I will get to work I suppose,' I sighed.

'Work, what do you mean?' he asked, tilting his head at me.

'Just show me where the damn kitchen is Jason!' I said, shoving past him.

'Okay, this way then,' his confusion continued, as he allowed me to follow.

Heading out of the room things were different, every room was bigger than the last. We walk down a long corridor, greeted by pack members as they bowed before me. 'Well this is new,' I thought to myself.

'Well duh, your there Luna,' Elsie said, as I rolled my eyes.

'Being there Luna means nothing!' I snapped, moving past them all I nod in response. Walking through the games room we made it to the kitchen.

'Luna, this is Mr and Mrs Symonds; they are the pack cooks,' he announced with a smile.

'Pardon me Luna, but can I get you something to eat?'
Mrs Symonds asked, I look at her confused.

'I have to prepare food?' I said, without a second
thought.

'No Luna you don't, that is our job,' she smiled lightly.
'We were hired to cook, as we are indeed chefs' she said.

'So you like cooking?' I said, in disbelief.

'We cook with passion love and appreciation, after all
those who cook together stay together,' she said, hugging
Mr Symonds, her words were oddly satisfying.

'So, what do I do?' I said, looking around the room.

'We eat!' Elsie said, in the back of my head, hearing her
saliva bubbling. 'I'm hungry!' she added, as I heard a
rumble coming from my stomach.

'Let us fix you something to eat,' she said.

I nod as I watch them whip me up a light fruit salad
which I devour in a second, realising I don't think I took a
breath between mouthfuls I sit back slightly, taking in my
surroundings. My hearing becomes tuned as I hear the
other wolves talking, my thoughts trail down the halls off
into the distance.

Focusing further I heard the tree's rustling and the birds
chirping, the Omegas are talking.

'Do you think she remembers us?' a worried voice
spiralled around my head, I know exactly who that is.
Getting up pushing myself away from the table I walk to
the sounds of the whispers, not fully knowing where I was
going it took me out to the garden training area.

'Mal!' I shouted, my voice strained.

'Dude, I think you can take that as a yes,' The Omega
said, taking a step back.

'You can do better than that, lets scare the life out of
this boy!' Elsie said, jumping around in my mind.

210

'Mal!' I roared, making him drop to the floor.

'That's better!' she said.

'I told you I would remember you!' I said, approaching him quickly. |

eat him!' Elsie said, as she bounced.

'Elsie I'm not going to eat him!' I replied sternly.

'Break his leg?' she said.

'Gosh remind me to seek counselling for you,' I said, unsure if she was joking.

'I don't need counselling, I need to hurt something,' she snapped.

'Anger management too!' I said, with a smile.

'What are we going to do then?' she huffed.

'Were going to bring him down a peg or two?' I warned.

'Ohh like a tent peg, were going to pummel him into the ground?' she said.

'Quite the opposite! why did I get the serial killer wolf?' I groaned, as I walked closer to him.

'Oh I like cereal, can we eat some now?' she asked, now fully distracted by her stomach.

'Elsie focus, will you?' I tutted at her.

'Fine!' she said, as we approached him.

'Remember me?' I whisper in his ear, feeling his temperature change. 'I told you I would remember you!' I snarled, smelling his fear as the sweat seeped out of his pores, until I couldn't contain myself any longer, a burst of laughter escaped my lips.

'Get up,' I said, allowing him to his feet.

'Is that it?' Elsie huffed.

'What was you expecting?' I said.

'A little more than just, get up dammit; we're going to have to change that. Bite his ass!' she said.

'Elsie I'm not going to bite any part of his manly parts,' I said in disgust.

'Manly parts, what are you five?' she said, laughing at me.

'No I'm just clearly not as vulgar as you are!' I said, noticing she didn't respond, my attention turned to Mal.

'What is Mal short for anyway?' I smiled at him.

'Malcom, Luna!' he replied, bowing before me, giving me a bright idea.

'Okay Malcom, we are going to learn respect. Today you are going to run in your wolf form, and you're going to run until you realise the mercy I have shown you, and the ridicule I have spared you. If only you showed me the same curtesy,' I smirk.

'Yes Luna,' he replied, shifting into wolf form, and running off into the distance.

'Well now, that was something I suppose; I still want to rip his puny head off!' Elsie said.

'Okay Elsie let's get you some food,' I said, as I started walking towards the house.

'Finally, I'm starved!' she replied, with a howl.

'You get grumpy when you're hungry,' I said, making my way back to the kitchen.

'Are those freshly made cookies I can smell?' I said, as I begin salivating.

All of my pack had smelt the cookie before we had, they each crowded around the kitchen waiting for their piece. Turning around they all stared at me moving out of the way as I entered, making my way past them one by one I reach for a freshly made hot cookie.

'Hmm!' I said, as the food danced around my taste buds. As I walk away the pack members jump on the cookies, snatching and grabbing at them.

'One at a time!' my thoughts projected outwards, stopping them in their tracks. 'We are not animals!' Elsie roared, scaring them slightly, one by one they took their cookies bowed and left.

'Maybe you should eat a lot sooner?' Jason said nudging me, letting out a cackle.

'Hmm Elsie, gets mad when she is hungry,' I said, as we both laughed together. Looking at Jason both our eyes turned white as we were being called.

'We're here!' Jason's eyes returned to normal, but my eyes remained tranced.

'Come to me my love!' I heard in the back of my head. Elsie began to howl and prance around with excitement, and before I knew it I was running.

Racing towards my mate for a long overdue greeting, bouncing over chairs and running past other pack members, I reached the front entrance crashing into Phoenix and gripping him tightly.

'Hello my love!' he said, melting my heart.

'Where have you been?' I said giving him a thump.

'Ouch,' he smiled, getting closer to my face, and kissing my lips.

'This is Valdor, he is the Elder of the ancient Galdorie pack,' he said, pointing behind him.

'Hello Luna,' he said without a bow, no one seemed to question it so neither did I.

'Hello, why is he here?' I whisper to Phoenix, strategically covering my mouth.

'I am here to train you, and to see what your abilities indeed are,' he smiled.

'Great, I never did like training!' Elsie scoffed, and I was inclined to agree with her.

213

'We will start tomorrow, for now at least I hear your wolf wishes to be alone with your mate,' he said sarcastically.

'Stuff our mate, let's get him!' Elsie said.

He smirks, 'Quite the fiery one, isn't she?' his grin becoming wider.

'He can hear us?' I whispered.

'Relax, we will kick his arse!' Elsie said confidently.

'I would like to see you try!' Valdor replied.

'Is he joking?' Elsie growled.

'I am neither joking, nor am I weak,' he smirked.

'Sure he's not, I could beat him,' Elsie said, as a fire ran through our stomach.

'Shall we put that to the test?' he said, rolling my eyes, I reluctantly agree.

'Right this way then!' he said, pointing towards the garden.

'Elsie, what are you doing?' I asked, as my feet started to skip.

'We're going to teach this punk a lesson!' she said, as my strides got bigger.

'I don't think this is a good idea!' I said out of fear.

'You should listen to your human, little wolf,' he laughed pointing at us.

'Right that's it, put them up bub!' she said, taking a fighting stance. Looking to my left I saw everyone gathering in the garden to watch the fight.

'Go on, Annie!' Echo screams from behind me.

Elsie lunged for him with her teeth baring, he moves out the way flicking us sideways.

'Elsie!' I yelled.

'Relax, I've got this!' she said lunging again, this time he brings his arm out, close lining us to the floor with a thump.

'Elsie, you're going to get us hurt!' I said, knowing she isn't listening.

Why did I get the crazy suicidal homicidal wolf?

'Hey, I heard that!' she replied.

'You was meant too, you crazy bitc... look out!' I yelled, as Elsie ducked out of the way.

'You need to control your temper!' Valdor said.

'You need to shut the hell up!' Elsie said, as she lunged again, twisting her body, clamping her mouth shut as she shifted us into wolf form. Now I had no choice but to watch.

'Training you, will be like training a puppy!' Valdor laughed. Elsie began running for him with speed catching his stretched-out arm in her mouth, he paused for a moment before bringing his fingers to her face as he shook them.

'Uh, Uh, uh!' he said, whilst waving his finger. Bringing his arm up he launched us above his head, with a wave of his hand he stopped us in mid-air, leaving us there like a dangling prize.

'Now then let's see, hmm you have all the great potential in the world Annabeth, but you need to control your wolf!' he said, pacing up and down.

'Control, what's he talking about; I'm going to scratch his eyes out' Elsie snapped, scratching for him.

'You need to think as one, only then will you work as one,' he said, tapping on his chin.

'Is he an idiot, where did Phoenix find him!' Elsie cursed.

'I don't know, but can you not anger him by calling him an idiot,' I said worriedly.

'Did he hear me?' we both look on at him.

'Yes, I heard you,' Valdor replied.

'Well that's that then, he's a demon,' she said, scowling at him.

'He is not Elsie! Hold on are demons real too?' I asked but secretly didn't want to know.

'Yeah!' she said with joy.

'They are not, and he is not!' I replied, in annoyance.

'Is so!' she said.

'Elsie, so help me!' I snapped, thinking of my next move.

'What I didn't bring him here,' she insists.

'If you two are quite finished!' he snapped, our attention drawn back to him.

'Now tomorrow we will train, and you need to be ready for what's coming; believe me child you think today was challenging, wait until tomorrow!' he sneered, his tone worried me, not Elsie though, nope it was like she created her own boxing ring in my head, as she played the eye-of-the-tiger on full blast from my memories, great my wolf now thinks she is rocky balboa.

'Owe I'm going to get him tomorrow, wait and see Annie!' she said, still punching the air.

Oh lord, I'm going to die aren't I.

After spending some time with Phoenix things started to heat up slightly between us before Ronan had other ideas.

'Mummy!' he shouted, honestly, I can't catch a break.

'Yes sweetie?' I yelled back at him.

'Can daddy read me a bedtime story?' he said, shoving a book in his father's face.

'Of course I can,' Phoenix said, scraping him up with one arm, carrying him to his room as Ronan rubbed his tired little eyes. He returns ready to continue what we started but my mind drifted, I had questions that I wanted answers to. He walked over to me whilst I was sitting on the couch, folding himself in half he sat down beside me stretching his arm around me pulling me in, my fingers automatically come up pressed against his lips, as I tried to create some space.

'Phoenix?' I said, leaning backwards.

'Yes my love?' he said, with a mischievous grin.

Okay this man is seriously going to give me another baby if he keeps sweet talking me like this.

'Can I ask you some questions?' I said, as his eyes look on in frustration, but he agrees.

'Why do you never talk about your parents?' I said, as his eyes narrowed, sadness was all over his face.

'They were taken when I was a child,' he said.

'By whom?' I asked, with horror in my eyes.

'By the Nafari!' he sighs.

'Who are the Nafari?' I said, searching his face I realised this was not something he wished to discuss.

'The Nafari, are one of the five founding packs of the world, but their leaders are not wolves,' he said, looking away from me.

'What do you mean? how can they be a pack if they leaders are not led by wolves?' I asked, digging a little deeper, trying to gain as much information as I can.

'The Nafari aren't a pack of wolves, but they do lead them, they're governed by a sadistic madman craving Alpha blood to sustain his immortality; never fully finding what he needs to make this permanent,' he said, as his body becomes tense, he slowly begins to clam up.

'So if there not wolves, then what are they governed by?' I asked, taking a deep breath in waiting for his reply.

'I'm tired, it's time for bed,' he said, taking my hand he pulls me towards our bedroom, getting changed we climb

217

into bed. Kissing me on the head he pulls me tightly to him, as we both drift off to sleep.

# Chapter 26
# The lone wolf

Upon waking it was time to start my training, sensing Phoenix was still sad from the night before made me feel awful. I brushed past him giving him a kiss on the cheek, his smile formed which made me happy. Getting ready I begin to think about last night, who are the Nafari? And what are they looking for?

'Mummy, can we go get some Ice-cream today?' he asked.

'No sweetie, mummy has to train today,' I said, as his face saddened. 'But we can get some from the kitchen later?' I said, in hope that his face would lighten once more. Having the desired affect his face lit up as he nodded frantically before Phoenix got him ready for the day. Going downstairs I made sure to load up on calories shoving everything in my mouth I could get my hands on, with a half-filled mouth and a ravenous wolf I leant backwards trying not to puke.

'Ready to train?' I hear a sarcastic voice echo behind me.

'We sure are!' Elsie said in haste.

Honestly, I loved my wolfs spirit, but I think I'm going to regret this.

'Right this way,' he said, again with the sarcasm.

I pull myself up off of my stool and follow him to the training matt outside, standing in front of us he urged us to take a seat opposite him.

'You need to centre yourself feeling the wind move around you, flowing through you and touching your soul,' he said, in a spiritual tone.

'Is he being serious?' Elsie laughed, as I shushed her, I attempted to close my eyes and concentrate.

'Feel it's movements touching your skin, and shifting direction,' his motions becoming more intense.

'Oh brother, this is boring; can we do something else?' she whispered, gently to me.

'Elsie, would you just!' I shouted, opening my eyes.

'Will you both be quiet, how do you expect to learn!' he snapped, pointing at us with a scrunched-up face.

Hearing Elsie mimic his voice in my head was I will admit a little funny.

'Is he looking at me?' Elsie said.

'Seriously Elsie, you need to learn to chill,' I said.

'I don't think I do!' she huffed.

'Oh Elsie, you most certainly do!' Valdor replied.

'Oi will you stay out of our head, it's rude to listen in on other people's conversations!' Elsie said.

He sniggered, 'Then you shouldn't make it so easy!' he said, as the corners of his mouth arose into a widened smile.

'Annabeth, did I tell you how much I hate him!' Elsie said, flipping him the finger, my finger might I add.

Ignoring her I get on with my learning, but after spending what felt like hours learning the movements, he then made us put them all together, left hand over right and right over left before bringing it into a circle.

'Wow! looks like you farted, and smoke popped out your butt! That was so little, does it smell?' she said, her laughter was contagious, making me giggle too.

'Elsie, it wasn't a fart; we did it!' I said excitedly.

'You did, but it was pathetic!' Valdor said, making Elsie angry. Why does he poke that bear?

'Right that is it, I've had it with him; I'm killing him,' she replied, rolling up my sleeves.

'You move straight to killing far too quickly, Elsie,' I said. I paused for a moment, hearing Jason coming up behind us with some refreshments, looking over I saw the ice clanging against the glass. A drink never looked so good.

'Echo, looking good,' he shouts, to her as she sunbathed.

'Go away dog!' she yelled, from the distance.

'Well can't say I don't try and be nice,' he said, handing me the ice-cold beverage I had been dying for. Before Valdor spoke to us in a different more saddened tone, 'Child you have to understand, the Galdorie don't have female wolves, unless they are bred but even then they are half breeds. I am one of the last humans of the Galdorie,' he said.

His persistence was admirable, and my attention was now fully on him. Why was he so sad?

'What do you mean?' I asked quietly.

'I mean a woman wolf created by the moon goddess is of value, as there hasn't been one for over one- hundred-years,' he said.

'Who am I of value to?' I said.

'To everyone, as we don't yet know what powers you possess other than telekinesis,' he said, as I shot him a worried look. Great I'm a walking trophy.

'Sarcasm is not a good trait at the best of times, how many people know about you?' he said, making me pause for a moment.

'My friends, my pack, and the Grayson pack,' I said.

'Another pack?!' he said, his eyes widened.

'Yes but we showed them!' Elsie said proudly.

'This is not good, what about your family?' he replied, stamping his foot. My eyes move frantically as I remember my family, I was not only scared for my current family but also my birth family.

'What was that thought, who are they'? he said, circling his finger in the air, trying to make me return to my previous thoughts.

'My family?' I said, lowering my head in frustration.

'They are not the people I see around me, does the other pack know of them?' he said, as his anger increased.

'Yes,' I said, averting my gaze.

Without another word his eyes glazed over and before I knew it Phoenix was by my side.

'You need to find her family, now!' he shouted, alerting Phoenix to his demands. Phoenix alerted the others, and they leave immediately.

'Go and be with your son, we've got this,' he said.

For the first time ever I felt Elsie's urge to run away, she shifts stretching her legs out pawing at the ground below us. Jason and Mal follow closely behind as we howl into the distance, after running for what felt like an eternity around the grounds we arrive back home. Shifting back I gather some clothes I left in a tree, quickly putting them on I rush to Julia and explained everything to her.

'I was worried about this!' she said, lowering her head.

'Why didn't you tell me?' I whispered, to not catch Ronan's attention.

'Let's go outside?' she said, as we turned, she directed me outside, her arm placed around me as we walked, with Ronan now skipping closely behind us.

'Why didn't you tell me from the beginning?' I sighed. I couldn't help it a feeling of betrayal washed over me, as I felt she was the only one I could rely on.

'Because I wasn't sure, you need to understand something,' she said, before Jason interrupted us.

'Annie, we found your family's home!' he said, with a hint of regret in his voice.

'That's amazing, where are they?' I said, with pure excitement, fully ready to see my family again.

'We don't know,' Phoenix's voice echoed from behind me, my head started to spin with the information.

'The house was in disrepair, your family are nowhere to be seen,' he said, as my mouth began to water, my stomach bubbling, as I feel heat rising as it burnt my throat, bending over I vomited on the floor letting out a loud scream. My knees buckle and I found myself falling, Phoenix rushed to me catching me as he cradled my struggling body, my legs kicking out as I try to fight his comfort.

'We don't know what's happened, but we will find them,' he said.

I knew something was wrong, the feeling of dread filled my stomach and chest for the past week, my sudden reaction to this made it so everyone piled through the door to the garden.

'Annie, you need to remain strong!' Julia said, trying to pull my attention, as my whales became out of control.

'Annie, calm down,' Echo said, in a reassuring tone.

'Can't you see she won't calm down Echo, she's distraught!' Ava replied.

'What do you know?' Pete shouted.

'You all need to be careful!' Valdor warned, noticing nobody was listening as my anger was rising, sitting back he watched closely. 'I really would take a step back if I were you,' he said, picking at his fingernails, rising to his feet, with his devilish smile growing.

'Everyone just shut up!' I yelled, sending out a gust of wind, throwing everyone backwards.

The only one remaining on their feet was Valdor.

'What the hell was that?' Olivia laughed.

'That was her!' Valdor said, pointing right at me.

'I warned you all, but at least we now know you don't just read minds,' he said, casually picking lunch out of his teeth.

'Please find my family!' I begged.

'We will all do our best,' Julia said.

'Hay, mummy why are you so upset?' Ronan said.

Looking out I saw these beautiful little yellow eyes staring at me, I pulled him in close not wanting to let him go.

'Never grow old my baby!' I whispered to him, Elsie howling in my head, feeling every ounce of pain I was feeling.

'Please just find them,' I whisper.

'I have a feeling they will find us and when they do you must be ready, you must control your temper. Maybe that's it!' Valdor gasped.

'What's it?' Phoenix asked.

'Yeah, what's it?' Ronan said giggling.

'Maybe we need to push your emotions,' he said, running his hands down his beard.

'Oh yeah, and how's he going to do that?' Elsie snapped.

'Like this!' he said, with a sickening smile.

Moving with speed he grabbed hold of Ronan's arm and dragged him closer, rising to our feet we take a fighting stance.

'Let go of my boy!' I yelled at him, ready to lunge for him, Phoenix now by my side.

'Uh careful wouldn't want me to break him now, would you?' he said, making me shift.

'Let go of our pup!' Elsie snarled, as she began circling him. Slipping his hand down he gripped Ronan's neck, my eyes darken with rage.

'Elsie, let Annabeth back out, or else!' he insisted, initially she did not listen.

'Elsie do it now or I will slit his throat!' Valdor commanded, reaching for Ronan's neck.

I began screaming in Elsie's head trying to get her to listen, watching as his hand slid down further.

'Do it now!' he commanded, shifting me back to human form.

'Do you love your son?' he said casually, I shot a look at Phoenix still in wolf form he nodded.

'Mummy, daddy help me!' he screeched.

My claws grow with my fists balled stabbing me in the hand as the blood dripped to the floor, reminding me this was no dream.

'Let him go!' I said, feeling myself about to shift again.

'Don't you dare shift! Do you want me to break his neck? What sort of parent are you!' he cackled.

'Shut up!' I snapped, feeling a different rage boiling.

'You want me to shut up, you want me to let go? Then do something about me or can't you?' he smiled.

'I said shut up!' I said, throwing my hands out gripping him in my web, as I watched him struggle.

He levitates up as I launch him towards the tree, winding him before I Slammed him to the ground, Phoenix jumped for Ronan putting him on his back, darting out of the way to safety. Valdor attempting to get up and dragging himself away for cover, it was a poor attempt, and he was going nowhere.

'Oh no, we're not done with you yet!' I said, as my arms stretch out, I begin pulling him towards me, his hands drag in the dirt.

Catching handfuls of mud in the palms of his hands as I dragged him to me, lifting him in the air I bring him face to face with us, our teeth baring, claws showing but we do not shift we hold our composure.

'Fascinating!' he clapped.

'Going to kill my son, was you?' I said, as I bounced him like a ball.

His smile widened, 'No, but it worked, didn't it?' his smile now filling his face.

'What's he on about? The absolute weirdo; Kill him!' I hear Elsie's voice in my head, my eyes glowed green, as the urge to kill was overpowering my sanity.

White steam flowed out of my body, my rational mind being overtaken by the urge to punish, luckily for him two little hands appeared Infront of me as I was about to end him with a single snap.

'Mummy it's okay, he told me to scream,' he said, catching my attention, as I dropped Valdor on his bottom.

'What?' I said, bending down to his level.

'Valdor was in my head, and he said to scream mummy daddy help me, but he wouldn't hurt me it was pretend,' he smiled, reaching for him I held my baby close, my eyes closed feeling my temperature lowering as I embraced his tiny frame, whilst glaring over his shoulder at Valdor in disgust.

'You ever use my baby again to get what you want, I swear on the moon goddess I will kill you myself, got it?' I screamed, waving my finger in his face.

'Oh yes, I've got it,' he replied, rubbing his bottom.

'Next time you won't be so lucky,' I warned.

His smug grin made me want to pummel his face into the ground, for what he had just put me through. But I am afraid that was going to have to wait.

# Chapter 27
## My heart and soul

The past few days have killed me, I ached in places I didn't think possible.

'He's pushing you too hard!' I hear Phoenix call from the bedroom door, his voice like music to my ears, opening one eye I peer over at him.

'It's fine, I can handle it,' I smile without sincerity.

'No you can't, look what it's doing to you?' he said, as he leaned up against the door frame. Gosh he was perfect. His voice turned to silence; all I could see was a shirtless god standing before me making Elsie wolf whistle in my head.

'I want to meet him!' she announced.

'Meet who?' I asked.

'His wolf!' she replied.

It suddenly dawned on me that I had only met his wolf twice, all be it due in a fight, but still none the less it was time. I look at him with loving eyes as we ask permission, hoping he will agree to shut Elsie up for once.

'We want to meet your wolf,' we project outwards, making him take a step back.

'You want to what?' he replied stunned.

'We want to meet your wolf, we wish to run with him,' I said, as our minds linked intertwining as one.

'Sure,' he said, shrugging his shoulders.

'What's his name?' Elsie asked, saving me the embarrassment.

'Woolfie!' he replied. Surely he wasn't being serious.

'Owe erm, what a lovely name,' I said, trying to hide my expressions from him.

'What? What sort of Alpha name is that, might as well of called him puppy!' Elsie howled with laughter.

'No my love, I am joking!' he said giggling.

'Oh thank God, there is no way we could be seen with you without a name change,' Elsie said.

'Elsie manners?' I snapped at her.

'I was merely stating what you was thinking,' she laughed.

'What's his name really?' I asked, hoping he would give a straight answer this time.

I waited patiently thinking his pause was for dramatic effect, I sat up right in the bed folding my arms, his muscular frame leaned towards me as his arms were above his head resting on the door frame.

'Oh lord!' escaped my lips.

'His name is Argorn, he is not always very patient nor well understood,' he said, slowly pacing towards me.

'I want to meet him!' she screamed, her voice becoming childlike. I could hear her thumping in my head, stamping on my last nerve.

'Will you just be patient?' I snapped, entering my mind to try and find her. 'Elsie honestly, you are worse than my child!' I said, confronting her irrational behaviour.

'I am not you've got your mate, now let me have mine!' she said, standing before me.

'Say please or learn some patience!' I stamped back in disapproval.

'I have been patient you have your mate, now I want to meet mine!' she wined, making me feel bad for her.

'Fine!' I said, as our bickering was getting ridiculous.

'Erm Annie, can you come back out now?' Phoenix said, breaking me from my trance.

'You really have to stop doing that, normally we talk to our wolf, but you looked like you went somewhere different?' he said, as I ignored him.

'Okay so we get Ronan ready place him in the nursery, then we run?' I said as he nodded, I leaped up off the bed, to go and wake our son.

I get up and move to the mirror in our room I hadn't noticed before how big it actually was, guess that comes naturally to the Genai family, looking around my room I finally took in my surroundings before my attention turned back onto myself.

'We need to look pretty!' Elsie said, suddenly my hand came up as she began erratically painting our face, reaching for our makeup products.

'You said pretty Elsie, not clown!' I said, lifting my hands trying to resist her.

'Relax trust the process,' she said, hammering me with a foundation brush.

'How can I trust the process when you're making us look like a drag queen,' I said, squirming in my seat.

'Yes but drag queens are beautiful you know, so quit moaning!' she said, reaching for the bright pink blush.

'He loves us as we are,' I protested.

This became counterproductive because as she was painting, I was removing with force.

'Will you leave it alone, at this rate we will look like clowns!' she said, taking over both my hands, giving me no option but to sit still. Waiting for her to finish was like watching paint dry, incredibly boring.

'And Wala!' she said, as if she was the next Picasso. Finally able to look at myself I gasped, somehow she made us look amazing. Not a blemish, no circles completely flawless and our skin positively glowing.

'I think if we move our face somethings going to crack,' I replied, not giving her the satisfaction.

'You're testing my patients!' she said.

'Who are you kidding Elsie, we both know you don't have any of those,' we both laugh.

But our laughter was broken by a knock on the door, as Phoenix peered around it.

'Ready my love?' Phoenix called, my feet becoming lighter than air I rush to him.

'We are yes,' we both responded.

'Follow me then,' he said, as we walk out of our room, down the corridor to the elevator, getting inside we pressed ground floor.

Stepping out we walked into Maria, she was not fond of me and didn't she let me know it.

'Phoenix,' she said, fluttering her eyelids at him, as an uncontrollable rage filled my core.

'It's Alpha to you!' he replied, giving me a little smirk.

'Of course, Alpha; hello Luna!' she hissed.

'Maria,' I replied, taking hold of Phoenix's arm, her eyes flash red, her cheeks pinken and her smile diminishes.

'Poor puppy!' Elsie said, making my smirk bigger.

'If there is anything I can do for you Alpha, I mean anything don't hesitate to call,' she said, batting her stupid eyes, and winking as she walked away.

'I hate her, surely we can kill this one?' Elsie growled.

'Hmm she is coming close!' I said, as Phoenix wraps his arm around me pulling me in closer, making us melt and forgetting our previous thoughts.

'Now my love, we run,' he said.

My thoughts trailed back to the woman in the diner, maybe her words didn't mean what we think they mean.

'What do you mean?' Elsie enquired.

'Elsie, if the first warning came true from her, maybe the second warning wasn't meant straight away?' I said.

'I'm not following,' she replied.

'If she said our troubles are only the beginning, then maybe she didn't mean with Luca?' I said.

'I think you had too much coffee this morning, you're spoiling this for me, now shh!' she said, as we continued walking out onto the grounds.

Getting to the lake I watch on as he undressed, looking away I blushed a little. Hearing movements I saw Mal and Jason coming up behind us.

'Need an escort?' Jason asked, as Mal stood puffing out his chest.

'No we're fine, I will call if I need you,' Phoenix said, in a dismissing tone.

'Valdor is looking for you,' Mal responded, my eyes lowered realising I might have to go and train.

'If Valdor ruins this for us then I'm going to put him in a hole and bury him, whilst using only my back legs to fill in that damn hole so it lasts longer!' Elsie said.

'I'm beginning to worry about you, you're a total psycho!' I scoffed.

'Later!' Phoenix said, making them bow before they walked away. This is going to be fun I thought, undressing fully I packed my clothes in a nearby tree stump ready for my run.

# Chapter 28
## The devil knows no bounds

As we change our paws hit the soft mud filled ground under us, the watery earth squidging between our pads as I pawed at it sinking the mud in deeper. Elsie begins to stamp with joy causing mud to spatter everywhere.

'You're such a child!' I said to her.

Shaking off our worries raising our neck and stretching out to finally see him, his wolf was shining in the daylight and staring straight at us without a single word.

'This is weird, is he going to say something?' Elsie asked.

'Elsie, say something to him,' I urged.

'But he's just staring maybe his wolf can't speak, or worse maybe it has a stutter?' she laughed.

'Or maybe you haven't shut up long enough for him to speak,' I snapped, trying to shush her.

'Maybe if you shut up then he would speak!' she said.

'Elsie this is getting us nowhere!' I yelled.

'Yeah, well you started it!' she said.

'Did not!' I insisted, knowing she was wrong.

'Did so!' she replied, pausing for a moment we hear a chuckle coming from behind us, we were bickering so much we hadn't noticed he had moved.

'Hello ladies,' he said, as he brushed past us.

Walking past us he flicked his tail across our nose.

'Oh my!' Elsie's jaw dropped, as she began panting heavily, dribble escaping the corners of her mouth, with her tale pointed and wagging frantically.

'Elsie, are you serious right now?' I said, as he approached us, her tale getting quicker as she lowered to the ground. Spreading herself out.

'Oh my word, you're totally gross,' I said, closing my eyes. For once she was actually lost for words, getting closer to us he nuzzled his head into our neck giving even me butterflies.

'Maybe we should leave these two alone?' Phoenix said.

'Agreed!' I said, as I slowly made myself scares.

We finally began to run, and I found myself wanting to stay a little longer, to feel the wind in our fur, the feeling of his touch on our face, the embrace his wolf had for her was divine.

I soon realised this was getting weird, slowly shielding myself off I decide to search my memories for answers, I was unable to let go of the notion of the Nafari. Why did they feel so familiar to me? Where have I heard that name before? Sensing I was running out of time I gave up for now, after searching for what felt like hours, I finally concluded I would have to consult the pack archives to find out the questions I needed to know.

Upon coming back to reality both Elsie and Argorn laid panting heavily on the ground, curled around each other next to the streaming waterfall east of the property.

'Uhem!' I said, with a little cough.

'Alright there are we, Elsie?' I said, as she ignored me.

'You did it didn't you?' I laughed.

'Did what?' she said, acting innocently.

'Don't play coy with me, you dirty little birdy,' I laughed.

'I don't know what you mean,' she huffs.

'Sure you don't do you have anything to say, Argorn?' I said.

'Nope, a gentleman never tells,' he said, suddenly his ears spike, as he turned his head to the distance.

Running towards us at an alarming speed, was five rogues closely followed by Boid.

'Run!' shouted Argorn, our feet separated planting firmly on the ground, freeing our mind and sending out a distress signal to the whole pack.

'I am done running!' we roared.

'Annabeth please!' Phoenix screamed.

'No!' I said, standing tall with my wolf.

'Go now!' Argorn yelled, as the stamps got closer.

'Annabeth, we are one and we've got this!' Elsie roared, before we knew it we was running.

Phoenix roared following closely behind me, both sides rushing towards each other neither ready to back down. We smash into each other, tearing at anything we could sink our teeth into, Elsie snarling gripping one Rogue by its throat as she smashed down on its neck,

bone-crushing screams and whimpers filled my ears, with one final bite the wolf was finished.

Letting go he fell to the floor, Elsie balancing on her front legs whilst kicking out at the wolf coming up behind us, two wolves now on me trying to pin me to the floor, snapping at my neck and growling.

One took a hold of my legs attempting to drag me backwards, bearing down on my leg we let out a yelp catching the attention of Phoenix, he ends his opponent before rushing to help us. Boid looking over he transformed back lifting his arms up, he sinks them into Phoenix's ribs crushing them, hearing a snap as Phoenix screams in pain. Hearing our pack coming was of comfort but I knew there wasn't time. Kicking both the rogues off of me I push out my arms dragging them upwards, my eyes glow red as I

235

look on at my mate barely moving. Rising them off of the ground I bring them close, I could smell their disdain for me, their anger radiating from their flesh mixed with a little fear.

'Why have you come?' we growled, in a tone that I had not heard before, but they remain silent.

Looking around Boid was nowhere in sight, as the stampede of our pack getting closer to us filled the air.

'Tell me!' I roared.

'We will never tell you anything!' his laughter came as a shock.

'You're going to have to kill us!' the other rogue spoke.

'She won't kill us; she hasn't got it in!' he said.

But I was in no mood for mercy, with that I flicked my wrist snapping both of their necks simultaneously, their bones cracked as their breathing ceased. Letting them go I let them plumet to the ground, my eyes flicker as my body becomes weak.

'Phoenix!' I whispered, looking on at him, as my world went dark.

Upon waking I was scared, not for myself but for my mate.

'Phoenix!' I begin to scream uncontrollably, to a worried Jason storming through the door.

'Annie please!' he yelled, as I pull the wires and the tubing from my arms.

Attempting to stand to my feet Jason tries to stop me, he places a hand on my shoulder for reassurance, grabbing him by the neck I launch him against the wall.

'Luna please!' he said, desperately clutching at his throat as I continue to squeeze, his taps getting heavier as he struggles for breath. Realisation hit me and I loosened my grip.

'Jason I'm so sorry, I don't know what came over me!' I said, trying to help him to his feet.

'It's okay, he's in the other room,' he said, pointing to the door, as he clutched onto his neck.

'Annie, he's really hurt,' he replied, my eyes widen in disbelief, going to his room I saw Maria by his bedside.

'What are you doing in here!' I said, as Jason came in behind me.

'Maria get out!' Jason spat.

'She's the reason he is hurt can't you all see, I would be a much better Luna!' she said, placing a hand on Phoenix's chest, we shift slightly.

'Don't make us tell you again, remove your hands off of our mate or we will have you banished,' Elsie snarled.

'Jason you can't be serious, she was a rogue how do we know she didn't do it!' she said, pointing her neatly polished finger at me.

Elsie took a hold of it snapping her fingers in the opposite direction, her bone-curdling scream filled the room as she wept, with agony written all over her face.

'Get out!' we snarled, holding her hand she rushed out of the room.

'Annie, what's gotten into you?' Jason said.

'I don't know, honestly I don't know what's wrong,' I said, looking down in shame.

'She is a bitch though I will give you that!' Jason laughed.

'I like him!' Elsie replied.

Looking over at Phoenix he had wires everywhere with bandages around his ribs and legs, I reached for him, that spark between us ignited. Jason reached for me sensing something was stopping him I got closer, we took a hold of his hand closing our eyes we felt the pain rush through us, thrusting us forward as we tried to remain on our feet, peering down we saw our veins blacken risen and pulsing as his pain entered our body. It was a pain I had experienced on many occasions.

Snapping me back to the time Luca's she wolf asked for a different meal and I foolishly declined, what a mistake that was. Grabbing a hold of my hair she threw me to the floor kicking and punching me, dragging me up again by my hair she slapped me colliding with my face she propelled me backwards, falling I hit my head on the kitchen counter knocking me out for days.

My thoughts transferred back to see my Phoenix looking back at me with a smile.

'Hello love,' he replied, my heart skipped a beat as I kissed his face all over.

'You scared me!' I whispered in his ear.

'Where is Ronan?' he said, as I turn to look at Jason, with Mal, Echo and Valdor standing behind him.

'Ronan is fine, he is downstairs with Julia,' he said, as Pete entered the room.

'Yeah funny story, we were the only people who could settle him,' Pete laughed.

'Thank the heavens! I will be better next time, I promise,' I said, looking back at Phoenix, his hand reaches for me, a slight smile arises as he drifts back off to sleep.

'Echo, how's it going?' Jason asked, as she walked right past him his eyes deflated.

'Give it time, Jason,' I said, knowing there is a reason he is drawn to her, his eyes glistening at me.

'It's her birthday soon,' he replied all giddy.

'You can feel it too?' he added, as he looks on at me in hope.

'Yes I can feel it too, just go easy on her,' I said, as he nods with appreciation.

'Now someone take me to my boy!' I ordered.

'In good time Luna, we need to talk!' Valdor beckoned. Knowing I wasn't going anywhere before I would talk to him was challenging, every ounce of me wanted to rush to our son. I nod returning to my room, closely followed by Valdor.

'Now there is something we must discuss,' he said.

'Is he sure this can't wait, I can smell our pup from here, I want a hug!' Elsie demanded.

'No Elsie, this cannot wait!' he said, as his anger startled us, he took in a deep breath before continuing. 'You're the one,' he said.

What is this some kind of Matrix movie, is he for real?

'Focus back Annie, he's getting mad!' Elsie said, as I look back over to him.

'This is no joke, you are a Galdorie!' he said, his voice becoming strained, like he was scared of something.

'Well duh, we know that,' Elsie muttered.

'Yes but what you don't know is I lied to you,' he said, filled with sorrow and regret.

'Owe how so?' I replied, sitting on the bed to steady myself, my interest peaked.

With permission he approached me, folding himself in half in the chair opposite.

'I lied to you about the female wolf, there in fact has never been one,' he said.

'So what does this mean?' I said, my uncontrollable anger rising again.

'It means you are the first, an original if you like,' he retorted, as if it were nothing.

'So how powerful am I exactly?' I said, squinting my eyes at him, I lean forward half covering my ears knowing I won't like what comes next.

'We don't know,' he replied.

Great what a relief, here I was thinking it would be bad. 'We do know however that the prophecy predicts that should a she wolf originate from a woman born of half human origins, that she would indeed rain victorious,' he said, throwing his arms in the air, as if it was the best news he had ever given.

'Half human, what do you mean?' I enquired, wishing to know more.

'I mean a woman born of wolf decent, with at least one mystical parent' he said.

I urge him to move away from me as the shock fuelled my rage, sweat began to run down my back as heat filled the room, the temperature rising drastically, pulling at his collar he took a step back as I began to steam.

'Annie, calm down!' he said, standing to his feet taking strides backwards, my skin began to burn, 'Control your wolf, Annie!' he yelled, my ears deafened as I could no longer concentrate, letting out a burst of energy knocking everything over in my room, sending it soaring in different directions. Letting out a little scream my memories flowed, as if unlocked by magic, the memories surged through my brain at speed, flashing me back to the day my mother died.

The day was an ordinary day and we had gone to the circus together as a family, my brother and sister had to stay home as they had the flu, so me, my mum and dad all went whilst my grandmother looked after them both. Heading home the night was dark with a slight crack in the window I could feel the breeze touch my face, and the tree's rustling in the background. Bringing me back to where it all had started, a memory I had long forgotten and forgotten for a reason. Something spooked them, knowing they were scared I could feel it on them. The car began to speed up and my mother was tapping on my father's arm urging him to go faster, seeing my fear my mother reached for me.

'It's okay angel,' she said.

She continued to look back at me, the fear remained in her eyes as she urged me to crouch further down into the seat. Suddenly the car slowed as my father began pumping on the breaks frantically, the car grounded to a halt and began flipping in slow motion. Our things were flying around the car as we rolled, rolling for a while before finally sliding on its side across the concrete below, finally stopping my mother reached for me again extending her arm as far as it would go, tears flicked from her eyes, staring into my soul as we laid upside down in the car. 'I'm sorry!' she urged before the door opened and she was torn at speed from the car before my very eyes, my father remain in his seat held in by the seatbelt, his head was bleeding as he remained still.

I mustered up all of my courage to peer out of my window, seeing a dark figure standing clasping his tightened grip around my mother's throat. My voice scratches unable to make a sound every fibre in my being screaming for me to help her, I remained still watching on in horror as my mother was dragged through the trees and disappearing at the blink of an eye. My father coming too as the tears dropped from my eyes and moistened my face, my eyes dead and my soul screaming. Getting himself out of his seat he pulled me from the car, walking in the opposite direction, holding his hand to my head to try and shield me.

Looking back, I saw something, it was a long handprint imbedded in the base of the car.

'Annie, Annie!' Elsie's screams.

'Annie, are you okay?' her concern caused a stray tear to fall from my eyes.

'What the hell was that?' she added.

'That was our memories,' I respond still stunned, I take a seat back on the bed, my hands shaking uncontrollably.

'Annie what is it?' Valdor asked, walking towards me looking into my cold dead eyes.

'My mother was taken!' I said.

'Who took her?' Elsie growled, in a low tone.

'I don't know, but what I do know is my father lied to me,' I said, staring into space.

'Maybe now might be a good time to go and see your son?' Valdor said, instantly lifting my mood.

Pushing past all of them I ran to where I could hear his little laughter, my heart thumping as I got closer to him. Stopping in the doorway I searched the room to see him playing with Julia, sneaking up to him I scooped him up off of the floor taking in his scent as I sniffed his hair, my heart warmed, my stiffened body relaxed as he curled his little arms around my neck.

'Mummy!' he said, filling me with joy.

'Hey sweetie, I missed you,' I said, longing for a hug.

'I missed you too, where did you go?' he asked, with his yellow eyes staring up at me.

'Nowhere important, I'm back now and I'm never leaving again!' I said, as those words brought out the pinkie promise I had been waiting for, my mood finally calming and my spirit soaring.

'Ronan?' I said, placing him down on the floor.

'Yes mummy?' his grin beaming, as I noticed he's missing another tooth.

'Never grow up, okay?' I said,

'Okay can we go see daddy?' he said, as my heart sank again thinking of Phoenix, how was I going to save this one.

'Soon baby, daddy will be back in a couple of days,' I said, I was so sure of this that I didn't feel it was a lie.

'Okay, but I miss him,' he said, as I kiss his cheek.

'I know you do baby, but Grandma Julia will be with us for a couple of days to give us company,' I said, as I look on at her with hope, she nodded in agreement.

'Now go and see if there is any cookies,' I said, my grin widened, as his little mouth moved quicker than his feet could, rushing to the kitchen he began smacking his little lips together.

'Julia, I need to ask you something?' I said, knowing she had been hiding something from me.

'Sure what is it?' she said, taking a seat leaning backwards, creating as much distance as she could, as if she knew what was coming.

'You knew, didn't you?' I said, as my look towards her narrowed, as I scanned her features.

'I didn't know for sure,' she said, as she began bouncing her right knee, I knew something was off.

'You say you didn't know but you certainly knew about this place, but how you're not a wolf?' I said.

'I do know about this place have done for years, do you remember the story of the woman who couldn't have what she wanted?' she replied.

Closing my eyes I search back to one of the first conversations we had, my eyes rapidly turning as I remember.

'Yes I do, she couldn't have the man she desired,' I said, my face saddened, as I realised it was her story.

'Yes well I may not be a wolf, but it was different in my day as human is considered weak to a pack,' she said.

'Is that why you favour Phoenix?' I said, searching for answers. 'Who is he to you?' I added as I watched the tears fill in her eyes, the regret showed as she avoided the question.

My roar frightening as I screeched at her, 'Tell me!' I said, standing to my feet, unable to control myself my pack members scurrying away to safety.

'He is my son,' she sighed, her words calmed me instantly, taking a seat beside her I reached out, for her to only pull away.

'There you go, are you happy now?' she said angrily.

'But how?' I asked, my look softens, as I approach her differently.

'Many years ago I was supposed to be his father's mate, however my mate's father had other ideas, separating us both off from each other once Phoenix was born. I was cast out, I am a rogue,' she said, bowing her head in shame and averting her gaze.

Of course it's all starting to make sense now.

'Does Phoenix know?' I asked.

'No I was cast out not long after he was born, ripped from my arms commanded never to speak to him again. His father would visit bringing me pictures off him once in a while, I followed his life so closely, but his father married not long after and she became Phoenix's mother,' she said, as I began to fidget, this news was too much for my head to comprehend.

'So he doesn't know you're his true mother?' I said.

'No I could never tell him, they had me bound to secrecy,' she said.

I found myself staring at her for a moment, I look at her frail frame wondering what was wrong with her, but deep down I think I knew.

'So Julia, how old are you?' I said.

'Wow Annie, that's rude!' Elsie snapped.

'I am fifty-three-years old, I was young and in love back then, so it was pretty much at first sight,' she said.

I stared at her again realising how old she looked now, if I would have remained a rogue the same would have happened to me, the thought shook me to my core.

'Phoenix has to know!' I yelled.

'No he doesn't, you leave it be Annie!' she pleaded with desperation in her eyes.

'I can't lie to him Julia, I am telling him!' I said.

'Please don't you will destroy the only mother he has ever known,' she said, rising to her feet.

'Okay I won't tell him, but you should he deserves that much from you both!' I said, as she shook her head angering me slightly. 'I'm going back up to see Phoenix, are you coming?' I said, nodding her head she followed closely behind me. The shock must have still been written all over my face, I wish she hadn't told me but equally I know I gave her no choice.

# Chapter 29
## The day things changed

It had been a couple of days since I found out the shocking news about Phoenix and Julia, I knew something was off, but I wasn't that sure. The morning was long my mind was in pieces, I sat closely watching over Phoenix as he slept, his wounds absorbing healing finally. I sat on the chair next to his bed guilt lined my face, pain laced my heart, I reach out for him stroking his face not wishing for him to wake yet.

'What are we going to do,' Elsie asked

'I don't know,' I replied, the door opened as they came to say goodbye, they had to head back to the hotel that had been short staffed for days now.

'We have to go now, Annie,' Julia said, still looking on, desperate for me to keep her secret, my feelings hurt striking a cord that everyone was leaving me.

'They aren't leaving us,' I hear the sorrow in Elsie's voice. 'They will be back,' she said, her low comforting voice bringing peace to my heart, the droplets fell from my face as I began hugging them goodbye.

'I will be staying,' Echo said, trying to reassure me.

'Yeah, you will!' Jason smiled brightly.

'On second thought,' she said, wiping the smile from Jason's face.

Coming up behind me Pete brought me into a long-held hug, my feeling of abandonment growing stronger as he held me tighter. I slowly wept some more as I watched them leave, my attention turned to Jason as he swooned over Echo, 'Patients!' I said nodding to him.

You see Echo wasn't yet eighteen-years-old, her mother and father left her young, and she had been alone ever since, the reason Jason is so drawn to her is she is in fact his true mate, her birthday next week will reveal all. I must admit I am looking forward to it.

It had been a couple of days and Phoenix was up and about resuming his Alpha duties; however, something was wrong, he seemed different more worried, increased security patrolling the perimeter and sticking like glue to my side.

A letter arrived in the mail; it was from the silver lake pack requesting our presence.

It had been years since I last saw them, to say I was nervous was an understatement, since the last time I was in their presence I had an agreement with them for Luca's pack.

'We're not going, I will want to kill him!' Elsie snapped, as a monotoned growl floated across my head.

'Can we just get through this?' I said, as I leaned across the kitchen counter,

'When do we have to leave?' I huff in annoyance, turning to look my man in the eyes, he was standing before me holding the letter. 'This evening!' he replied.

'Great what are we going to do?' Elsie asked.

'What about Ronan?' I asked, not wanting to go back to that pack house, knowing I had been keeping Julia's secret, that I had originally planned to unveil.

'Ronan will have to stay with Julia, meaning I get you all to myself,' he smirks at me, leaning on the counter beside me.

'Oh lord,' his smile made me weak, like he had suddenly relaxed then it hit me.

'Will all the packs be there?' I said, as he nodded.

247

'You can't start a war here as Alpha Valencia lives there, that would be suicide!' I insisted, trying to hold his attention.

'I won't start anything my love, I will however be smug as hell,' he said, leaning further into me giving me a kiss.

'Mummy, daddy!' Ronan said, as he launches for us, we kneel to the ground, our arms stretched out wide ready to embrace him.

Thankfully we didn't have to leave that soon, so I had Phoenix spend the morning with our son, I went to the pack library to consult the books, Valdor had left a couple of days ago but oddly has yet to return.

Walking into the library to me was pure bliss silence speaks louder than words, looking on the shelves I find what I am looking for. It was a brown book laced with string bindings, you had to wear gloves just to touch the pages as the book was ancient and friable. Looking up in the book I searched for more on the Galdorie, I didn't find much else other than the normal prophecy when I looked into the Nafari, well that was a mistake. Slowly my fears became a reality, the prophecy didn't mention them at all, but as I looked at their prophecy it stunned me, the more I use my powers I become like a beacon drawing them to me.

'What are we going to do about this,' I thought, to myself forgetting about my wolf.

'Well we could always kill him,' she laughed.

I honestly sometimes am not sure why I bother.

'Yes we could, that's if he doesn't crush us first!' I said, trying to shove her aside.

'We don't have time to be afraid, remember we get alone time with our man this weekend!' she said.

Putting the book away I took of the gloves snapping them off of my fingertips, rubbing my fingers into the palm of my hand feeling the powder on them.

'So much for powder free!' I smirked.

Walking back to our room I hear a commotion coming from outside, I run downstairs to see Valdor standing in the hall.

'I need to talk to her!' he shouts.

'Valdor we are going away, this is going to have to wait!' Phoenix said, in a dominating tone.

Valdor continues to yell at Phoenix when Phoenix finally roars.

'It can wait, Valdor!' he yells dismissing him, Valdor attempted to barge past him.

'Valdor I'm warning you, it can wait until we get back!' he said, gripping hold of his arm.

I was dying to know what he has to say but equally not wanting to disappoint my mate, I closed myself off from the thoughts and walked back to our room continuing to pack ready for our time away.

'Mummy do you really have to go?' I hear this sad little voice come up behind me.

'Baby, we will be back before you know it,' I said, with a half-smile.

'But where will I stay?' he said, in a sweet voice, pulling at my heart strings.

'You are going to stay with Julia and Pete,' I said, as his smile formed slightly, as I packed his clothes into his little rucksack.

'Okay it's time baby,' I said, Phoenix coming up from behind him bringing him into a bear hug, lifting his shirt blowing little raspberries on his tummy.

His little giggled echoed through the room, a sweetened song I hoped would never end, picking him up and placing him on my hip he looked at me holding onto my stomach he said, 'Mummy somethings wrong?' he said, as my eyes widen with shock.

'What's wrong sweetie?' I replied, whilst he continued to hold me.

'You will see,' he replied, with a little giggle.

Is he trying to give me a heart attack! Thinking nothing more of it I started walking out the house, and right past Valdor who stood guarded by two omegas ready to silence him should he so much as look at me. I so desperately wanted to know what he needed to tell me, I silently walked past him out the door biting my lip and chewing my cheek to prevent myself from speaking.

Loading our stuff in the car brought back flashing images, giving me a pitted feeling in the bottom of my stomach, the closer I got to the car the stronger the feeling became.

'I don't think we should get in there,' Elsie said, as a bad feeling coiled around the pit of our stomach.

'Wait get him out of the car now!' I yelled, Phoenix rushing to do as I said.

'Everyone get back!' I screamed.

But nothing happened, I closed my eyes again searching for that feeling, it began to roll and twist in my stomach.

'Roll the car and let off the breaks,' I commanded.

'Now don't you think you're being a little dramatic?' I heard Mal's voice come up behind me.

'Do it!' I ordered, as Mal approached the car letting off the breaks, it began to roll down the drive.

'Maybe our feelings are wrong?' Elsie said.

250

Suddenly a loud earth-shattering bang exploded the car 10ft in the air, as it engulfed into flames before our very eyes. Picking up our son I shield him from the scene before him.

'How did you know?' Mal said looking at me, making me shrug back at him.

'Check all the cars!' Phoenix demanded, putting my hand on his shoulders, I attempt to sooth him.

'This had to be someone here, no one would have gotten in,' I said, looking at Phoenix, knowing we now couldn't trust anyone was daunting.

'Jason!' I said, receiving a dull expression from Phoenix.

'Jason is my oldest friend he would never!' he said, his face becoming angry.

'No I mean have Jason check the cars!' I said, as I watched his eyes lighten and his body relax.

'That's a better idea!' he replied, his eyes glaze as he mind links Jason, I stop him.

'We want to try, what do we do?' I said.

'You need to concentrate on Jason and him alone, remember what he looks like marking it to memory, then when you think you have it whisper to him,' he said.

I take a deep breath in allowing my body to relax, listening out for him I soon pinpoint his location.

'Jason,' I whisper, but he doesn't reply, he is currently leaning against the fridge pestering Echo.

'Jason!' Elsie screamed,

'Now was that totally necessary?' I said, as we felt his heart skip.

'Yes Luna,' he replied

'Come out the front to us now, we need you,' I said, before we knew it Jason was by our side.

'Hey Annie, how can I help; wow what the hell happened here?' he said, pointing his finger towards our burnt-out car.

'Someone planted a bomb on our car, my son was nearly injured,' I sigh.

Looking at Phoenix knowing I need to tell him the truth, it was something I had been hiding for weeks now, something I knew he wasn't going to like.

'We need you to check our car for us,' Phoenix said, Jason was stunned as he pointed at himself.

'Right away,' he said, as he got to work.

I must say he checked every inch of that car, if it weren't for that weird feeling we would all be dead now.

After getting the okay from Jason we approached the car again this time with caution, the feeling didn't present itself this time, so I agreed it was okay.

'Jason, you're going to need to come with us,' I said, as he shook his head with pouting lips.

'But it's Echo's eighteenth birthday tomorrow,' he wined.

'Well Romeo, you're going to have to wait,' I smirked, leaving the car door open, trying to show him inside, he clamped onto the sides of the doors, he was strong, but we were stronger.

Wrapping my arms around his torso lifting him from his feet pushing him in as I slammed the door behind him, his faced pressed up against the glass hearing the handle thrash as Phoenix locked the door upon entry. He was not a happy Beta, but his happiness was going to have to wait.

# Chapter 30
## A day on our own

It had been forever since me and Phoenix got to spend time alone with each other, we knew our son would be safe with Julia but as we dropped him off I couldn't help but feel the worry pouring from her.

'Please don't tell him!' Julia pleaded, pulling me to one side.

'I can't not tell him he is my mate, I will however give you time to think of how you're going to do it,' I said, as I touch her shoulder.

'Ronan, we have to go now baby,' I shouted, trying to get his attention.

Coming over to us Ronan gave us a big hug goodbye, I sniffed his hair as my heart began to ache.

'Bye mummy, bye daddy,' he said, his upbeat little attitude gave me hope, that new beginnings were coming.


We soon set off and the journey was tiring and longer than I remembered, we had been on the road for what felt like an eternity, the sun soon disappeared as a darkened cloud shielded it from view. We began approaching a place I use to call home, soon realising we had to pass through Mystic River gave me the chills.

'How we doing back there, Jason?' I smirked, hiding my torment.

'Yeah great,' he replied, with a sour face.

I was sure his arms would be hurting by now, as they were so tightly folded across this body.

'Lighten up Jason, you will be home soon you

love-sick puppy,' Phoenix scoffed, I raised my fist for a bump from Phoenix, looking out the window I felt a tap on my knuckles as he reciprocated.

Entering a town I barely remembered was scary, this was not a town I recognised, everything was in ruins and the town was destroyed.

'What the hell happened here?' I said.

'Surely this isn't Mystic River?' I added, but no one answered me.

But to my dismay it was as I spotted the half standing fountain I once gazed upon with my father, my thoughts turned to sadness, noticing a town that use to be so full of life, but now it was a mere relic of its former glory.

My thoughts turned to my friends that I once lived with, my fear for their safety was gut wrenching, Shay and Orion were my two closest friends.

The journey proving too much I leaned on Phoenix for support, my eyes closed, and I slowly drifted off to sleep.

Feeling hot breath on my neck and a pinch on my chin, as his soft lips caressed mine.

'Morning my love, it's time to wake up,' he whispers. My eyes open with a groggy feeling about me, I stare upon him, I honestly didn't look cute in the mornings, but he loved me anyway. Reaching up I rub my eyes.

'Are we here already?' I said, he nods getting out the car, I stared and watched him closely.

Opening the door he reaches out his hand and I take it, there is something so mesmerising about a man who opens the door for you, a sign of devotion and respect. We were greeted at the entrance by staff, with bitter stares and shown to our room in the hotel.

'I have taken the liberty of requesting a certain room,' Phoenix said, winking at me, my eyes narrow as I wasn't sure he completely remembered our entire encounter. Walking up to our room my surroundings became familiar, walking into the room he kicked off his shoes into the middle of the floor.

'Owe I remember now, who's boats are these?' I said, as we erupted into laughter.

He started to stalk towards me with those lustful eyes, ready to take what he had been waiting for.

'There isn't time, later!' I said, batting his grabby hands away, in a playful manor.

'Fine!' he said, with a pouty face.

When suddenly we hear a banging on the walls, listening closer it was a bitter Jason.

'If I'm not getting any, you're not getting any!' he shouted, our laughter growing, as we settle in trying to get ready for the meeting with all the Alphas.

Going downstairs to the lobby I begin to fidget. What on earth was I going to do? I began frantically picking at my fingers, unsure as to why I felt so uncomfortable.

A sickness arose within me, that sweet bitter taste in my mouth rising as the saliva formed abruptly, I took in a deep breath pushing it back down again. I hadn't felt this worried in a long time, Phoenix takes my hand as we entered the lobby, his hand reached for mine as our fingers interlocked.

'Don't worry,' he said, as his smile comforted me for a moment.

Walking in the room I could feel all eyes on me, including one in particular, Orion was present, fighting the urge to run to her was harder than I thought. Breezing swiftly past her I bow my head at her, Luca growls at me from a distance causing Elsie to growl back, catching the attention of Alpha Valencia.

'Hmm I don't remember you having a wolf?' he laughed.

'Yes sir,' I said, nodding out of respect.

'We had a deal, or did you forget?' he mumbled.

'No Alpha I didn't forget, but I am no longer a member of that pack,' I spat.

'You mean no longer Luna of that pack,' he smirked, looking right at me, Luca's hands clenched.

'I was not,' I said, as he glared at me.

'Don't lie to me child!' he said in a threatening tone.

'Don't threaten me, Alpha!' I replied angrily.

'We had an agreement!' he said.

'Yes we did but I was made a rogue by my pack, so I was unable to fulfil my duties further!' I snapped.

'Hmm yes well as decided the Grayson's and their pack did not live up to their end of the bargain, so the treaty became void because of your absence,' he said, taking deep pleasure in his words.

'This was not my fault, this was his!' I said, pointing towards Luca, making him half change.

'Don't you dare change in here mut!' Alpha Valencia roared, making Luca take a step back, his breathing heavy and his nostrils flaring.

'Now I wish to be alone with you,' he said, his hands come together as he steeples his fingers in front of him. I try not to look on at him as I advert my gaze.

'Out all of you! you too Alpha Genai!' he demanded, with a slight warning to his tone.

Phoenix looked on at me taking hold of my hand gripping me tightly, I nodded in approval and he left closing the office door behind him.

'Now then, we need to talk,' he said.

His eyes zoomed in on me as he looked me over tapping his partially changed hand on the desk, I look on ready to defend myself if necessary, he laughed, and his menacing face softened.

'Relax will you, you're putting me on edge,' he said, as his lightened tone confused me.

'Erm?' I said, looking around the room to see if I'm being punked, like I'd be on the cover of wolf magazine or something bizarre like that.

'Honestly your face is a bit of a picture,' he smiled softly. What in the hell is happening?

'I said I would deal with you and only you remember, I kept my word but now I wish to talk to you about something else,' he said, leaning into me, 'I know you had no wolf when you was last here, which would make you my dear a Galdorie,' he said, as my eyes widen, gripping the edges of my seat. He's going to kill me.

'Relax no one will hurt you here, however I wish to make you a deal,' he said, as my grip loosened slightly.

'What, what do you want?' I replied, my fingerprints embedded into the chair.

'Annabeth, do you have to sound so weak? Up the tempo please!' Elsie said.

'Not now Elsie!' I said aggressively.

'I want you to pledge allegiance to my pack, in return we will come when called and do as you wish?' he said. My smirk arose slightly knowing I now had the upper hand.

257

'I want you to call Orion back inside,' I said, my eyes glistened, as I got a bright idea.

'Do we have a deal?' he said, extending out my hand I shook his, making the deal of a lifetime.

'We will come anytime you call,' he nods, as the doors open bringing in Orion, I signalled to have the door closed again as a worried Luca clung to the door frame outside as the door shut in his face.

'Hello Alpha,' she bowed.

'Hello Orion,' he replied, leaping from my chair I smothered her with hugs, she responded by pulling me in squeezing me tightly.

'I missed you so much!' she whaled in my ear.

'And I you. Orion, listen to me,' I said, bringing her out of our hug, and looking at her face to face.

'Do you want to come with me?' I asked, as her eyes flickered, she looked on at Alpha Valencia, clicking in her face I snapped her back to me.

'Do you want to come home with me?' I asked again with hopeful eyes.

'Yes,' she nodded, frantically.

'Then so be it,' Alpha Valencia responded.

'What about Luca, he will kill me!' she said, taking hold of my wrist.

'That won't be a problem he is being escorted out as we speak, no deal and no treaty for him you are free my dear!' he said, her eyes flood, as she throws her arms around me once more.

'We need a drink!' I laugh, pulling her in deeper.

'Yeah just not like the last time we was here,' she replied with laughter.

'Orion tonight we are both going to go crazy!' I said, as we both look at Alpha Valencia, he nodded for us to leave.

I dragged her up to my room to help me get ready, barging through our door we walked in the room to a half-naked Phoenix.

'Oh lord, did he come with the room?' she said staring at him.

'No that would be my mate,' I said swiftly, letting her know he is off limits.

'Oh well that's a shame,' she replied, causing Phoenix's face to redden.

We both giggle like girls as he falls off the bed reaching for his pants, another knock coming from next door as a warning.

'Don't even try it, keep your hands to yourselves!' he said, his voice muffled, as the walls took the brunt of it. We laughed again but this time harder, our sides begin to split and our faces beginning to hurt.

'This is going to be a great night,' Orion laughed.

'Yes one I've waited for, for what seems like forever!' I said, clutching at my sides, as Phoenix ran to the bathroom.

After getting ready we go downstairs, I couldn't help but think this was not going to be the last time we had heard from Luca, but my thoughts drifted again as a very handsome man walked out of our bathroom.

His scent giving me goosebumps, as a bang on the door caught our attention.

'You two better not be!' Jason said, through the door, we both smirked as he entered the room.

'Woah hot Mumma!' he said, in a boyish tone, causing a warning growl from Phoenix.

'Okay, okay I'm sorry!' he laughed, holding his hands up backing away slightly. I wrap my arm around Phoenix's as we begin to leave the room with Orion close behind us. She was an absolute vision, I could see why she was my decoy Luna as her elegance was unmatched, outshining mine even now but I didn't care I adored her more than I did my own sister.

Getting downstairs I skip the small talk with the boys, grabbing hold of Orion I dragged her to the bar.

'Two tequila slammers please!' I said.

'Here get that down you,' I added, handing her a shot, she put her tongue inside, and pulled an awful face.

'Well what the hell did you do that for?' I said, as I watched her shiver whilst poking out her tongue.

'That is so gross!' she replied, taking a seat on the bar stool beside me.

'Well you're not supposed to lick it, you're supposed to shot it!' I laugh uncontrollably at her.

'Oh, no thank you!' she said, pushing it away.

'Do it!' I growled, knowing I had an unfair advantage. Tilting her head back lifting the glass up she downed it, mistakenly holding it in her mouth for a second before she swallowed it, she gasped for breath as her face pinkened.

'It's like a fire hydrant exploded in my stomach!' she said, reaching for breath.

'Yeah good, bartender two more of those stat!' I laughed, ordering another round.

After many more of these and when we finally couldn't see straight, I felt two arms come from behind me scooping me off of my stool. Whilst me and Orion sung the words to the macarena badly, I don't think anyone really knows the words to that damn song. Jason picked up Orion as she squished his cheeks and pulled on his ears. To tell you the truth I liked drunk Orion.

'Tomorrow Orion, we go home!' I laughed, as I then looked my mate in the face, whispering etching him to come closer, only to scream in his ears.

'I will tell you later!' I smiled.

'Maybe you could say it louder?' he said.

Soon realising he shouldn't have said that as I took a deep breath in, his eyes widened in fear as he quickly placed a finger on my lips to shush me.

Getting back to our room I felt him remove my shoes and my earrings before placing me into bed, pulling the covers over me and turning out the lights.

'I have something to tell you,' I said.

'Shh my love, tell me in the morning,' he said, turning out the lights.

The room began to spin and my body temperature rising, probably trying to deal with the amount of alcohol I had just put into it.

'Can we go on holiday soon? when are we going to get a cat?' I whispered, his laugh was contagious.

'My love we are technically dogs, what makes you think getting a cat would be a clever idea?' he chuckled, sitting on the bed beside me.

'Owe yeah, maybe a rabbit then?' I said, trying not to throw up.

'Darling, still dogs,' he laughed, cupping my cheeks.

I lay still for a moment contemplating my next move, all I could think of was please don't ever leave me.

Opening one eye I look on at Phoenix standing to his feet and undressing before me, he truly was a god of a man, he looked back over at me.

'I will never leave, you are my heart, and you are my soul,' I smile in response.

Oh lord that horrible feeling arose again, am I going to throw up? My mouth watered as I arose to my feet. Rushing past him I ran to the toilet, to my surprise nothing happened, thank the lord.

'Nice one, very sexy!' Elsie laughed, her howls began to hurt my head.

'Elsie, hey how's it going. Do you want a cat?' I said.

'Go to bed you mess, I'll see you in the morning!' she said, as I eventually passed out.

# Chapter 31
## The morning after

Waking up in bed to the burning sun raining down on me through a crack in the window, however I was not entirely sure how I got here. My breath smelt like death and my head felt heavy, realising It was time to leave I gathered up our things, throwing off last night's clothes attempting to have a shower.

'Maybe it's better you wait till we get home?' he sniggers. I must admit it wasn't the worst idea.

'Now my love tell me, what did you mean last night?' he said, coming out of the bathroom, I sit on the bed twiddling my fingers.

'Just tell him already!' Elsie screams at me.

'Well, now don't be mad,' I said staring at him.

'I kind of said to Orion she could come live with us,' I whispered closing one eye.

'Oh thank god, I thought it was something more serious,' he said.

'You mean she can come?' I replied with surprise, he nods, and I leap from the bed into his arms.

'Have I told you how much I love you?' I said, as he grins back at me.

'Not lately,' he said, earning him a light slap on his chest. Blinking rapidly I got distracted by my surroundings as I began looking around my room, it looked like we had been burgled in the night.

'What on earth happened here?' I said.

'Well that was you, that was you; Oh and that was you!' he said, lifting me onto his lap, as he pointed around our room.

'Oh my goodness, why didn't you stop me?' I said, placing my hand over my face, realising what I had done. Firstly in my wisdom I re-arranged the room the way I wanted it, I destroyed a table by falling onto it, I moved the bed into the middle of the room, and lastly, I chucked the rug under the bed because I didn't like it.

'I tried to stop you, but you're not easy to reason with when you have half a gallon of shots in you,' he said.

I laugh uncontrollably causing a little snort to escape my lips, the shock of that alone made me laugh more, I started to wheeze looking at him.

'Oi is it time to go home yet?' I hear coming through the walls.

'Yes,' I replied, soon followed by a knock at the door.

'Happy to be leaving?' I said smugly.

'Can we go now!' he snapped, his pouty childlike expression made me laugh again.

'I think we will stay for breakfast?' Phoenix responded, making Jason stamp his feet.

'No!' he yelled.

'What's wrong Jason, not hungry?' Phoenix added.

'Nope!' he replied sharply.

'Owe he's hungry for something, just not food,' I said, with another little snort, as I moved towards the door.

'Oh come on, please can we go home?' he begged, almost coming down onto his knees.

'Fine we can go you load the car, and I will go and find Orion,' I said, as he rushed past us to the bags slinging them all onto his shoulders. This boy wasn't messing around! I walk out of my room and made my way down to Orion, knocking twice to get her attention. Opening the door, she looked as sick as I felt.

'Hey, it's time to go,' I said quietly, as she held onto her head.

'Gorr she looks awful!' I hear Elsie chuckle to herself.

'Is it morning already?' Orion groans, her hair was standing on end, with her mascara smeared around her face and lipstick dragged down her chin.

'God, she looks like death cooled down,' Elsie said.

'Elsie, you mean warmed up?' I said, hearing her tutting.

'No I mean she looks like crap!' she said.

'Orion, you have Cheetos in your hair,' I said, examining her more closely.

I was so jealous where in the hell did she get those.

'Oh well that's disgusting isn't it,' she said, as she flicked one towards me, making us both laugh instantly holding onto our heads, as she picked the rest from her hair, looking at it as if she was still going to eat it.

'When will you be ready?' I quickly said.

'Ready? where are we going?' she said.

'Orion, we are going home,' I smiled, her grin joins mine, as she begins jumping.

'I didn't think you was serious!' she said, almost leaping on the spot.

'Oh I meant it and you need to get ready, Jason's getting grumpy,' I said.

She turns on her heels pacing through her room taking wider strides towards her belongings, coming back towards me excitedly she grabbed hold of my arm dragging me inside.

'Well at least you didn't change your room,' I said, as she turns looking at me confused.

'What do you mean?' she said, tilting her head to the side.

'Nothing,' I smile back at her.

Temporary insanity or maybe it was the last tequila shot that messed me up? Who knows. I look on at her as she frantically packed what little she owned into her black suitcase, leaning over her nightstand she pulls out a pair of jet-black sunglasses.

'I will be needing these today,' she said, as she placed them over her squinting eyes.

'Yes I only wish I had thought of that!' I said, as the door swings open, revealing a very impatient Jason.

'Can we go home now?' his anger evident.

'Yes Jason we can go now,' I said.

He pushes past Orion snatching her bag from the bed and throwing it on his back, rushing back out the room whilst hoarding us like sheep.

'What's his problem?' she questioned.

'Hormones,' I replied.

'Might as well sling us on those shoulders!' Orion retorted, what a witty thing to say I must admit.

'Yeah, yeah get moving!' he said, in an annoyed tone, ushering us towards the elevator.

We took the elevator right down to the bottom, when the doors open people began to bow at us.

'Erm how much did we drink last night?' Orion said, giving me a nudge.

'I don't think we drank that much, maybe they think we are someone else,' I said, as quietly as I can out of the side of my mouth.

'Are we royalty, maybe we were knighted or something,' we giggled like little girls, whilst Jason still shoved us towards the entrance.

'Will you quite shoving me!' Orion spat.

266

'Well will you move your abnormally short legs and let's get going!' he replied.

Jason decided he could wait no longer; he scooped Orion up throwing her over his shoulder as she began kicking and screaming

'Put me down you big brute!' she yelled, as she slams her fists into his back.

'You had your chance,' he said smugly.

I tip toed lightly behind them trying to keep up, my hangover made my head pound, going out into direct sunlight was torture. Bringing my hand up to shield my eyes as the car pulled up outside, the sun felt like it was burning my retinas and my brain.

Climbing in quickly I sat draped across the chair, Jason reaching forward strapping me in to not delay him any further.

'Jason relax, she will be waiting for you when we get back,' I said, as he slowly begins tapping his foot and shaking his leg. This boy needs to learn to relax.

Orion climbs into the front seat, slumping herself in the chair and putting in some earphones.

'So Orion do you think you're going to like this life?' I asked, with joy, still not fully believing this was happening.

'It's been a while since I could just relax,' she said, lifting her hands up, and resting them behind her head.

My thoughts darkened as I realised most of her life she was a decoy, what a horrible way to live.

Phoenix put his arm around me and pulled me close, he reached for his bag and pulls out a bag of chips, dangling them in my face with a smile.

'Oh I love you so much!' I said, snatching them from him, I open them watching Orion's nostrils flare as she sniffs the air, taking a handful I pass her the rest.

267

'Oh my gosh, they are like little pieces of heaven,' she said, chewing loudly.

'Eww can you please close your trap; I can see the food mid digestion!' Jason snapped in disgust.

This was going to be a long journey home.

Stretching out I put my leg over Phoenix's as I leant back against the window, pulling out his phone he attended to emails, and I drifted peacefully off to sleep.

My thoughts turned dark, as a fight between two worlds emerges, I couldn't see their faces, the only face I could see was my mothers and she was telling me to run. The sky turned black, cloudless, and completely empty. Hope was gone and my world estranged. A fire ignites turning the earth around me to thickened black tarry mud, light scatters of gravel fly through the air bouncing off of the ground below, embers floating past my face turning to ash before my eyes. My mothers voice echoing in the distance, I blink twice as I yell back for her, a dark figure approaching with talons showing. I begin to run in slow motion looking back I fall into a road, the figure catches me curling its hands around my neck, squeezing the life from my body his breath potent and ungodly.

'I've been looking for you!' his voice deep, and as his long tongue protrudes, he ran it across my face in an up and down motion, 'I will see you soon!' he said, his scary menacing tone terrified me.

'Don't be afraid!' the creature spoke, 'Be very afraid!' he said, loosening his grip for a second before pulling me closer, 'In the dark of the night, I'm going to find you!' his tone ferociously strong.

The black ooze rushing from his lips down the side of his face, spitting at me with every word he spoke when suddenly.

'Ahh!' I screamed, clamping onto my neck, as I jolted upright flinching at Phoenix's touch.

'Annabeth, what's the matter?' he said, as he shook my shoulders slightly, with my eyes streaming I sit further forward, my hands shaking as I trembled in my seat.

'Annie, it was a dream,' Phoenix said, as he desperately tries to calm me.

'That didn't feel like a dream!' Elsie replied, as

I reached for Phoenix pulling him closer.

'Something's wrong!' I said, making his grip tighten around me.

'You're fine my love,' he said.

'No something is really wrong!' I snapped.

'My love please relax, we will be home soon,' he said, as I let go of his arm, sliding close to the window watching and waiting.


Our journey home was unsettling, leaving me on the edge of my seat the entire time. Getting to Mystic River the car grounds to a halt as I fell forward held in place by my seat belt, jolting my neck out of alignment.

'What's wrong, why are we stopping?' Phoenix commanded, Orion and Jason's heads blocking our view of the road.

'A tree, Alpha!' the driver responds.

Jason got out of the car to investigate, after a few seconds he climbed back in.

'We won't be getting home that way, it's all blocked off,' he replied.

'The only way home is through there,' he added.

As I sat looking out my window, I see the axe embedded into the tree stump that had been cut with absolute precision.

'What does this mean?' Orion asked.

'Well it means the only way home is through Rogue city,' Jason responded.

At first I thought he was joking but the look of concern growing on their faces was evident that he wasn't. Orion began to heave, rolling down the window she threw up over the side. Ordinarily I would have found that funny, but this was no ordinary moment and no ordinary day. Taking a left we began our journey, the driver automatically locked all the doors making us feel like a prisoner in our own car. The silence was overwhelming as darkness surrounded us, we make our way through the deserted city, bins with small fires lit in them lighting our way as the daylight slowly faded. There was no one around, normally when a rogue feels threatened, they all come running but not this time.

'I don't like this,' Elsie said,

'No neither do I,' I said, trying to catch the driver's attention.

'How much longer till we are out?' I asked but he didn't respond. 'Excuse me, how much longer?' I shouted. Finally turning his head he replied.

'Not long now,' he smiled, turning back around.

I could see the end of the road but barely, a foggy misty cloud drifting past shadowing the exit, looking further into the distance I could see shadowy figures dipping in and out.

'We need to move, now!' I yelled, as the driver slammed on the accelerator.

Rogues were coming from all directions leaping onto the car, clawing at the roof top trying to get inside.

'Move faster!' Phoenix yells.

I let out an almighty scream, hollowed and meaningful, the car grounded to a halt screeching across the gravel. The driver continues to accelerate, as the wheels spin without movement, hearing talking coming from behind us, I knew it was Boid.

'What the hell is he doing here?' I question, as we try and think of a plan.

'Alpha, what do you want us to do?' Jason asked, patiently waiting for instructions.

'We need to get out of here!' Phoenix yelled.

'Jason, we need a distraction!' he added.

When suddenly the car begins moving backwards, my thoughts going haywire as I realise I would probably never see our son again, closing my eyes I slowly try and remember what he looks like, remembering his scent gave me comfort.

'Hurry!' my thoughts moved me as the footsteps moved closer to the car, it was like listening to the grim reaper approaching without anyway of stopping it.

The sounds get closer as I saw Boid coming up from behind us, yelling coming from all directions as I see angry starving wolves shift back to human form. The Rogues begin chanting, as if victory was fast approaching. What are we going to do? I search around looking for some form of exit but there was nothing, I look around the car as the voices become muffled, slowed down as if it were a dream. I closed my eyes in hopes that it was, but when I opened them again the situation we were in was very real.

# Chapter 32
## What lies beneath

My brows begin to sweat, and my breathing becomes heavy, water dripping down my face as the air in the car diminishes.

'What are we going to do, Elsie?' I cry out to her in my head.

'I don't know I'm unsure if we can take all of them at once, but I'm willing to try,' she growled.

'I think we should at least try but on one condition Phoenix doesn't come with us, Ronan will still need at least one parent,' I said, as Phoenix clung to my arm, his words muffled as I didn't take them all in.

'I love you,' I whispered, removing his hand from my arms, I punched him in the face rendering him unconscious.

'Annabeth, what the hell!' Jason yelled in shock.

'Jason, I'm going to get out, and you're going to drive him home,' I said calmly.

'We won't leave without you!' Orion yelled.

'You will do as you are told, Ronan needs at least one parent!' I roared, making them cower in their seats.

'Now let me out!' I snapped, noticing no one was listening, I shifted slightly. 'Let us out!' we said, as the doors unlocked.

I reached over kissing Phoenix, his softened lips giving me butterflies, 'Take care of our son,' I whispered, hoping he could hear me.

I swiped his hair to the side noticing his lip was bleeding from where I punched him, licking his lip his wound sealed, I took one last look at the man who gave me hope that love really still existed, the sickened feeling knowing I was never

272

going to see him again caused droplets of tears to fall from my eyes. I said a final goodbye before I opened the car door, swinging it open I took out a rogue to my left, yells and laughter erupted from the distance as I slammed the door behind me, I unhitched the bonnet allowing the car access to move.

'Sacrificing their Luna, how coy!' I heard a familiar voice come from behind them.

'Hello Annabeth,' hearing his voice made me sick to my stomach.

'Luca!' I said, rolling my eyes and biting my cheeks, I looked upon him through gritted teeth.

'Move!' I yelled, as the car began to leave.

Looking back briefly I sighed in relief, my loved ones would at least be spared.

'Now sweetheart, you've got some explaining to do!' Luca said, as I closed my eyes sending out another distress signal, to my amazement nothing happened, maybe this is it and I just have to accept it.

'We don't have to explain anything to you!' Elsie rumbled from my core.

'Oh you don't? you stupid girl! Now then, let's get down to business,' Luca said, stabilising himself on one leg, as he rested the other on a piece of steel pointing at me, his army closing me in.

'How did you get a wolf?' he said, I shrug my shoulders. Nodding his head as one of his minions punched me in the gut, bringing me to my knees.

'More importantly how did you trick me, my darling mate?' the words caused sick to rise to the back of my throat as a sharpness crossed my face, the burning after effect made me close an eye.

'Also heard you had a baby, you whore! I know it's not mine,' he nodded, another blow came from my right.

'Might have to pay a visit to the little brat!' he snarls, my eyes snap up, as I look upon him.

'You wouldn't even get close!' I said, with a grin.

'Annabeth, stop fighting me and let me out, I will tear his throat out!' Elsie said, readying for battle.

'Where are my family?' I said, looking at them.

Boid and Luca look at each other before looking back at me.

'You're family, how should we know?' Luca replied.

'Yeah they are probably still where we sent them!' Boid said. Realising they had no clue where my family were, I begin to laugh as the blood drips from my mouth, the taste of killing him was too much. He was my demon and what do we do with demons, we send them back to from which they came. My eyes begin to glow and my skin radiating a white mist, I knew what was coming another blow to my ribs fuelling my anger. An anger I had held back in fear for my family, but since he didn't know where they were its game on.

My laughter growing as my tone lowers, taking in as much oxygen as I could master letting out a banshee like scream, I launched them backwards, a wave shooting out in different directions, closing my eyes I take a deep breath, looking out to the horizon I saw my mother.

'Run!' she yelled, her screams bouncing off of the wind. My eyes widened realising I had seen the scene before me before now, getting myself up I don't hesitate, I run for the car as I chase my family through this darkness.

'Jason, Phoenix, Orion; wait!' my mind link strong Phoenix finally awake.

'Stop the car now!' I hear from a distance, the car stops the doors fling open, running I could hear my breath as I get closer to him.

Two hands come up from behind me, feeling his fingers embed into my ribs I let out a yelp as he pulled me backwards and lifted me into the air.

'Jason get him!' I screamed, as Phoenix attempted to run to me, Jason tackled him to the floor dragging him back to the car, slamming it shut from behind him.

Boid slams me into the ground with force.

'I'm not supposed to kill you, but ah well what the heck.' he grins, his eyes still fixated on me.

'Annabeth let me out! he's killing us!' Elsie screams.

'You're not a warrior, you are a stupid human rogue whore!' Boid spat.

Lifting my hand I grab his wrist, my eyes burst open as I look him in his face.

'We are not a Rogue!' I replied, sending him rolling in the air, as he hit the ground.

Getting up I try and run to the car as he grips a hold of my ankle dragging me down further away from safety, looking through the back window I saw Phoenix's cries as Jason kept him pinned. Holding out my arm I reached for him, looking back I brought my foot up and slammed it into Boid's face, knocking him backwards and loosening his grip. Managing to climb to my feet I drag myself forward, my strides getting bigger as the taste of serenity was getting closer.

'No!' we yelled, my wolf by my side.

The other rogues stopped in their tracks, another continual wave emitted from my body, turning around I ran to my car, climbing through the window as the car moved forward.

Phoenix bringing me in to a hug, I sniffed his hair.

'Why didn't you change?' he said, shaking me back and forth.

'We didn't need to! I will always have her back, don't worry.' Elsie said, showing her face, he looked at me in amazement.

'We know what to do now!' I said, bringing him in to a hug. 'I need to end this!' I added, as he shook his head in disapproval.

'I can't let you go back out there!' he said, grabbing on to me for dear life, I go to open my door.

'Don't make me punch you again!' Elsie smiled.

Opening the door a crack, I hear a rumble coming from a far, I climb out of the car I start to shift.

'Now that's more like it!' I hear Luca's voice traveling through the wind.

Taking a firm stance, I get ready to pounce, suddenly wolves where everywhere a fire ignited just like my dream, the ash flicking settling around me.

'Annabeth, go home! We've got you!' I heard through an open mind link.

It was the silver lake pack and I have never been so happy to see another pack in my life, nodding my head I change back climbing back into the car, we begin to move when I see a fight erupt from behind us, they all began closing in on Luca and Boid completely ambushing them.

'Wait!' I roared, as I looked through the back window, watching their fate, as they become surrounded by Alpha Valencia and his pack.

'Look away, Annabeth!' I hear Phoenix call to me.

But I would not, that man has caused me so much heart ache that I was going to watch as he took his final breath. Not blinking not moving a muscle his neck snapped before

276

my eyes, thinking I would have some kind of remorse for him that I would feel something, but I didn't not even a flinch my heart remained cold, like an icicle I could now unfreeze as I was finally free. Looking on I saw two figures cowering in the background.

'Stop!' I instruct.

'Annie, we have to move!' Elsie said.

I realised my cries alerted the silver lake pack, but I couldn't leave them there.

'I said wait!' my voice more forceful, opening the door I yelled for them. I saw Paddox and Shay weak and trembling, I signalled for them to follow.

'How do you know we can trust them?' Jason asked.

'They are my oldest friends,' I said, sending word ahead of time, I alerted the pack to their presence and ordered them not to be harmed.

'Orion, what the hell happened to your pack?' I asked.

'Silver lake happened the treaty ran out. Luca however didn't change as agreed, we was run out of our homes and became rogues,' she replied with sadness.

My eyes closed as I realised this was my fault, I was to blame and no one else, my stubbornness did this.

'We need to help them!' I said.

Phoenix shook his head in a disapproving manor, I laid my head on his lap, my wounds beginning to heal as he ran his fingers through my hair.

'Woman if you punch me again to get what you want, I'm going to lock you in the tower, got it? And what about our son, you could have been killed!' he sighed. Knowing he was serious I nodded laying back down as I wept a little in his lap.

'We're going to be okay,' he said, leaning down to my ear level as he whispered to me. Finally falling asleep, I cling to him for comfort.

# Chapter 33
## An eye for an eye

Waking up I was finally home at last pulling up to the hotel I step out the car, stretching out my stiffened legs pulling my arms up over my head. Unfazed by the past I keep moving, scared if I stop I might give up. Walking towards the hotel the hardened gravel crunched below my shoes, the breeze drifted past me lifting my very soul. The door opens as I see two little legs fly towards me, my wounds on my face had healed in a matter of hours but the rest was going to take time. He mowed me down with one singular hit causing me to wince slightly, but I didn't care I pulled him close to me.

'I missed you,' he said, searching my face confused, as I started to cry, pointing his little fingers at me he began flicking them off one by one.

'Mummy, what's wrong?' he asks, as Phoenix falls to his knees, he runs his hand through Ronan's hair.

'I missed you both!' he said happily.

'We missed you too baby,' I said, bringing him in again for another hug,

'Mummy you're crushing me!' Ronan said, as he patted my back repeatedly for me to release him, absolutely not this boy was going to just have to deal with it.

Julia came out of the front door, her eyes saddened as she looked on at Phoenix, looking back at me she nods.

'Phoenix, can I borrow you a moment?' she asks shyly.

'Of course you can, is something wrong? Has he been bad?' he asked, looking at Ronan.

'Oh no nothing like that, I just need a word?' she said, rather sheepishly, nodding he followed her inside.

279

Is she going to do it? Will she finally reveal her ultimate secret? I stayed outside with Ronan waiting for the others to arrive. I felt bad, after all I did make them run the entire way here. Shay and Paddox arrived.

'Wait here a moment,' I called to them, both nodding at my instructions.

Giving it at least a few moments I enter the hotel, walking towards the kitchen I see his fists curled under into a ball as he sat in a chair by the table.

'Why didn't you tell me?' he asked, as that tightened fist relaxes, stumbling to his feet he brings his arms up, causing her to flinch slightly.

He wraps his arms around her, pulling her tightly into his chest, her body relaxes as she embraces him.

'You're not disappointed?' she asked, making me pick up my son and cradle him. I remembered her story, but I wasn't crying because I was sad, I was crying because I was happy that her story now had an alternative ending and a happy one at that.

'Mummy, you're doing a lot of crying today, you sure you're okay?' he said, as he poked his little fingers in my eyes to widen them, bringing my hands out I tickled him softly looking at his father.

'We have to go Phoenix,' I said, knowing it would now be hard for him to leave.

'Can't we just stay for tea?' he asked.

'Oh come on!' I hear an irritated voice beckon from behind me.

'Jason it's fine go home, you've done more than enough,' I said, dismissing him.

Holding his hands together thanking his lucky stars, I watched him shift as he ran out of the hotel and through the trees.

'Let's hope Echo isn't in heat,' I laughed slightly.

'And who might these be?' Julia gestures to Orion, and the two shaking wolves behind her. Their fur looked matted with thick grease lining their coats, my heart wrenched as I got a better look at them.

'It's okay, no one will hurt you here,' I instructed, my eyes illuminated, as they slowly shift back.

It dawned on me just how much the years must have taken its toll on them.

'Annabeth?' Shay said, still in a haze, her mood instantly lifting when she realised it was me.

I've missed you both so much!' I said, holding my arms open for them. I thought they would come to me, but they did not, with my feelings slightly hurt I stepped towards them, both dropping to their knees they bowed before me, I walked towards them lifting them tall.

'You of all people should know you don't have to do that,' I said, as I brought them into a huddle, one by one they accepted it.

'Why didn't you come to me sooner?' I asked.

'We didn't even know if you was still alive,' Paddox said.

'Also you left so abruptly, we thought you didn't want to see us anymore,' Shay said.

'Of all the people!' I snapped, realising I was frightening them.

'Of all the people in the world you two where my only friends not only would I trust you with my life, but I also love you with all my heart,' I said, as hope filled their eyes.

'I will never leave you again!' I added.

Phoenix come up behind me holding our son's hand.

'Orion, Shay, Paddox, this is our son Ronan,' I said, in hopes they would finally understand.

'You have got to be kidding, go you,' Shay said, in her usual preppy attitude.

'When did this happen, also how is he his?' Orion asked.

'The party, he is six' I replied.

'Six and a half,' Ronan tutted.

'You absolute stop out!' Shay toyed.

'I'm so happy for you,' Paddox said.

'Thank you,' I replied, my smile sincere, as I look upon their faces.

'Well then there is nothing left for it, you will all have to come home with us!' he said with a smile, causing a sigh of relief from all parties.

'Do you mean it?' Shay asked, as she bounced a little.

'But we are rogues?' Paddox said, lowering his head to the ground with shame.

'Not anymore you're not you are family, but you are going to need a bath,' I said.

'Why a bath?' Paddox replied, as little sniggers come from Phoenix and Ronan.

'Because you stinks,' Ronan said, jokingly as him and his dad toyed with the others.

'Okay I will give you that little man, we certainly could do with some touch ups,' Paddox said, lifting his arm up and waving his hand in front of his nostrils.

'Right well, I believe you had better come with me,' Julia smiled, as she showed each of them to a room. Hearing the blissful moans coming from each of their rooms as they took a bath brought back serious memories, ones I had long forgotten.

Knocking on each of their doors I asked them to join me downstairs, one by one they both descended the stairs. Ava was stood waiting in the kitchen as she plated up the last of the food, Paddox eyes bulged the minute he saw her.

'Uh oh,' I said with a grin.

'Mate!' he said, making her drop a plate, he walked towards her, I could see his palms were sweating.

'Hi my names Paddox, what's your name?' he said, wiping his sweaty clammy hands on his shirt, before extending his hand.

'Ava, nice to meet you,' she said.

'Oh lord these two will need a room, Julia. Preferably one of the back rooms, and one they can't destroy,' I said, laughing slightly at the situation.

'Hmm right you are, best go and move his things then,' she chuckles as she leaves the room.

Shay pouncing on the chair her eyes popping as she dives into the feast, slamming the food into her mouth driven by hunger.

'Slow down Shay this isn't the only meal you will ever get, I will cook for you myself if I have too,' I said, trying to offer her reassurance.

'Maybe they would like to stay here for a while?' Julia announced, walking back into the room.

Realising the only company she had would have been Pete, I felt the need to ask everyone else too.

'Would you like that, Shay?' I asked, as she shook her head.

'My place is with you, Luna,' she said instantly.

'Paddox?' I said, but I think I know what his answer is going to be.

'Yeah go I will be fine here,' he said, waving us off, as he looked back at Ava completely in love.

'Well that settles that, think it's time we all went home; Mum can you come and see us tomorrow?' Phoenix asked, as Julia's expression changed, her pulse becoming erratic as she nods with glee.

'I will see you tomorrow,' she replied.

After saying our goodbyes, we all climbed into the car to go to our final destination, Ronan quizzing Orion on the journey home.

'So are you my sister?' Ronan asked.

'Yeah if your mum had me when she was six,' she laughed.

Ronan was smart but he did not get the joke. Hearing them begin to bicker made me laugh, it would appear we now have two children to look after.

Looking over at Phoenix I could sense something was off about him.

'What's the matter?' I asked.

'I have a mother, did you know?' he replied.

Those words caused a worried lump to form in my throat, I nodded in shame.

'I did know yes, but I wanted to give her time to tell you herself,' I said, placing my hand on his.

'Is that what you wanted to tell me previously?' I shook my head, telling him now was going to be even harder under the circumstances.

'No,' I said, taking a hold of his cheeks, 'I've been lying to you, I know why that pack came to our aid and I'm afraid we might end up owing them for it,' I said, as he ran his fingers through my blonde hair.

'A price I will gladly pay!' he said happily.

# Chapter 34
## To run or not to run

Finally we are home, unwinding the windows I stick my head out letting the wind blow through my hair, what a wonderful feeling. Looking on I saw the pack was already assembled awaiting our arrival, bringing my head back into the car I stuck my arm out taking in the soft breeze as I let it flow all around my hands.

Phoenix still attending to his work with Ronan curled into a ball across my legs, a strange feeling washed over me making me sick to my stomach, lifting Ronan I placed him on Phoenix before opening the window further and throwing up outside, my mood shifting when Phoenix touched me.

'Get off!' I snapped, as he reached for me.

'Okay my love, I'm sorry,' he said, lowering his hands, as we approached our house.

Getting out the car my mood was still shaky, as I began feeling all my emotions hitting me at once. What the hell is this? Surely I'm not feeling bad for that man who tortured me and put me through hell?

Pete comes out from the back of the crowd, as he waves at me with a beaming smile.

'Look at his smug grin,' I cursed.

'Annie, what the hell is wrong with you?' Elsie asked, I dismissed her quickly, my rage fuelling as we approached everyone.

'Hey Annie,' Pete said, making me want to hit him, with his sarcastic tone.

'Great day isn't it?' he asked, his smile beaming at me.

'Oh yeah, what's so good about it Pete!' I spat, folding my arms in front of me, trying my best not to throw up.

'Uh oh!' he said to me, making me angrier.

'What!' I snapped at him fiercely.

'You're pregnant!' he said, angering me more.

'No I'm not you idiot, I'm just hungover!' I snapped, as he folded his arms together, he looked back at me.

'Well if I was you, I would go and see a doctor, because I think you are,' he smiled politely.

'Oh don't be ridiculous!' I said.

'If anyone knows what your like when your pregnant Annie, it's this guy right here,' he said, pointing at himself, Phoenix now standing beside me.

'Well you have been through a lot, might be worth just getting you checked out anyway?' he said, as his words soothed me instantly.

'Fine but I'm not pregnant, I would know,' I insisted, the sheer notion completely winding me up.

'Okay well that settles that then, we will go straight to the infirmary,' he said, pointing me towards it, as if I had become stupid all of a sudden, touching my shoulder I shrug him off. Walking past Pete, I hear another smug ass comment.

'If she is pregnant, run!' he whispers, to Phoenix thinking I wouldn't hear him.

'Hey stop that, I'm not flipping pregnant, and I don't need your help to the infirmary either!' I said, pushing his hands away. His sighs where really getting on my last damn nerve. Pushing past them I walk to the infirmary, Valdor waiting for me guarded by two Omegas as the desperation in his eyes increased.

'Annie, we really need to talk!' he said, waving at me from the hall.

'Yeah, yeah, I just have to deal with something first!' I said, as my determination and stubbornness to prove them wrong, clouded my interest in what Valdor had to say. Swinging the infirmary doors open it clanged as it slammed against the wall, unapologetic I looked on.

'Hello Luna,' the doctor said.

'Hello apparently I'm in need of a physical,' I said, as my sarcasm radiated from me.

'My name Is Dr Giolin,' he said, as I accidently scoffed at his last name, trying my best to compose myself and contain my laughter.

'Something funny, Luna?' he asked politely,

'Nope, absolutely nothing,' I said, curling my lips under, to prevent my impending laughter from escaping.

'So what seems to be the problem?' he asked, as he gestures for the chair in front of him, moving forward I slumped in the chair as I picked the skin on my fingers.

'Ouch!' Elsie yelped in my head, 'Would you just tell him already, before you completely flay us!' she snapped.

'See my annoying brother thinks I'm pregnant, I need to prove him wrong!' I said, in a bitchy tone.

'Uh I see, okay well please fill this cup up,' he said, as if this was my first rodeo.

This wasn't going to be difficult as I was desperate for the loo, I snatch it from his hands launching myself out of the chair.

'The toilet is just through there,' he said lightly.

His politeness was making me feel bad, going in I did my business and walked back out to the doctor.

'So Luna, how long has it been since you had intercourse?' he asked, as embarrassment filled my face.

'Erm, not long,' I responded, the redness heated my ears, I now looked like a hot mess.

'I see, and when was your last period?' he said, causing me to pause for a moment, trying to recall but I couldn't.

'Oh I'm actually not sure,' I replied, sitting back Infront of him, I watch as he takes my pee and dips a stick in it.

'Don't worry we don't need to wait this is pretty accurate,' he replied, dunking a strip in my urine like a biscuit. Fear washed over me as my stomach pitted rendering my body numb, I watched as he mouthed the words. 'You're pregnant, congratulations,' he said.

Oh this has to be some form of sick joke, with everything that was happening I could have killed me and our unborn child.

'Let's see how far along you are shall we?' he said, pointing towards the bed.

'Take it this wasn't planned?' he added, I shook my head as he exposed my stomach, pouring a gel on my abdomen that felt like ice.

'This will be a little cold,' he instructed, as he smeared it on my exposed stomach. A little cold, where had he been storing this, at the back of the flipping freezer?

'Okay I see them now,' he said, my eyes widened, as I laid holding up my shirt.

'What do you mean them?' I said, my disbelief growing, thinking he's trying to trick me.

'Here is baby number one, and there is baby number two,' he said, turning the screen towards me, his smile was wide.

I could honestly have punched him; I bring my hands up to my face and smack them onto my forehead.

'What's wrong?' he asked with worry.

'Nothing doctor, it would appear I owe someone an apology,' I said.

'Right you are then, we will need to schedule a series of appointments,' he said, as if I didn't already know.

Yeah great I thought one destroyed my body, but two? Oh lord someone help me, no wonder my anger was raging quicker this time around because I had two in there making my blood boil. Getting up from the chair I stop and look at my feet.

'Farewell old friends, it will be a while before I see you again,' I said, as the doctor chuckled behind me, turning back I shoot him a look, he coughs covering his mouth. what is he four?

'Right we will need to book those appointments now, please see the nurse and we will get that sorted for you. Have a blessed day, Luna,' he said softly.

My smile was grim as I stared at him before leaving the room in a hurry.

After seeing the nurse, I was now more than ever fired up, walking back to the kitchen I see Pete and Phoenix having a catch up as they make an excited Ronan some lunch I approached with caution.

'Hey preggers, you alright?' Pete said, so very sure of himself.

'Yes I'm doubly alright,' I said, as their confused faces made this too easy.

'Can't we just tell them already?' Elsie howled, with excitement, I shake my head a little.

'What did the doctor say?' Phoenix asked, as he mistakenly stopped prepping Ronan's food.

'Daddy hurry, I'm starving!' he said, stroking his little belly and stamping his foot.

'Well it's double the trouble I'm afraid,' I said.

'What do you mean woman spit it out!' Pete said, as their annoyance at me was becoming quite clear.

'Annabeth, just tell them!' Elsie begged, as I paused for dramatic effect.

'We are having twins!' I blurted out, as both their jaws dropped to the floor.

Phoenix dropped Ronan's sandwich as he moved over to my face, pulling me towards him.

'Daddy!' Ronan yelled, as Pete takes over.

'Eww you didn't wash your hands, uncle Pete!' Ronan squealed, in the background.

'Okay cool it kid!' he said, as he rushes over to the sink to wash his hands.

'Do you really mean it?' Phoenix asked warmly, my smile growing as I hold up a peace sign, grabbing hold of me he yells.

'I'm going to be a daddy again!' he yelled, raising me in the air for all to see.

'Oh how embarrassing!' Elsie said, which I ignored. She wasn't ruining this feeling for me, as previously I never got it. Wrapping my arms around him, I could feel his warmth towards me, as he twirled me around in circles with pure joy written on his face.

'Uh yeah that's nice, but could you put her down and deal with one crazy child at a time?' Pete said.

We both laughed as he lowered me to the floor.

Walking out of the kitchen we go to assemble the pack, ready to announce our joyful news.

'I really, really need to talk to you!' Valdor shouted, his desperate tone catching our attention, Phoenix nods as the guards release him.

'I need to tell you the other half of the prophecy, you need to make sure you don't become pregnant,' he said, placing his hands together, like he's praying.

'I consulted the witch from the wood and...' he goes to say before I interrupt.

'Valdor, we're already pregnant,' I said, as those words made my stomach flutter.

The words we are pregnant though are not accurate, I was pregnant, and I certainly was going to feel every second of it, as my thoughts drifted to the swollen ankles the mood swings, the aches that came with it.

'Oh god,' I said, out loud as I recalled the searing pain from childbirth, like needing to take an enormous poo but worse, the size of a watermelon!

'How many?' Valdor said, with worry in his eyes.

I smiled and held two fingers up at him, his shock and fear was baffling to me.

'You're sure?' he replied, pacing slightly, our worry now growing.

'Yes we are quite sure, why?' Phoenix said.

'We didn't know the whole of the prophecy!' he said, as he began shuffling on the spot.

'Hey guys what's up?' I hear a familiar voice calling for us, walking up to us was Jason and Echo hand in hand.

'Oh hello, lovers,' I said, causing Echo to blush, turning her head to the side I noticed her neck, I saw the mark strong and fresh.

'Well you two didn't waste any time now did you?' Phoenix replied, causing Valdor to scream at us.

'You don't understand, the key to the bloody prophecy is twins!' he shouted, throwing his arms in the air.

'The prophecy can only come true if there are twins growing, the power of all three of you combined will make it radiate and your powers will become deadly. The prophecy states that any human woman, made Galdorie who bears twins will rein hell on earth. That should she be consumed, the world will change, as it will alter space and time, power will shift from good to evil,' he added, as his words made me feel sick.

'So what are we to do?' I asked.

'You need to destroy one!' he said, firmly without hesitation.

'We will not be doing that!' Phoenix said, as Jason and Phoenix stood in front of me, blocking me from Valdor.

'Then it would seem we had better get ready for the fight of our lives, he will be coming for them before they leave your body not allowing you to become separate entities,' he expressed, as I took a seat on the couch trying to figure out a way out of this mess.

'So that must have been why our dreams told us to run?' Elsie said, as I felt a warmth stroking my hand, looking up it was Ronan with Pete right behind him.

'It's okay mummy, we protect you!' Ronan said, his words warmed my heart, as I sat looking at those beautiful yellow eyes.

'Would be us wouldn't it?' I replied, pinching his cheeks.

Julia walking through the door with some freshly baked goods with Paddox, and Ava right behind her.

'Wow this place is awesome,' he shouted, looking up at the ceiling, I half smile at him.

'I should have stayed here!' Paddox laughed.

'Right Valdor, what do we do?' I said looking at him.

'We need to leave!' he urged, as I sat shaking my head.

'I will not leave my home!' I said with absolute certainty.

'Annie we must run, if the Nafari heard your cries like the rest of us did then they already know about you?' he said, still urging me to leave.

'You all heard my screams?' I said.

'Yes we were all ready to leave when you sent out a soothing wave of calmness!' the guard said.

They were all coming for me. I fought back the tears as I realised a second ago that I'm a bit of a crier, I needed to appear strong Infront of my pack.

'There is one more thing Annie, they have your family,' Valdor said.

My fists tighten with rage as my claws dig into my palms, blood oozing from them as it dripped down my palms onto the floor.

'Annie don't,' Julia yelled.

'I need to get them back!' I snapped, raising to my feet.

'That's what they want, you have to wait!' Valdor urged.

'I will leave the waiting to you Valdor!' I said, as my thoughts become irrational.

'Annie, they will kill you then they will kill your family, please listen to Valdor!' Julia pleaded.

'What are we going to do?' I said, shaking my head.

'We are going to train, we will be ready Annie!' Jason shouts, causing everyone to agree with him.

They have my Family but I'm going to get them back, it has been too long since I last saw them that I will not be giving up on them now.

It became clear the war had been waged and the fight was now on, what had become painfully clear was the Nafari now know of my existence. They will be coming for me, and we need to be ready.

'We will be ready!' Elsie said.

'The world will tremble before us!' she added.

There's that crazy wolf I know and love, our world was changing multiplying and all that was left to do was wait. Believe me when I say we will be ready.

# Chapter 35
## The Prophecy

It had been a couple of months since I learnt of the true prophecy, and if he wanted my children, he was going to have to go through me.

I laid awake all night tossing and turning unable to settle, the aches and pains coursed my body unable to sleep on my back any longer, I rolled over to see Phoenix staring straight at me.

'Hello my love,' he said softly, as my core heated, his eyes became lustful.

'Oh no, this is how we got here in the first place, we don't need to put anymore in there now do we!' I said, as his laughter was like a blissful song, a long-awaited serenity.

'We could always put just one more in there, so we would then have an even number of children when they come out,' he said, as his playful jokes moved me, completely in the opposite direction.

'Oh yeah, how about we put one in you and see how hot you look?' I toyed, folding my arms together.

'I would look as radiant as you do my love,' he smirked.

What a total creeper he is trying to make me forget being pregnant so he can get lucky, well I can tell you now it's not going to work.

'Time to get up, in three, two, one!' I said, counting down the seconds as the door swings open.

'Mummy, daddy!' Ronan yelled.

'Makes me try and remember how I got you pregnant in the first place, with such a warm welcome in the mornings,' he whispered, trying to hold back his laughter.

Phoenix got out of bed and moved towards the bathroom to go and brush his teeth, with a smiling Ronan climbing in the bed beside me.

'Mummy I made this for the babies,' he said, shoving a rainbow picture under my nose, still wet might I add. Phoenix returned from the bathroom, taking one look at me he erupted into fits and giggles.

'My love, have you seen your nose?' he said, as his laughter at my expense was growing.

'No why? What is the matter?' I said, with a blank expression.

Without replying he handed me my hand-held mirror from the bathroom, looking into it I saw a nicely shaped rainbow formed across my nose with hints of glitter through the corners.

'You look ridiculous!' he said, as his laughter continued, he dropped to the floor and proceeding to roll around holding his sides.

'Well mummy I think you look cute!' Ronan said.

'Well I must also admit, you certainly have looked better!' Elsie laughed.

'Yeah thanks, you do realise if I look like this then so do you?' I replied smugly.

'No that look is all yours, it has got nothing to do with me,' she replied quickly.

'I thought you always had my back?' I asked.

'Not with this I don't!' she said, as her laughter echoed.

Well isn't this great not only was I getting fat, but I now look like a rainbow, and the only thing that was missing was the leprechaun at the end of it,

my own thoughts making me giggle slightly. Phoenix leaned over handing me a dampened face cloth, I scrubbed my face getting rid of the paint, but the glitter remained. Great now I look like a flaming glitter ball.

How the pack and Valdor are going to take me seriously today I will never know. Getting up I staggered to my dresser pulling myself up to eye level, peering over I was horrified by my reflection.

'God we look a mess!' I said, reaching for my eyes.

'Yeah where the hell is that so called pregnancy glow anyway, because I don't see it!' Elsie replied.

'Elsie, you didn't see me the last time. Believe me when I say there is no glow, only the need for food and rage comes from me when I'm pregnant!' I said annoyed.

'Does that mean I will get angry too?' she asked, but in a tone I didn't like,

'More than likely, but that is not a license to be a murderous cow!' I said, quickly putting her in line.

'Oh, but it is!' she replied, her tone concerning, as she was clearly plotting something.

I got dressed for the day with the fatigue weighing me down, all my muscles aching as I find it hard to resist the urge to just go back to bed. All my muscles resisting as I stretch them out, warming them up ready for the day ahead, I must admit it was easier when I was up and walking, as standing still meant my muscles cooled down and stiffened instantly. Finally emerging from my room, I made my way downstairs to the kitchen, to see

Mr and Mrs Symonds waiting for me, with a cup of evilness that is a vitamin enriches shake that smelt like vomit and tasted like it too.

'For your growing babies,' Mrs Symonds said, shoving it under my nose, with an evil smile.

I wretched as she shoved it further towards me spilling a little on my lip. I took it in hopes I would be able to dispose of this poison before I would vomit it back up, allowing me to relive this experience twice. Mrs Symonds handed me a bowl of freshly cut fruit, I blinked at her as I looked over my right shoulder to see the other pack members eating a full English.

My mouth watered as dribble escaped my mouth.

'Can't I just have a piece of that?' I said, as my eyes bulged from their sockets.

'What some of this?' Pete jokes, as he took a bite out of his bacon, I growled at him, as he shifted off his seat hiding in the back as he finished his meal.

'Come now you can have some eggs but that is it, the doctor's orders remember?' Mrs Symonds insisted.

What kind of doctor would tell a hormonal pregnant lady that she can't have bloody bacon? Furthermore, a doctor who isn't brave enough to tell said pregnant lady himself, shouldn't be giving orders at all.

'Yeah but remember what you did when he said you couldn't have peanuts anymore?' Elsie said quietly.

'Elsie, that's not fair you know we crave those!' I snapped, completely annoyed with my breakfast.

'Ladies if you are quite done!' Valdor said sternly.

'Oh great, who let him in!' Elsie muttered.

'Have you two forgotten the imminent danger you are in?' he said, with a disappointed tone.

'Valdor, how could we forget as you remind us daily!' Elsie said, hoping he would go away.

'Clever wolf aren't you, but you won't be so clever when your dead now will you?' he spat.

'Valdor do you want some breakfast?' Mr Symonds asked.

'No time, we have work to do!' he said, clicking his fingers at me.

'Oh that had better not be at us?' Elsie spat.

'Come on let's just get this day over with!' I said.

'But he clicked his fingers at us?' she said in disbelief.

'Listen here you, I am in no mood for your games today. So Valdor, I suggest you tread carefully, or we will make you regret it, got it?' I said, pointing at him.

Elsie made an appearance in a flash, poking our tongue out at him and soon disappearing when his expression changed.

'Right you are, maybe today we will try something simple perhaps?' he said.

'Lead the way then,' I sighed, rolling my eyes.

Walking out the back he led us away from the training area, further and further out of sight.

'Where is he taking us?' Elsie asked. 'He's leading us to our death isn't he!' she added.

God my wolf was always so damn tetchy. He stopped abruptly Infront of the stream outside, closing my eyes I could feel my pack on guard ready and watching my every move.

'Here we are, we will be trying levitation today,' he said, pointing for me to sit opposite him.

'Can we not learn something else today, my brain is already hurting,' Elsie sighed.

'No we are learning this!' his eyes widened in anger.

'God why is he always so grumpy!' Elsie huffed.

'Because my dear, if you wish to die then you're going the right way about it!' he said.

'Did I mention temperamental as well?' she laughed.

'Elsie, I am in no mood for you today, will you just do as you are asked for once in your life?!' Valdor snapped.

'Would you too give it a rest; my head is already splitting as it is!' I said, shouting at them both.

'Well he started it, being all morbid and stuff!' she replied, in a lowered tone.

'Morbid you're one to talk, if I didn't know you better, I would say you're a serial killer!' he said.

'Again, with the cereal!' she groaned.

'Not cereal as in food you twit, serial as in a serial murderer!' I snapped.

'Well what are we supposed to be doing then, because I'm getting bored of this!' she moaned.

'Will you block her out already, she is testing my patience!' Valdor instructed.

'Annabeth, don't you dare!' Elsie screamed.

'Sorry it's just for a moment, you can come backout later,' I said, trying to calm my mind.

'Annabeth, don't you even!' Elsie roared.

I closed my eyes shutting my mind off from my wolf, it was an odd but deeply satisfying moment of peace. I placed her in a box in the deepest part of my brain, she is going to be so mad when she comes back out, I wish I could say it would teach her a lesson, but I doubt it.

We can't even shift to run off her excess anger because of the babies. I'm sure she will be okay.

'Shall we proceed?' Valdor asked.

'She's not going to be happy when she gets back out!' I said worriedly.

'Yes well tell her she should mind her manners then!' he insisted, whilst unfolding the corners of the blanket.

'Erm have you met her before? You tell her!' I said, not wanting to feel the wrath of my wolf.

'Oh no, she is your wolf my dear you can have that honour!' he smirked.

His words annoyed me as I knew she was going to be so angry with me, but if we are going to win this battle,

I needed to concentrate without the constant bickering going on around me.

'Now to levitate something you have to focus all of your energy on it, remember something will not simply move just because you asked it to. You must free your mind, focusing only on the object at hand. Notice its pattern, the way it looks. Mark it to memory then move with it,' he instructs, showing me the movements.

'Move with it? How the hell do I do that? Do I need to walk?' I said, trying to stand to my feet.

I must admit I didn't think that was a stupid question, but Valdor on the other hand did.

'Ouch!' I said, rubbing my head, as he found the nearest stick and hit me with it.

'You're not an idiot, so do not act like one!' he said, hitting me again.

'Ouch! That was not a silly question, I don't know if I'm supposed to move or not!' I yelled, earning me another whack on the head.

'Okay I get it, I don't need to move. Why couldn't you just say that?' I said, lifting my hands which also earnt me a whack across the knuckles.

'Use your damn words!' I yelled, growing tired of his punishments.

'My child how will you learn if you do not listen?' he said, in a condescending tone.

'By not being concussed maybe?' I replied sarcastically, looking upon his scowling face I took in a deep breath, I closed my eyes and tried to concentrate.

'I'm back!' I hear in my head, as Elsie comes through the door, I barricaded her in.

'Okay Elsie, if you're going to stay then we need to concentrate, because he keeps whacking me with sticks!' I said, in a childlike tone.

'Annabeth, you are a true Alpha, will you get a bloody grip?!' she snapped.

'Well why don't you bloody try then?' I huffed.

'Alright then I will, move over!' Elsie said, showing herself as she half turned.

'Right what do we need to do?' she asked, with unusual patience.

'You need to visualise the object in front of you, see its movements feel its vibrations and lift it remembering something will not simply move because you ask it too. Feel its energy then focus on it, sound easy?' he joked.

'Too easy! Right Annabeth, I'm going to need you for this!' she said, soon appearing side by side, we closed our eyes, adjusted our position leaning forward with our eyes still closed, we imagined the branch considering its size colour and edges.

'You're doing it, you're really doing it,' Valdor said.

Opening our eyes Elsie was still present, pushing me out of the way as she took over.

'Teach you to banish me to the dark!' she said, looking right at him.

Narrowing her eyes with a flick of her nose, she sent the branch flying towards Valdor. Standing to his feet he moved backwards falling into a muddy pit, as she proceeded to whack him with it the stick.

'Okay, I've got it!' he yelped, as the stick connected.

She stopped in triumph letting him up to his feet, thick mud clung to his clothes as she let out a roar of laughter and finally letting me back in.

'Valdor, why didn't you stop her?' my confusion growing, as he was exactly like us, but in this moment he was powerless.

'Because I don't possess the same abilities as you,' he said, with a saddened expression.

'What's that supposed to mean?' I said, as my confused expression grew.

'It mean's my dear I may be a Galdorie, but I don't have all the abilities, I possess the ability to read minds and to levitate small objects. But you, well you are something different all together,' he said, with amazement in his voice.

His words shocked me, I stood looking around as my pack looked on in fear. How was I going to explain to them that I am not a threat?

Closing my eyes I inhale the fresh air, in my mind I caused a small tornado to form, it was small, but it ran in circular motions, and my emotions ran higher as the tornado got bigger.

'What the hell was that?' I hear Valdor say, opening my eyes to his jaw wide open.

'What was what?' I reply blankly.

'How did you do that?' he said, furrowing his brows at me.

'Do what?' I said, with little patience.

'You made a tornado appear?' he said.

'I just thought about one,' I said, shrugging my shoulder.

'You're not supposed to be able to do that!' he gulped.

'Why not it wasn't that good, surely other Galdorie can do that?' I said, in a dismissive tone.

'No they can't!' he said, as his jaw dropped further.

'Okay I think that's enough for today,' I snapped, as I stomped off back to the pack house, to see Julia coming up the drive.

'Hello Annie,' she said happily.

'Hi!' I said, storming past her.

'Oh angry pregnant lady alert,' Pete said jokingly.

Ignoring him I carried on towards the house, an alarm sounded through my head, it was like a ringing in my ears as I cupped them to silence it.

'Something is wrong!' I yelled, as screaming reached my ears.

Turning I run in the opposite direction to see Shay coming back over the wall, I watch on as she tried to pull herself up before dropping to the ground the other side. Looking over my shoulder I saw Ronan running out of the house, I scoop him up with Echo close by my side.

'Take him!' I yelled, handing him to her.

'Yes Luna!' she replied, running with him in the opposite direction.

My feet rush to Shay quicker than my mind could keep up, her body limp as she desperately tries to move.

'Stop, Annabeth!' I hear Valdor calling to me, arrive by my side. He snaps me back forcefully.

'Valdor, get off of me she is hurt!' I screamed.

Reaching into his pocket he pulled out a glove, putting it on before he reached for her, pulling down her collar revealing a bite mark on her neck that sent her veins a wild red colour, with a green mist emitted from the wound site like a puff of smoke.

'What the hell is that?' I asked.

'Poison from venom, you cannot touch her stay away!' he said, pushing me backwards.

'She is my friend! Who did this to her? Shay where are the others?' I said, realising she was not the only one out on patrol.

'Gone!' she replied, in a fading voice.

'Get her to the pack house, now!' Valdor screamed, holding me back, as they picked my paralysed friend up from the floor, with her veins pulsating and bright red.

'Annabeth, you can't help her!' he instructed, as I watched them take my friend away.

'I can help her, what happened to her? If you want me to stay away, then you had better tell me!' I said, screaming in his face.

'There is a reason the Nafari are in charge of wolves, and why the pack allows it,' he said, still holding me.

'Tell us!' Elsie demanded.

'It is because the Nafari's bite is incredibly toxic to werewolves, don't you understand! That's why it's so important for you to learn! So you can beat them and restore order back to the Pack members they enslave!' he said, shaking me slightly.

'Well why the hell didn't you tell me!' I yelled.

'I tried, I told you it was of grave importance that you trained!' he said, trying to reason with me.

'Yes but you didn't tell me this would happen!' I replied, feeling a warmth run up my arm.

It was a spark I knew all too well, reaching for him I pulled him close.

'It's okay my love, we will take care of her,' he said, stroking my arm.

Taking in his touch I inhaled heavily with closed eyes, snapping them open I look at Valdor with fire in them.

'You said they can only merge absorbing another wolves' powers!' I said.

'Yes and it is true they take what they want from you, but they don't just absorb your powers they absorb your essence your reason for living,' he said.

Taking a moment, I look at Phoenix worry filled his face as he stroked my arm.

'Then we had better win then!' I replied, looking Valdor in the face, with sheer determination to win and beat the Nafari for good. This wasn't going to be easy, but the fear I had bubbling inside me was worse.

'We had better get to work!' I said with confidence

# Chapter 36
## My life

Remembering my life before this world wasn't so easy anymore, trying to remember my family and the way life use to be, was like a fading memory. I remembered my father's face and my brothers even Payton's, but I couldn't remember a time where we were happy.

A life I had previously allowed myself to forget, that I found myself sitting and reminiscing. Remembering my little brother playing freely in the garden, it was a summer's day with not a cloud in the sky and not an ounce of wind to cool us from the blazing sun, he ran around in circles trying to catch a butterfly, his playful screams were music to my ears. Awoken from my thoughts I was brought back to my current reality, sitting in my chair I hear the words.

'Annie, Shay is asking for you,' Phoenix said, bringing me to my feet, I barged past him, as I dashed out the room.

I hadn't until now been allowed to see her, it had been four days since the incident. I wasn't about to argue.

Leaving the room, I was greeted by pack members bowing before me with fear on their faces as they glanced in my direction, I stopped still looking around as they all continued averting their gaze, walking to the middle of the hall I mind linked them all simultaneously.

'Come,' I said softly, as they all gathered before me.

'I know you are all scared, but you need not be afraid of me. You are my people now and I will never hurt you but will however fight with you and for you always for the good of the pack. You are my family, and we don't hurt family! I will be here for you all the time you are here for me. Please

306

trust me, I would die before I let another one of you get hurt,' I said, as I looked out at angry faces.

'Believe in me, as I believe in all of you!' I said, as the faces I looked upon soften. Guards pounded one hand on their chest as a sign of approval, others followed as it was the Genai way, it was a warrior's tribute to other warriors!

'We stand with you Luna!' I hear from the back as Jason appeared.

'From now, and for forever!' he yelled, his voice strong and mighty, I nodded before turning around and heading for the infirmary.

'Nicely done, Annabeth' Valdor said, coming up behind me. 'They will follow you to the ends of the earth now, this is a power you will soon need!' he added.

Ignoring him I continued past him, with my mind completely focused on my friend. Getting into Shay's room was daunting, she was encased in a bubble of plastic separating her from everyone else. I stared at my friend looking upon her frail frame, her veins now green with wires and lines draped across her everywhere. Opening her eyes, she reached for me pulling down her oxygen mask with her other hand, I moved forward to a hardened grip holding me back.

'You can't touch her!' Valdor insisted.

'Watch me!' I said, slapping his hands away, he reached for me again.

'Touch us again, and we will break it!' Elsie said, opening a claw ready to attack, holding up his hands he steps backwards away from us.

Opening the zip we step inside, as I reached for her, but she responded by holding up her hand to stop me, I froze unsure of my next move.

'I tried to come sooner, but they wouldn't let me,' I said, reaching for her again.

'Annabeth, you can't touch me Valdor was right!' she coughed, spluttering before me, as she laid trying to inhale fresh oxygen, to fill her lungs with.

Holding a tissue to her mouth, she attempted to hide the thickened black mucus that drained from it with every cough she did. Her wheezing was too much for me to bare, her chest rattled indicating she didn't have long left; the death rattle was going to take her from me too soon and I wasn't ready for it.

'Shay, please tell me what to do?' I pleaded, as my eyes saddened, staring at her for instruction.

'There isn't anything you can do,' she replied, putting her mask back on taking in more oxygen, 'My days are numbered, it has been a pleasure knowing you, I have loved you like a sister, and I will continue to love you long after I am gone,' she smiled, gripping my heart.

'Why can't I touch you?' I said, trying to reach for her again.

'Because this is a different kind of Poison, I overheard him say before he bit me, that he laced his fangs with a locator, if this touches your skin he will know exactly where you are!' she said, struggling for breath.

'Who is he? And if it is designed to locate me, can it not locate you?' I said, watching her shake her head.

'I didn't catch his name and no, it is specific to power, your kind of power. I managed to get away in time before they could track me, running in circles meant the venom acted quicker but it was the only way I could avoid showing them your location. They will be tracking me for days, which is why when I am gone you must put me back. I'm sorry but I had to warn you!' she said, as I still tried to fight the urge to comfort my friend.

'I'm nearly done. Say goodbye to... Say goodbye to Paddox for me,' she said, as I watched the tears fall from her eyes, onto the pillow beneath her head.

'Shay please, if you would just hold on!' I pleaded, as I watched her take her last breaths.

Her eyes flickering as she jolted slightly, the corners of her mouth blackened as she gasped for breath, it was as if she was drowning and there wasn't a thing I could do to stop it.

'No!' I howled in a harrowing voice, my screams heard everywhere alerting the pack to my distress. Phoenix coming up behind me as he scooped me backwards, I clawed at him trying to get him to let me go. My friend was gone. I was losing everything I held dear to me, everything I loved. Who was next?

Pulling me out of the room Phoenix dragged me to the hall, Paddox looking at me with disbelief in his eyes as the tears reddened my eyes and the puddles filled as water fell.

'Tell me she's not!' he said coming for me, 'Tell me she's okay!' he added, trying to move my hands away from my face.

'Paddox, please don't!' I said, trying to resist him.

He pulled my hand upwards revealing my face, my anguish evident as the tears laced my eyes.

'Paddox, I'm so sorry!' I said, causing him to rush to her room.

My eyes blinked for a second thinking that she might be okay, only to be met with his faithless screams burning my ears, a scream I feared I would never forget but it is a scream I feared I would hear again.

Lowering myself to a sitting position on the chair I recalled that preppy girl I first met, so full of life. She knew what she wanted to be, and exactly where she was going. Meeting me would appear sealed her fate, she was destined for greatness but was robbed of her happy ending all because she met me. Stumbling to my feet I screamed.

'We need to move her,' I said, as Paddox come back out of her room wiping his face.

'What do you mean we need to move her?!' he said.

'She told me she was poisoned with a tracker; the witches of Columbia will be able to locate her!' I said.

'Let them come!' he said, puffing out his chest.

'We can't put the rest of the pack in danger Paddox!' I said, trying to calm him.

'So you want to throw her out like trash!' he spat.

'No she will be buried a warrior, with honour and dignity!' I said, as the doctors in suits prepared her body.

'I can't let you do that, Annabeth!' he said, walking towards me, I looked at him hurt.

'I'm afraid you don't have a choice,' I said, as the pack members surrounded him.

'But this I can do!' I said, taking his pain.

'When we have won, I will bring her back here and we will bury her right, I promise Paddox!' I said.

Drying his eyes, he nodded at me as they took her body through the hall out the back, stopping them I placed a hand on the body bag.

'We will meet again my friend!' I whispered.

I watched on as they wheeled her away, my heart breaking with every step they were taking, I recalled a time when she made me laugh. Searching through my memories of her it was a time I had yet to speak about before now, she was attempting to turn on my shower in my old house when we were getting ready for that wretched party, but the house was so old and fragile that she broke it clean off, meaning I couldn't have a shower.

'Oops, this belongs to you,' she smiled, awkwardly throwing me the nob for the temperature control.

'Shay!' I laughed.

'What? It's not my fault it broke, it's this old house your dad should have brought a newer one!' she played. Our laughter filled my heart as the memories flowed back to me, making it hard for me to breathe.

'Calm yourself, we will see her again,' Elsie said, attempting to comfort me.

'When will we see her again?' I replied distraught.

'She will live on in our memories, we will see her again but not yet!' she insisted.

I calmly walked back to my room wishing to be alone, Julia holding on to Ronan as he attempted to come for me. Pete picked him up whispering something in his ear. Returning to my room I remained silent, disbelief was my first stage of grieving.

# Chapter 37
## Denial

I remained in my room for the next few days, closed off from the world and closed off from my family. Images plagued my mind as I recall her taking her last breath before me, I cursed the moon goddess for taking her away from me so soon, she should have lived a long and happy life. I laid unable to sleep because every time I closed my eyes I saw Shay, im sure it was my mind playing tricks on me, I saw her ghost appearing everywhere preventing me from resting.

'You did this to me!' she said, every time I close my eyes. 'This is your fault!' she added, as the blackened tarry blood oozed from her mouth, she spat at me waking me from my dreams. The horror that surrounds my dream cycle was inevitable, closing my eyes again I try and think of happier times, but they become overshadowed by my grief. Phoenix stands before me.

'You can't stay in here forever,' he said, his kind voice having no impact on my current state.

'I just need to sleep,' I whispered, desperate for sleep, drained of energy, and my willingness to engage vanished.

'Here the doctor prescribed you this, I can't listen to you scream another night my love, you need help!' he said, as I snatched the pills from his hand, downing them with a pint of water on my bedside cabinet.

'Leave me alone!' I responded, as my eyes quickly became drowsy.

'Please come back to me,' he said, his voice echoing as my eyes closed, my cheek tingling from his touch.

My dreams became white as I sifted through the clouds, I was floating, falling through them with Elsie right next to me.

'Elsie?' I said, as my voice echoed into the abyss.

'Annabeth, why are we here?' she asked, with a worried tone to her voice.

But I did not have the answer, we began falling at speed as the light turned to darkness, looking up we could still see the light above our head as we fell into a pit of despair.

'Annie, where are we?' I hear my wolfs whimpers as I tried to find her.

'Annabeth!' I hear a voice echo into this deep void, a voice I did not recognise.

'Who's there!' I yelled, only to have my voice yell back at me.

'We are the knowing!' the voice echoed.

'Gosh my head is messed up!' I laugh uncomfortably.

'You are in grave danger; you need to get up, you need to get ready, for he is coming!' they said.

'Who is coming? All I want to do is sleep!' I said, with pure exhaustion.

'We have foreseen your future; your babies will be taken should you not be ready. The power within you is strong, a desired power by all,' the knowing said with intent.

'Then we shall run!' I said, with confidence.

'I am afraid it is too late for that if you do not train you will not be ready. Then this will be all you know, darkness for eternity is what awaits you!' their tone becoming more serious.

'If you're all knowing tell me, do I win this war?' I said, hoping for the right response.

'We cannot tell you your immediate future, doing so will alter the course of time, changing it permanently for the

313

worse. We can but act as a warning, instructing you of which you already know you should be doing,' they said, offering me no comfort.

'So much for the knowing!' I scoffed.

'This is not a time for jokes! You shall see the pain and rath of thy own actions. Heed our warnings, for you will not get another! Go to where the lights touch the earth, do it alone. You will see your family there, find them, find them!' they said, fading into the distance.

The darkness fades as I was awakened and ready, listening to my instincts I rush out my room, running downstairs I make it to the kitchen, I was about to tell them all what I had dreamt before realising none of them would let me go if I did. My heart was racing, as the air felt as if it was thickening around me.

'My love, are you okay?' Phoenix asked, looking at me.

I swallowed my thickened saliva as I nodded back at him, watching him play with our son was something I longed for. Opening my eyes as if for the first time, I watched the smiles on their faces form. It was as if they were before me in slow motion. I was seeing them, every part of them and I knew what I had to do. I was going to go, I've had my training, and I was ready.

'We can do this, but we must go tonight!' Elsie said, I nod as I stood looking at my family. I spent the remaining hours watching them. I had planned on leaving without a fuss, but I had to decide how I would do it.

Patrolling officers were out day and night, getting past them was certainly not going to be easy.

Looking on at my family we decided to play a board game, they of course did not have a chance because I was the biggest cheater going and they knew it.

314

'Erm, I will be banker,' I said, earning me a look.

'Oh I don't think so, you always cheat!' Phoenix said, laughing at me.

'I do not!' I said, in total denial.

'You so do!' Elsie laughed.

'Mummy, you are a cheater!' Ronan smiled, twiddling his fingers. What a little traitor.

Our laughs carried on through the afternoon as Ronan had me playing something called swing ball, followed by water gun fights much to the cleaner's dismay before we settled playing gods of war on his PlayStation. It was an oddly satisfying game, I of course didn't get it, I just followed the instructions of an incredibly competitive Ronan. Running my fingers through his hair it was finally time for bed, after settling him in I walked downstairs heading for the garden. Going out to the garden I watch patrol carefully; it was Mal and Jason's turn, and they ran like clockwork. Looking back at Phoenix, I knew I couldn't say goodbye to him, I knew it would be too risky, but something saved me, finally the world was working in my favour.

'I have to leave for a couple of hours,' he said, as he looked at me.

'Where are you going?' I said, twiddling my fingers.

'Are you worried about me?' he smirked.

'No I'm just wondering where you're going?' I said.

'Relax I must go to the construction site to formulate a new plan, apparently, we are building on an ancient burial ground. So, we either must move the site or exhume the bodies,' he said, casually as if it was nothing. Great that is all we need, more bad luck.

'Okay please be careful, you shouldn't mess with that kind of stuff!' I said, out of respect.

'Relax, I'm going to propose we move the site over,' he said, lowering his hands, to ease my tension.

'We don't need any ancient Sharman curse you know!' Elsie sniggered.

'Trust you to laugh at something like that!' I huffed.

'Can we go already? And bring a coat or we are going to freeze! I cannot shift remember,' she said, I nodded as I watched Phoenix leave the room.

My expression changed as I realised he didn't kiss me, looking back I saw him coming back through the door in a hurry.

'Almost forgot something,' he said, as my smile brightened, he leaned into me, and this is how I wanted to remember him loving and attentive.

'Goodbye my love, see you later,' he said, turning and heading towards the door.

As he left I waited a couple of moments before I saw him officially leave, I whipped my head around grabbing the remaining things I needed for my journey, leaning down I grabbed my bag I had already half packed under my bed. I had secretly packed some food and supplies for my journey too; it was going to be a long road ahead of me. Slowly walking downstairs, I paused checking my surroundings, all the pack members where asleep apart from the patrol officers. Going out the back I got down low using the bushes as cover, I ran from one to the next avoiding being seen. My breathe heavy as I tried to cope with my ever-growing bump, I was not really thinking of them, I was thinking of my family, of my losses knowing this would not end unless I ended it.

Getting down low with a baby bump was harder than I remembered, leaning forward to catch my breath as it took the wind right out of me, I pushed on with determination on my side.

I made it to the wall, looking up it was bigger than I remembered, with a sheer 10ft drop the other side.

'Going to need you for this one, Elsie,' I said.

'On it!' she said, as we shifted slightly, she leaped me over the wall without so much of a scratch.

'I hope we're making the right choice!' she said to me.

'We are, it is the only way!' I replied, as we began our journey.

Held back by our fear but pushed on by our pride we make our way forward, shamefully unafraid of what is on the other side.

# Chapter 38
## For the ones we love

We walked for hours which meant Elsie did nothing but moan the entire time, even though she wasn't the one walking and carrying two extra humans might I add. No she hitched a ride in my head, but still had the audacity to keep asking if we're their yet.

'Walk to where the lights touch the earth!' I recalled, the last message given to me by the knowing.

'Are we there yet?' she groaned, in my ear.

'No, we aren't,' I replied, as my thoughts silenced for a moment.

'So are we there now?' she said, in an irritating tone of voice, one that made me want to throttle her.

'Do you have anything helpful to say?' I snapped.

'Yes when will we be there, our feet hurt!' she said.

'Elsie, our feet hurt because we are pregnant not only because we are walking, plus you're not even walking I am remember!' I said, completely irritated with her.

'Can't we sit for a moment, I'm so hungry!' she said, letting out our tail slightly, digging it into the ground to try and stop me.

'You are quite literally worse than my child!' I replied, absolutely seething with her. Sadly, deep down I know she was right; we should try a little harder to be nice to each other. Suddenly I heard something alarming,

It was a rustling coming from beside me.

'Who is it!' I yelled, with no answer.

The rustling continued slowly becoming louder, standing to my feet I leapt into the bushes much to my dismay there was nothing there but a package.

'Don't touch that, what's wrong with you!' Elsie said, as I picked it up.

'Elsie, stop being a cowardly wolf! We're already in danger, what's a little more going to do?' I said, trying to make her realise the gravity of our situation.

Placing the package in both hands I noticed it was wrapped professionally in a yellow shirt with a silver badge on it, I searched my memories wondering where I had seen this before, my eyes fluttered for a moment, when I soon figured it out.

'Katrice!' I said, clutching onto it.

'Let me have ago!' Elsie said, as she sniffed it.

As we examined it more closely, I noticed blood spatter on the collar.

'Elsie, we need to find her, now!' I said, as her nose began sniffing the air.

We ran through to the woods as the scent ran us off the trail, pulling us around in circles until the trail ended.

'Where to now, Elsie?' I said, as we stood for a moment, wondering where to next.

Our eyes looked down to see a freshly turfed soil, an uneven patch from the rest of the ground, raised slightly with bugs rolling through it. We held our ground for a moment listening out for a heartbeat for any signs of life, but nothing not even a faint pulse was present. My stomach bubbled and pitted as I prayed nothing was in this shallow hole. Falling to our knee's we began to dig frantically, partly shifting our claws protruded, digging our nails into the freshly dug dampened soil flicking it behind us, as we dragged it backwards with our claws.

'Come on dig!' I begged, as we dug faster.

Soon revealing a hand beneath the soil, the bruising revealed on the hand as I dusted the mud off was purple and red mixed in with a pale complexion.

'Annabeth, she's!' Elsie said, with shock, unable to finish her sentence.

'Don't you dare say it, we don't know it's her!' I moaned, desperately still trying to dig.

I dug a little more revealing her face, leaning over I wretched as the sight of her mangled body, this was too much for my brain to comprehend. Her eyes were completely glazed over, the visible bruising around her arms and neck with bite marks and cigarette burns across her body. Her face barely recognisable and her mouth wide open and her face scrunched up, suggesting she died screaming. Her lips were grey with hints of purple lining her cupid's bow, the torment written all over her face was undeniable.

Trying to move her wasn't easy as she was as stiff as a board where rigor mortis had set in, which only made things worse as the state of her decomposition depicts that she was alive just days earlier, meaning I could have saved her sooner.

Looking around I noticed not a drop of blood was around her, her body has been sucked dry. Anguish washed over me as the sorrow ran my emotions.

'Why her, where is my family!' I wailed.

'Annabeth, we have to go!' Elsie said, trying to bring me to my feet, urging me to carry on.

'We can't just leave her here!' I said, as my cries turned into screams.

'Annabeth, we will come back for her!' she said, as I slowly began to lose it, Elsie took over our body for me, lifting me from the ground.

'We have to keep going, Phoenix and Argorn will know we are missing soon!' she said, carrying us all.

'Please we have to help her!' I said, as I watched her leave Katrice out in the cold.

'Please go back and cover her up, what about the animals,' I begged, screaming for her to turn around.

'No!' she said, stomping down the path.

'Elsie!' I cried.

'We are animals, the sooner you except that the better!' she said, and her response appalled me.

Closing myself off from her I went deep into my mind, remembering what Katrice was like and how I treated her in the beginning.

'How could anyone do that to her,' I thought, as my mind went dark, and my thoughts became numb.


Elsie eventually let me regain control after we were far enough away from Katrice, she didn't let me regain control of my legs, to prevent me from rushing back to her, my wolf knew me better than that.

'Elsie, are we nearly there?' I whispered.

'The lights touch the earth on Castle Donnay,' she said, pointing into the distance.

'So is that where we have to go?' I replied, out of frustration and pure exhaustion.

'Yes, that's where we have to go,' she said calmly.

Castel Donnay was no man's land and not a single person in the world are allowed to cross its barrier, those who have however have never been seen again.

The legend behind it was that it was governed by a monster, a home to a tyrant and ruthless murderer. Scouting around I sent out a distressed signal, looking up I saw it was heavily guarded, even in the dark of the night if you knew what you were looking for then you would find it.

The moonlight was a dead giveaway as our eyes glistened beneath it, making us visible to each other. Turning my bag around I pulled my sunglasses out of my backpack and put them on, shielding my glowing eyes from the moon and anyone who would see them. I waited in the cold dark night for any form of help, but nothing came.

'Elsie, are you ready to be brave?' I said.

'Yes, let's do it!' she replied.

Getting up we stormed towards the castle alerting them to our presence, wolves jumping and attacking from every angle, freezing them on the spot I launched them in different directions. Unfazed fuelled and ready. Startled and cornered as they all stampeded towards us, before we knew it, we were fully surrounded. My ears twitched as I heard a clapping echoing off the mountains.

'Bravo my dear, bravo indeed,' his voice was poised and posh, like he had lived for hundreds of years, allowing people to be lulled by his incredibly strong British accent. I scowled at him as he circled me, making sure to not take my eyes off of him at all times.

'I told you I would find you my dear, but it turns out you have found me, how very unfortunate don't you think?' he sniggered.

'The only thing unfortunate will be your head hitting the ground!' Elsie growled.

'Oh so very sure of yourself, are we?' he tutted.

'Where are my family!' my growl growing deeper.

'Didn't you find Katrice?' he said, with a menacing smile, when her name was mentioned it brough a lump to

322

my throat. 'Oh did I touch a nerve my dear? I would hate for your family to meet the same fate!' he hissed.

'Where are they?!' I snapped, my desperation was shining through.

'Bring them!' he ordered, as the double doors flung open, revealing my father and a boy I barely recognised. If it weren't for his eyes, I wouldn't have known the boy before me.

'Ethan?' I questioned, receiving a nod from him.

'Annie?' he said.

My father looked old, his hair was completely greying, the bruises lined his face as he looked on at me, some bruises were old but some were not, his eye was half closed due to the swelling, wanting to hug him was overpowering my judgment. I paused looking on past the guards.

'Where is Payton! What have you done with her?' I screamed.

'Absolutely nothing, she is right here!' he said, as the crowd parted ways.

'Hello Annabeth!' I heard, resisting the urge to lunge for her, she was fine not a mark on her.

Her dress was black and lined with silk, her complexion pale, death was too good for her was my initial thought, she was now undead just like her spoilt dead soul.

'Payton, what are you doing!' I yelled.

'Sister, you have your mate and I have mine!' she smirked, as the corners of her mouth cracked, and her smile widened.

'Payton, you cannot be serious! What have you done to my sister!' I yelled.

'I did not do anything to your sister, I gave her a choice. And well let's just say she chose wisely,' he hissed, like a venomous snake in the night.

'Payton what about Dad and Ethan?' I said, as my voice began to break.

'What about them?' she said, slily as I stared at how quickly she dismissed our family. Our only bond to each other broken, she was a mere shadow of her former self. She always was a selfish cow!

'Listen closely my dear, give yourself to me and I will let your family go. Do we have a deal?' his voice bellowed from within him.

'You will let them go and leave my family alone!' I said, as my body began to shudder.

'You have my word!' he smiled, revealing his teeth.

I have to say the word of an evident vampire didn't in my book count for much, but what other choice did I have. At this point he had me and he knew it, he waved for me to come closer, closing my eyes I start to step towards him secretly wishing my sister would stop this.

'Another smart girl, I'm beginning to like this family!' he snarled, pointing towards me.

His voice made me angry because we should know what to do. But in this exact moment, we were clueless, the overwhelming feeling of being drawn to him was like he had tied a noose around our body and was pulling us in.

'Annabeth, we have to get out of this somehow, you heard the prophecy!' she screamed at me.

'We can't, my family is at stake,' I said.

'Annabeth don't do it!' my father screeches, earning him a punch to the face.

I flinched for a second as I watched my father take a beating, slowly making my way over I stand before him.

'What's your name?' I said, as he smiles back at me.

'Oh my dear you hurt my feelings, surely you have heard of me?' he said, as he looks me in the eyes.

'No? well my dear my name is, Orpheus,' he announced proudly, taking a step to his left.

'Orpheus, I've heard of that name, it means darkness of the light!' Elsie whispers, in my ear.

'No need to whisper with your wolf my dear, I have consumed many of your kind, so I know what you are thinking!' he said, tippy toing with excitement.

'But I will admit, never have I come across something quite as radiant as you my dear!' he added, scratching my flesh with his talons.

The blood dripped onto his sharpened fingernails as he brought his hand up for a taste, his eyes redan as he shudders with glee.

'Oh you taste divine, I'm going to enjoy this!' he said, gripping hold of my throat, his hand opened revealing his sharpened claws ready to strike.

Unwilling to fight back out of fear for my family I accepted my fate, hearing cries roar from behind me as my brother and father attempt to fight back.

'It's okay, we are ready,' I smiled at them, as I watched them attempting to fight for freedom.

Returning my eyes back to him, his hand comes crashing down but does not penetrate before pushing me to the side he yells back at me.

'You were supposed to come alone!' he snapped.

Stopping I look behind me to be met with an army forming. At the head of that army was my mate, Jason, Mal, Echo and Valdor by his side, it was not only my pack but to my surprise the half-moon pack and the silver-lake pack joined as one, making our forces unmatched. I looked back at Orpheus as he backed away from me.

'Get them!' he commanded, as they sprang into action. A fight erupted as they crashed into each other, clawing snapping, and biting one another with such force you could hear bones breaking. Phoenix ran to me I looked around and growled forcing the guards to let go of my family.

'I will be back for you, and you will be mine!' he smirked.

'You can't have my children!' I shouted, causing him to laugh in response.

'My dear, it was never about your children. They would simply have been a bonus, no I wanted you. Your mother was an excellent addition to my power as will you be, until such a time be careful of your dreams my dear. You never know what they might tell you next, Payton come!' he said, with a warning. Clamping my fists together we get ready to fight. Rising to my feet with my mate by my side, Orpheus escaped with his life launching himself into the air and taking my sister with him.

'I will get you, mark my words!' he said, before he disappeared into the night.

My attention was now on the scene before me, broken beaten and lifeless bodies appeared in heaps. A wolf approached from my left, grabbing my mates arm I launched him towards it, sending the wolf flying in the other direction. Gaining composure, I closed my eyes and let out a roar, it rumbled through the floor dividing them from my pack.

'Enough!' I screamed, letting out a wave of power, stopping everyone in their tracks.

I looked to my left seeing my father holding my scared brother tightly.

'You are not animals! You will behave in a manner that brings honour to our kind, and honour to your people!' I announced to them all.

'Annabeth, are you okay?' Phoenix said, as he latched onto me, I ignored him momentarily.

'You are all now free wolves; you are free to leave, or you are free to join me. We will spare any other packs the same fate, we will rise, and we will conquer!' I said, as the wolves around me cheered and clapped.

Looking at my father I realised he now knew of our existence, which also meant he now couldn't leave us. Explaining this was not going to be easy.

'Dad, Ethan, please don't be afraid of me,' I said.

Dad walked towards me with his arms open wide, bringing me into a bear hug. My eyes flowed as I took in his dusty chalone, it was faint, but it was still there, pulling him back out of our hug I looked over at Phoenix.

'Dad this is Phoenix, he is my partner,' I announced, to him with pride.

'Nice to meet you,' he replied, putting out his hand.

'Ethan?' I looked on with sadness, as he didn't approach me at first.

Holding out my hands in hope he would come closer, I had waited for this day for so long. Opening his arms wide he jumped me, I have never been so happy to receive a long-awaited hug in my entire life. Pulling him backwards I ruffled his hair as I searched his features.

'Not the little boy I remember!' we laughed.

Opening his mouth he spoke for the first time, his voice was deeper which took me by surprise.

'Not a boy at all,' he said.

'Well no, it would appear you are not,' I laughed.

'What happened with Payton?' I said, as I looked at this sadness in my father's eyes.

'Just as he said, she made a choice,' he replied.

Holding onto both their hands I looked on, my heart now whole and full of joy. My father looked down at my stomach, as his attention shifted now fully on me.

'Are you pregnant?' his eyes sparkled.

'Yes, these will be my third,' I said proudly.

'Third, you mean you already have two?' he asked.

'No I mean I already have one, but I'm carrying two,' I replied, rubbing my round tummy in circles.

'You don't say, when can we meet your first?' he said with joy, reaching for my stomach.

'His name is Ronan and soon, you will have to live with us for a while. You can resume your job for us?' I said, as he nodded.

'Dad, I'm so sorry about Katrice,' I said, as his eyes filled at the mention of her name.

'Did you see her?' I said, as he shook his head at me.

'No my darling I didn't, in truth I wouldn't have wanted to, I will remember her just the way she was, so please spare me any details,' he said, I nodded, knowing I couldn't explain even if I wanted to, it was too gory, and if I'm being honest, I wished I hadn't even seen her like that myself. Jason and Mal approached us.

'Hey cool eyes little man,' Jason said, looking at Ethan, with an envious tone to his voice.

'Thanks, I guess,' Ethan said, shrugging his shoulders.

'Hey where can I get eyes like that?' Mal asked.

'Well first of all you've got to get sent to the slammer, where they tell you that you will never see daylight again,' he said, telling his story, and spinning his web of lies to Jason and Mal, who are currently hanging off his every word.

'Oh, come on!' I laughed.

'Shush, we wanna hear the story?' Mal said.

'You boys already know the story, Riddick?' I said. They blinked at me repeatedly as if they all had no clue what I was talking about.

'Oh brother!' I said, amused at their stupidity.

'Annabeth, would you be quiet, I want to hear the story!' Elsie snapped.

'You have got to be joking, it is quotes from a film!' I said, trying to get her to see reason.

'You're just jealous!' she said, listening in closer.

'Right I think it's time we all went home now, you guys too if you wish,' I said, as Alpha Valencia approached.

'We will be leaving now Luna, I will call in the favour when I need it the most,' he smiled, as I nodded. Leaving this place was the least of my worries, knowing Orpheus was still out there waiting and plotting, was much worse than anything else I could face. Having my sister meant he had the added advantage over my family, luring them out would be all too easy even if she were now a vampire, my father would always care for her, which meant I had to keep them safe and far enough away from her. He was going to pay for what he had done to my family. Taking them home, well taking them home was a risk I was going to have to take. My day was closing, but my journey, well, my journey is just the beginning.

**THE END**